The Ambrosia Project

THE CLANDESTINE DAWNING OF THE GODS

HALLIE PARKER

Copyright © 2022 by Hallie Parker

All rights reserved.

Cover Design: The Red Fox Creative
Editor and Interior Designer: Jovana Shirley,
Unforeseen Editing, www.unforeseenediting.com
Character Design: @maggies_artt
Map Design: Siren Songs Boutique on Etsy

No part of this book may be reproduced or used in any manner without the written permission of the copyright owner, except for the use of quotations in a book review. For more information, contact hallieparkerwrites@gmail.com.

This is a work of fiction. Names, characters, businesses, places, events, locales, and incidents are either products of the author's imagination or are used in a fictitious manner. Any resemblance to actual persons, living or dead, or actual events is purely coincidental.

ISBN: 979-8-9873236-2-5

Content Warning

- Profanity
- Mental illness
- Sexual scenes and situations
- Underage drinking
- Consumption of illegal substances
- Compulsive eating
- Cheating
- Grooming
- Mentions of murder

THE AMBROSIA PROJECT SERIES is loosely based on the Greek Olympian gods and goddesses. Please be aware that it is not fantasy, fan fiction, or a literal retelling.

This series is intended for mature audiences only. Reader discretion is advised.

Playlist

"Young God" by Halsey
"Tiptoe" by Imagine Dragons
"Counting Stars" by OneRepublic
"I Feel Good About This" by The Mowgli's
"Team" by Lorde
"Walking on a Dream" by Empire of the Sun
"Something Big" by Shawn Mendes
"Bones" by Imagine Dragons
"Just Getting Started" by Hawk Nelson
"Young Blood" by The Naked and Famous
"Good Life" by OneRepublic
"Bel Air" by Lana Del Ray
"It's Time" by Imagine Dragons
"Young Volcanoes" by Fall Out Boy

Incoming Students,

Before you embark on this retelling of our origin story, it should be understood that the history lesson in your hands is indeed the tale of how our gods and the world in its current state came to be. However, it is important to keep in mind when you turn the page, at this time, they were all mere mortals, such as many of you—entirely unaware of the existence of such divine souls living and waiting inside them.

Please be advised that you are about to encounter occurrences of temporary—and accidental—immortality, godlike abilities, and the existence of other celestial beings. However, the subjects of this story had been conditioned, like many mortals, to turn a blind eye to these instances. When our narrative begins, circa 2014 AD, only a small handful of gods were aware of their true being and therefore had to stay hidden. Most of the gods, including those making up our pantheon, had no idea the ways their lives were about to change.

We understand these are most unusual circumstances—for students, such as yourselves, to have insight into a character's storyline before even they are aware. Please take care with this information, and should you encounter any of the surviving gods, we kindly ask that you refrain from mentioning their beginnings. It's still a bit of a sore spot for many of them, but we believe with another hundred years or so, time will have healed these wounds.

Thank you,

The Republic of the Last City-State

March 1, 2014

Dear Mr. Alexander,

On behalf of Parthenon Studios, in conjunction with Olympia College, I would like to thank you for your scholarship application. As you know, this application is for the flagship group of this scholarship program, beginning August 2014. After careful review and consideration of your application, we feel that you would be an excellent choice to receive Olympia College funds for your university expenses—including tuition, board, books, et cetera—in exchange for showcasing your student life on a new reality television show, to be produced by and aired on Parthenon Studios.

The next step is for you to fill out and return the enclosed forms for you to receive funding. Please do so by August 7, 2014, in order to ensure your funding for the fall semester. You are expected to move into your assigned dorm no later than August 14, 2014, as classes begin on August 18, and your network orientation and the first filming session will take place on August 20.

If you have any questions or concerns regarding this letter, please feel free to contact us at your convenience via the contact information provided to you with this letter.

We feel confident in our selection of you for this program and are eager to see how your influence in the program will change the world. We look forward to working with you, and we thank you for applying to Olympia College and Parthenon Studios for your scholarship.

Yours sincerely,

Dwayne Kronos

OLYMPIA COLLEGE
Undergrad Student
2014 - 2015
ZACHARY ALEXANDER
STUDENT ID B00712945
INITIALLY ISSUED 8/1/2014
EXPIRES 8/1/2015
IF FOUND PLEASE RETURN TO
SCHOOL OF BUSINESS

OLYMPIA COLLEGE
Undergrad Student
2014 - 2015
KAI NEWPORT
STUDENT ID B00413769
INITIALLY ISSUED 8/1/2012
EXPIRES 8/1/2015
IF FOUND PLEASE RETURN TO
SCHOOL OF SCIENCE AND ENGINEERING

OLYMPIA COLLEGE
Grad Student
2014 - 2015
DAMON MONTCLAIRE
STUDENT ID B00628949
INITIALLY ISSUED 8/1/2013
EXPIRES 8/1/2015
IF FOUND PLEASE RETURN TO
SCHOOL OF GRADUATE STUDIES

OLYMPIA COLLEGE

OLYMPIA COLLEGE

OLYMPIA COLLEGE

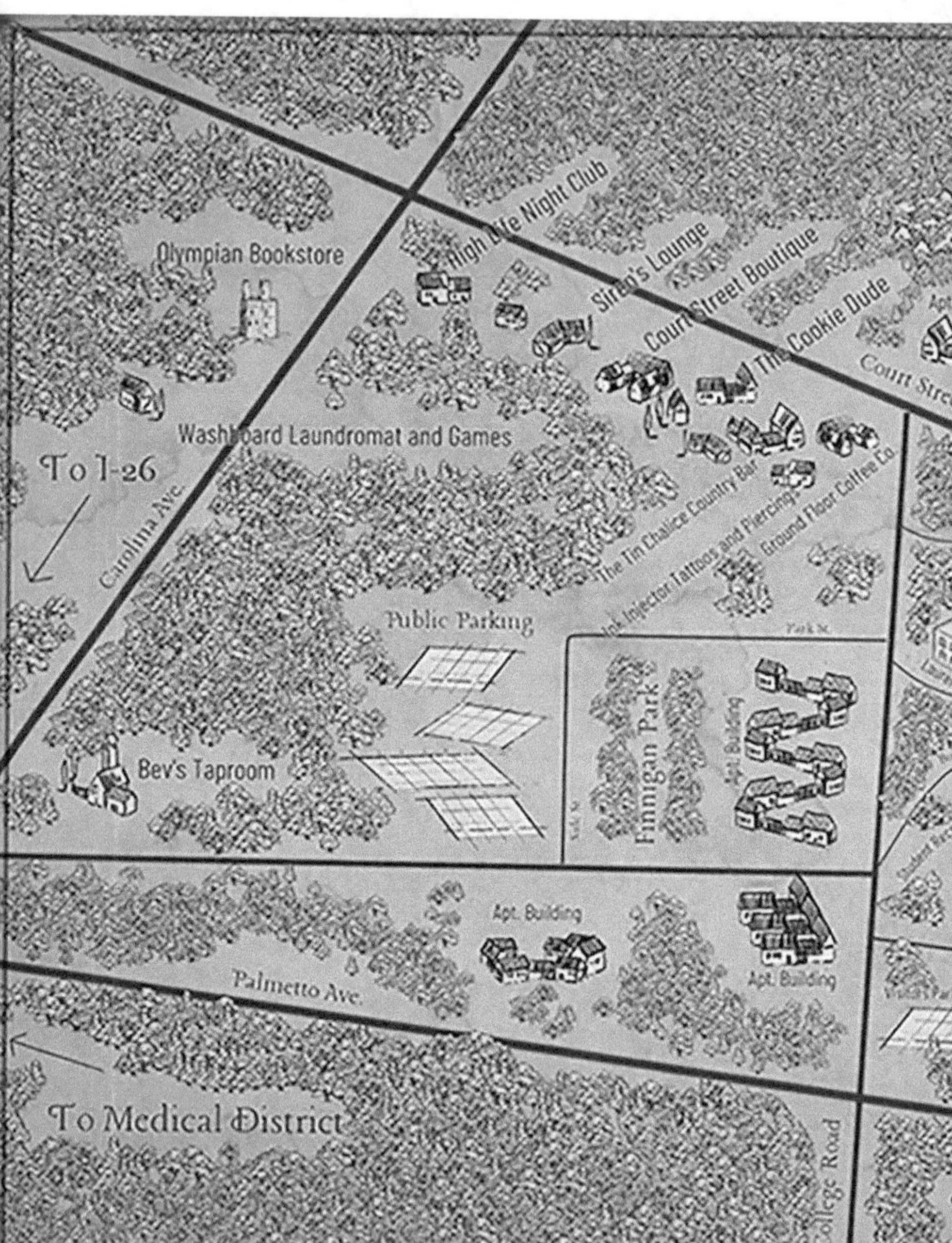

Olympian Bookstore
High Dive Night Club
Siren's Lounge
Court Street Boutique
The Cookie Dude
Apt.
Court Stree
Washboard Laundromat and Games
To I-26
Carolina Ave.
The Tin Chalice Country Bar
Ink Injector Tattoos and Piercings
Ground Floor Coffee Co.
Park St.
Public Parking
Finnigan Park
Apt. Building
Park St.
Bev's Taproom
Apt. Building
Apt. Building
Palmetto Ave.
To Medical District
College Road

lympia College

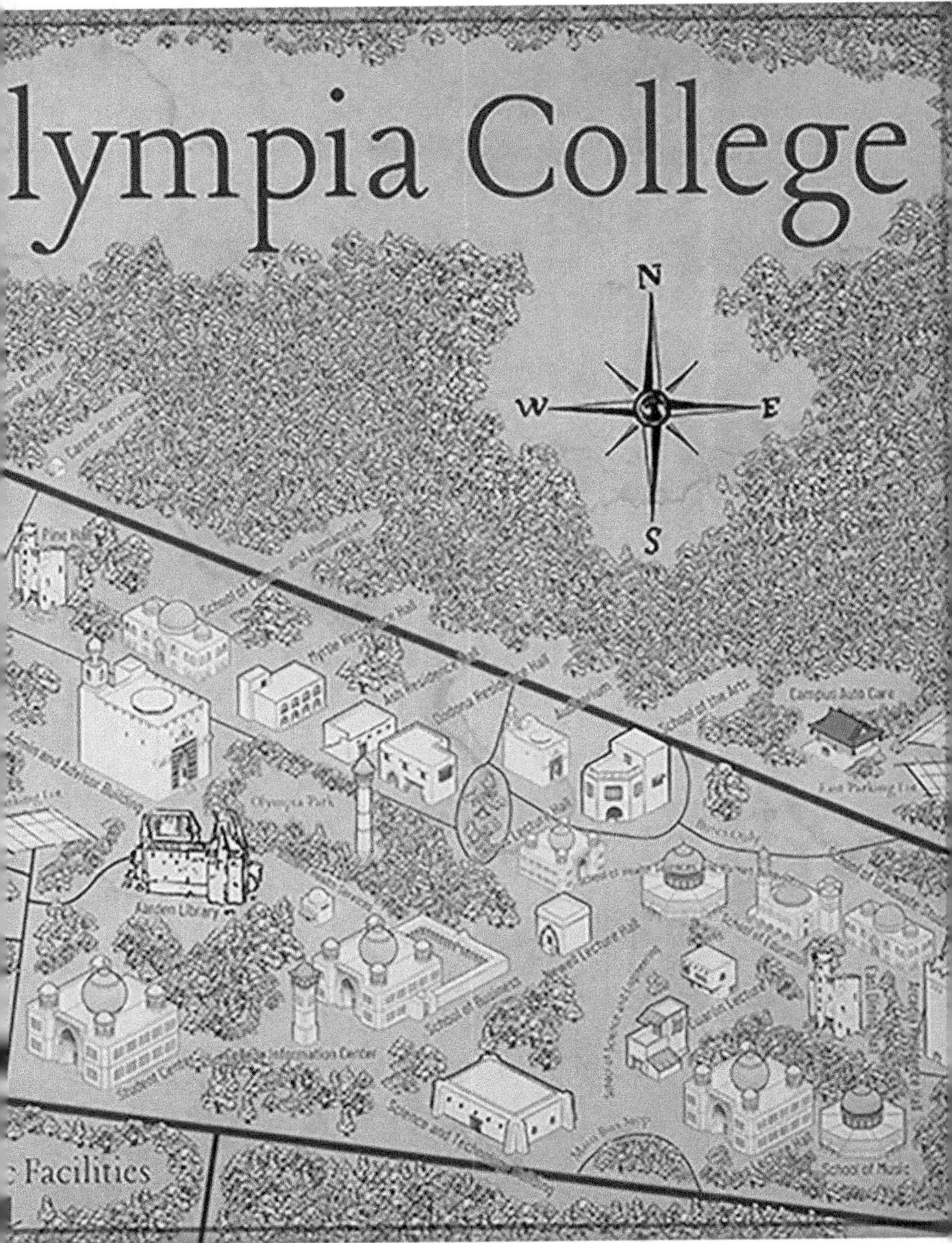

Prologue

Beginning in the late *1980s and lasting into the early 1990s, the world experienced a plethora of strange phenomena. Civilians witnessed everything from natural disasters, to plagues, to increasing divorce rates, to famine.*

Volcanoes that had been dormant for years were suddenly erupting, and floods and tsunamis devastated small islands and coastal cities. Smog hung heavily in places it never had. Tornados spun up in cities where twisters never should have been possible.

Clean drinking water was suddenly hard to come by, and it was not uncommon during this time for droughts to last for multiple months at a time. Farmers were left baffled by how little they were able to harvest, which led to food shortages and increasing prices when it was available.

Unrelated to weather, the rates for teen pregnancy and sexually transmitted diseases skyrocketed. Homelessness became increasingly prominent while crime rates rose around the globe, and cemeteries filled up fast and ran out of room. Countries were constantly on the brink of war, and global trade practically halted overnight. Inflation rates rose, and international travel declined steadily all over the globe.

Every devastating event that could happen did. Scientists, researchers, and experts in their designated fields gathered from around the world to analyze data, but no sound conclusions were ever drawn. The string of events dwindled down after several years, and they eventually gave up looking for logical reasons and attributed everything to global warming.

Minor instances still occur today, but not as often, and they do not claim as many lives as they once did. Scientists fear that they will never know the cause of these bewildering circumstances, and many fear that they might happen again, possibly with a more intense level of severity.

Chapter 1

HE WAS TALL AND COMPLETELY bald. The fluorescent light reflected off the top of his head as he walked into the conference room on the top floor of the Student Center. He didn't introduce himself to the six students in front of him—he didn't need to.

"Welcome, welcome. Thank you all for making it to our first meeting of many. I'm assuming you all know who I am."

The redhead nodded.

"Mr. Kronos," the blond-haired boy answered. Well, *boy* wasn't the right word. He had turned eighteen less than a month ago.

The man nodded. "That's correct. I'm the CEO of Parthenon Studios, Dwayne Kronos. I attended Olympia College too—of course, that was a long time ago," he added with a chuckle. Nobody laughed, as expected. "I'm very excited about this joint program the seven of us are going to be starting this semester. If things go well, we could be doing this for a while—well after you graduate."

He took a moment to take in the six young adults in front of him. Males on the left, females on the right. The two freshmen were in front of him, the juniors in the middle, and the two graduate students were third in line on each side.

"Does anyone have any questions before we get started?"

Again, no one responded. *That'll change.*

He directed his attention to one of his female colleagues on the opposite end of the room. "Has the remainder of the paperwork been signed?"

"Yes, sir," she answered without even glancing down at the clipboard in front of her.

"Wonderful. Now, would you all prefer to go around the room and introduce yourselves to each other before we break off for individual sessions or just dive right in to the interviews?"

A few nervous glances passed back and forth across the table, but still, no one spoke.

He clapped his hands together. "Okay then, we'll just get started."

"Um …" The redheaded girl began to raise her hand.

"Yes, Miss Hargrove?"

"Do we have to do the interviews?"

He knew there'd be at least one—he had just assumed it would be Mr. Montclaire, who had given him some push back. "As stated from the very beginning, the interviews are a requirement to be in the program. The whole premise of the show is to showcase different students as they experience life while attending Olympia College. The scholarship money is awarded as a form of payment, covering tuition, books, room and board, et cetera. You also already signed the legal documentation, saying you'd comply with doing the interviews. So, yes, Miss Hargrove, you do have to do the interviews."

The girl pulled her long braid over her shoulder and began fiddling with the ends of her hair as she slunk down in her seat.

"Does anyone else have any questions?" he asked again as he forced a smile on his face. Not bothering to give them much time to answer, he gestured to the woman at the back of the room, holding a clipboard. "My production manager, Rhianne, will be talking with you all, so she can devise a schedule with you to conduct future interviews. The room next door has been set up for the individual sessions, and you can all wait here until it is your turn."

He turned to the blond-haired boy. "Mr. Alexander, you're up first."

The following interviews had all been performed on an individual basis but were edited together.

Kronos: Let's just start off simple—what's your name, where are you from, and what are you studying at Olympia College?

Zach: I'm Zach Alexander. I'm from DC, and I'm a business major for now, but I might switch to poli-sci. But I'm really just waiting to go to flight school after I graduate.

Hanna June: Hi, I'm Hanna June Pruitt! Most people just call me HJ though. I was born down in Jackson, Mississippi, and then my family moved to Charlotte, North Carolina, when I was five, but *then* we moved to Bethesda, Maryland, right outside the DC area, when I was twelve. My parents and the Alexanders—Zach's family—well, they decided when we were little that we should get married, so mine moved to be closer to his, so we could be together—ain't that sweet? We've been together six years now—I know! [*laughs*] Oh, and I'm a family studies major and a psych minor.

Kai: I'm Kai. Kai Newport. I, uh, I grew up on a houseboat. So, I don't really have, like, a home state. But, uh, my license is from North Carolina. So, I guess that counts. And ... sorry, what was the last part?

Kronos: Your intended major.

Kai: Oh yeah. Um, marine biology. But it's pretty hard. Like, I'm probably gonna fail out ...

Amber: Amber Hargrove. I'm from Omaha, Nebraska, originally, but I moved to Charleston, South Carolina, when I was in fourth grade. I'm an enviro sciences major with a minor in women's studies.

Damon: Damon. New York. Forensic psychology.

Kronos: What was your last name again, Damon?

Damon: Montclaire.

Kronos: Any relation to New York Governor David Montclaire?

Damon: Why do I have to answer questions you already know the answers to?

Kronos: Because it's not for *me*. It's for the viewers. I need you to explain so that the audience knows who you are.

Damon: I don't want the audience to know who I am.

Kronos: [*sighs, turns to the crew members behind him*] Just edit all this out, please.

Dawn: My name is Dawn Avery Sutherland. I've lived here in Olympia, South Carolina, my whole life. I graduated with my undergraduate from OC two years ago in educational leadership, and I'm finishing my master's degree in architecture this semester.

Kronos: Do you take part in any extracurricular activities?

Zach: Yeah, I'm rushing a frat, hoping to get a bid from Zeta Upsilon Sigma, so that'll take up a lot of time. And if I choose the poli-sci route, I feel like I should join the Political Leaders Club. And then I'm dating HJ, so that pretty much takes up all of whatever free time I have.

HJ: Yes! I was basically guaranteed a pledge from Eta Rho Alpha 'cause my mama and Grammie were both sisters! We just finished recruitment last week! And I was also one of the four freshmen to make the dance team back at tryouts in May!

Kai: Uh, not really. Sometimes, I would volunteer at some of the beaches with cleanup crews, so I don't know; maybe I'll do that again. Otherwise, I like to go out on my boat when it's warm. [*shrugs*] Probably gonna have to get a job somewhere …

Amber: No, I don't have time for extracurriculars.

Kronos: Why not?

Amber: I go home most weekends to take care of my dad and sister. [*pauses*] They don't ask me to! It's not like a chore for me. I enjoy it.

Damon: No.

Kronos: No?

Damon: No.

Dawn: I work at a tutoring center a few days a week, but I'm really just trying to focus on finishing my master's—I only have this semester left! There's a lot more work involved than a bachelor's, and then if I get accepted into the PhD program online, I'll be able to pick up more hours while getting my doctorate.

Kronos: Describe your perfect day.

Zach: Probably sleeping in, definitely no schoolwork. FaceTime with my family. Hang out with some of my friends. [*laughs*] I don't know why, but I really love, like, a crazy thunderstorm in the middle of the day that only lasts for, like, thirty minutes, and then the sun comes back out. I love that. But then, you know, [*clears throat*] like, take my girl out to dinner and then … you know … take her home after.

HJ: I'd like to get up without an alarm. Honestly, I'd like to just spend the whole day with Zachary! [*laughs*] I'm, like, totally that girlfriend that's, like, obsessed with her boyfriend. I just love bein' with him. What I'd really like to do is for us to drive down to Charleston, do some shoppin' on King Street, have a picnic, take, like, super cute photos for Instagram, and just hang out with him all day.

Kai: I'd like to wake up back on the boat. I don't know why, but I can't really sleep on land. Maybe it's because I spent my whole life literally being rocked to sleep by the waves. I don't know. I'd do some fishing, lots of surfing if the waves were good. Smoke a joint. And if this is a fantasy, then I'd have a girl there too.

Amber: Oh, that's easy. I'd be back at home. I would do some cleaning and then grocery shopping early in the morning. Then, I'd grab Fleur, and we'd go plant shopping. We could spend all day in a garden nursery. We both do our best thinking while surrounded by plants and flowers, so we'd most likely just hang out there together for hours. Probably return home late afternoon, and I'd make dinner for the three of us. If Daddy was still awake after that, I'd really love to go out for ice cream that night to this place he and Mom used to take us when we were little.

Damon: I'd be back at my apartment, studying and researching my intended career field, not doing this interview.

Kronos: That's what you'd do for the whole day?

Damon: I'd stop to walk and feed Spot.

Kronos: Who is Spot?

Damon: My dog.

Kronos: You—your dog's name is Spot?

Damon: [*silence, eyebrows furrowed*]

Kronos: We'll come back to that.

Dawn: I'd spend the morning tutoring the kids I help, maybe volunteer with the food drive downtown. Then, I'd go home to my parents' house. My daddy would have a huge bonfire going in the backyard, and we'd invite the rest of our family over—maybe the neighbors and some family friends. Mama would be in the kitchen, making all my favorites—her macaroni salad, s'mores cream pie, anything I can think of. We'd spend hours talking with everyone, and then after they all went home and we cleaned up, me, Mama, and Daddy would go inside and eat the second s'mores cream pie that Mama had made, you know, just for us, and we'd watch some old home videos.

Kronos: Last question. If you could change one thing about yourself right now, what would it be?

Zach: [*long pause, then leans back in his chair with a smug look on his face*] I wouldn't change anything.

HJ: I'd like to be done with college! I know I just started, but Zach and I are gettin' married after we graduate, and I just really don't want to not be married to him any longer than I have to be! [*laughs but cuts it short, drops shoulders, and stares off into space*] Or maybe my nose …

Kai: I wouldn't be in college.

Amber: I'd like to be able to have my family closer, so I could still live at home and be able to take care of Daddy and Fleur.

Damon: I wouldn't be doing this interview.

Dawn: Nothing. I like myself exactly the way I am. [*smiles*]

Chapter 2

KAI

AFTER SCHEDULING THEIR INDIVIDUAL INTERVIEWS, Kai was the first one to leave. He'd taken the latest slot possible—sometime in the middle of September. Dwayne Kronos had said that it would be "right after episode four airs"—whatever that meant.

This show isn't going anywhere. Nobody is gonna watch this.

He had been relieved when Amber had asked if the interviews were mandatory because if she hadn't asked, he was going to.

We even think alike.

If his long legs hadn't carried him out of that conference room, he might've made the mistake of asking her out. Again. For the fourth time.

He just couldn't help it though. When he looked at her, he actually felt calm. Not necessarily happy, but just more comfortable in his own skin, and that was something he hadn't felt in a very long time—since he'd come to school at Olympia, honestly.

What was strange was that as soon as he headed back home, that all went away. He was outgoing around both people he had grown up with and total strangers. He was eager to help people but also knew when to take a step back and have time to himself. He could talk to anyone about anything, but especially his mom. Whereas, at school, he felt like he basically turned into a nonentity. But as soon as there was water in his view, everything changed.

What worried him was that he thought maybe Amber didn't want to go out with him because of the way he acted.

Can't blame her though. No one wants to date someone who's visibly depressed.

The worst part of it all was that he couldn't stop thinking about her. He'd seen her in their orientation group, and that was it—game over. Luckily, they'd had several classes together their freshman year since the school was fairly small—just over five thousand students.

Kai had wanted to just stay home and go to community college. That was what made sense to him, and even his uncle Kris agreed. He wasn't sure what he wanted to study, and his mom needed help with her business. Cleaning yachts for the absurdly rich along the entire edge of North Carolina *and* the bottom tip of Virginia Beach was a tedious job, and his mom did it all on her own—the scheduling, the accounting, and of course, the cleaning.

Kai had always just accepted that he'd inherit the business one day, and truthfully, he was okay with that.

But early in his senior year of high school—not that he actually went to a real high school since they traveled all year from Sandbridge down to Ocracoke and homeschooling was really the only option—Leticia got a call while they were in the middle of cleaning opposite ends of the Sumpters' 70.2 M cruiser. Not only did Kai not hear the conversation, but he wasn't even aware that it was happening.

Fifteen minutes later, his mom was running toward him, squealing like an excited little girl, waving a piece of paper. She read her scrawled notes back to him, informing him that there was a man named Dwayne Kronos who could get him into college. He had somehow gotten Kai approved for financial aid for two years at this tiny liberal arts school, Olympia College, which was landlocked, in the middle of South Carolina.

"Mr. Kronos is working on getting this scholarship program approved, but he said that's going to be another two years before it actually begins. But once it does, you're already in it! All your books, your classes, everything will be covered! And Mr. Kronos said that if you get good grades during your first two years, you know, before the program starts—and I know you will—he will pay back every cent that financial aid is owed. *Every penny.* You can go to college, baby! You can actually go, and you won't have that horrible student debt haunting you forever. This is exactly what we hoped for!"

For the first time in his life, his mom was happy crying. She was jumping up and down, and the smile on her face seemed to be stuck there. She wanted this for him *so* badly. How could he possibly tell her that he didn't really want to go?

This woman had done everything for him. She'd raised him almost completely on her own. Uncle Kris came to help when he could, but ever since he'd retired, he wasn't consistently around. And not only did she manage her own business, but she was also the one homeschooling him. Truthfully, as he got older, she didn't need to be as involved as she had been when he was younger, but still. Managing a teenager's education and business at the same time was a lot, and she never complained.

So, how could he possibly let her down?

Once a contract for the arrangement had been signed by both his mom and the mysterious Dwayne Kronos, he felt slightly better. However, throughout the whole process and even in the years to follow, Kai had never met the man.

Until today.

He'd even pulled Kai aside as soon as the stupid interview session was done. "It's nice to finally meet you. How's your mom doing?"

Kai made small talk with the man in charge because he knew his mom would want him to even though the whole thing still made him uneasy. He had so many questions he wanted to ask Dwayne Kronos, but he was surrounded by strangers—and Amber.

Between the two guys—who he unfortunately shared a biological father with—the blonde girl who kept tossing her hair and smiling at the camera like she just belonged there, the oldest member who exuded peace, and the redhead he had the worst possible crush on, it was just too much. He had shown Rhianne a screenshot, which he'd taken before the semester started, of his schedule and mumbled that he wanted the last interview. She had handed him an appointment card with *September 16, 2:45 p.m.* printed across it in the neatest handwriting he'd ever seen.

As he walked across the west side of campus toward the dining hall, he couldn't help but overthink about the answers he'd given earlier. He was already dreading the next interview session. It was all so fake and forced. Not that Kronos was reading off of cue cards or anything, but he assumed Kronos would be during the one-on-one sessions—unless he memorized all the questions he had for them.

Kai had already decided he hated wearing a mic pack as the sliding doors opened for him. He threw some sweet potato fries into a to-go container, grabbed a premade meatball sub, swiped his ID card, and continued his trek to his RV.

As excited as his mother had been about the scholarship program, she'd also been realistic, knowing that Kronos could come back and say at any point that it hadn't gotten approved. Kris took it upon himself to read through the contract, having been an environmental lawyer just a few years back before he retired. He solemnly informed his sister and nephew that if that was the case, the entire contract was null and void.

And even if it were approved, there was still the matter of the student loans for the first two years. Olympia College required freshman and sophomore students to live on campus, but after that, they were free to move into any housing they chose. Leticia had made it clear that she did not want Kai to even apply to be a resident advisor.

"It would be a great opportunity for you, but you need to make sure your grades stay up, so if this does all work out, Mr. Kronos will pay back those loans, and you don't have to worry about them, baby."

Again, he couldn't argue with her.

Which was exactly when Kris had stepped in and offered for Kai to use his old RV. He was immediately on board—until the question of where he was going to park it arose.

The former head of maintenance at one of the state universities a few cities away, Mr. Caffrey, had apparently gotten into a pretty big workers comp deal years ago, and Kris had handled his case and won the man a few thousand dollars. Which might not seem like a lot, but he was able to retire and keep his pension and his timeshare in Palm Beach. He had been over the moon when Kris called him up and was more than willing to let his nephew park the RV in his driveway. There was no rent or lot fee to pay and no contract to sign, surprisingly, considering his uncle had orchestrated the whole thing. All Kai had to do was mow the grass and water his plants once a week and occasionally feed his cat when he went out of town.

He had all the privacy he wanted, and Mr. Caffrey never mentioned the smell of marijuana coming from the little vented windows of the Airstream.

He hadn't realized how zoned out he was until the chime of his phone brought his focus back.

Amber: I didn't know you were in the program.

Kai: Really? Kronos told me you were

Amber: When did you speak to him?

Kai: We didn't actually talk, it was just in an email

Did he have a hopeless crush on Amber? Yes.

Did he feel comfortable telling her that he'd known about this whole thing for the past three years? Not at all.

Amber: Huh, that's strange…

Kai: Yeah

Kai: Yours was the only name he told me though. He said two of them were grad students, and two were incoming freshmen

Amber: Wonder why he didn't share that with me…

Kai: Idk

Amber: Well, anyway I'm glad I recognized at least one person.

Kai: Me too

Amber: Having you there will make it a little more tolerable.

Amber: So, thanks.

Kai: You're welcome

Why is she so weird?

Like, she always does this.

She says things like she's glad to have me there, but I guarantee the next time we see each other, she won't even talk to me.

And then she'll text me and tell me she's sorry she's being weird and that she does want to spend time with me, but her schedule is weird because of her classes and because she drives to Chucktown every weekend.

So, we'll just keep texting.

And things will seem like they're going somewhere ... until she makes it clear that they're not.

And then a few awkward weeks or even months will go by until it happens again.

I just need to ask her out. Something she can't say no to. And we just need to talk. Because I think—no, I know—that if I can get her to just let her guard down for, like, a minute, she'll see that this will work. And it'll be good.

Fuck, it'll be so, so good.

But who knows when that'll be? Because now, I have to worry about cameras being around. Maybe. I don't know. No one's gonna watch this stupid thing anyway. What kind of name is The Olympians? *Like, that's our fucking mascot. Stupid.*

Kai unlocked his door and swung it open. He stretched his long legs out on the small couch that was crammed into the space and opened a beer. Every once in a while, Mr. Caffrey would leave a twelve-pack on the counter for Kai. "I never did this," he would grumble before retreating to his living room to watch reruns of The Love Boat.

His phone buzzed again.

Unknown Number: What are you doing rn?

It was a girl he had met last semester. She would come over once or twice a week, and they'd get naked.

Kai would rather have Amber ... but she didn't want that.

Kai: Come over

Just because he couldn't be with the girl he wanted to be with didn't mean he shouldn't be with anyone. At least for a little while.

Chapter 3

HANNA JUNE

Hanna June did all she could to not skip out of the meeting. How many college freshmen got their dream sorority bid *and* aced their first reality show interview in the same week?

She grabbed Zach's hand as they left the Student Center and headed back to their dorms. She'd wanted them to be in the same building—that way, it would be easier for one of them to stay the night. But when the residence assignment bids had opened earlier that year, she was in cheer practice, and by the time she had gotten out, the closest she could get was the next building over.

Junior year, we'll be allowed to move off campus, and we can finally live together.

Some of her new sisters gave her an excited, "Hi!" or an enthusiastic wave as they crossed paths.

Greek life was something that both she and Zach had planned on being involved in, even before they applied to college. It played a big part in why they only applied to schools down South. Zach had briefly tried to convince her of applying to Penn State, but she had reminded him of the brutal winters up there, and it had quickly been taken off the table.

Did she want to go to a bigger school? Absolutely. But were there any other colleges offering to make her a TV star? Scratch that.

Were there any other colleges offering to make anyone a TV star? No. The choice had been obvious, and Zach felt the same way.

The two of them had been the last to leave, having been told by Rhianne before the interviews started that Kronos wanted to speak directly with them together.

"Now, I don't want the others knowing I'm telling you this. Something tells me they'd be okay with it if they found out, but it's the principle of the whole thing. Understand?"

She and Zach eagerly nodded along. The other four didn't seem to really want to be in the spotlight at all. Which worked out for them because they weren't really into the idea of sharing it.

"You two are going to be my stars. Yes, it's an ensemble cast if you really want to put a label on it. We're making a reality show here. You watch reality TV, don't you?" He didn't pause to let them answer. "Think about *Keeping Up with the Kardashians*. There's no star of that show. They all share the spotlight because that's how they want it to be. They take turns being the subject of an episode or two, but ultimately, they need the whole group of them to make it the phenomenon that it is. But *you two* …"

The look he gave them was that of a proud parent. A look Zach had never been given by either of his parents and Hanna June had only seen twice—the first when their families saw her and her future husband together for the first time, and the second when they placed the crown on her head as she won Miss Maryland Teen. Actual tears had run down her mother's face. It was an image she'd never forget.

"You two are my headliners. That's the best way to think about it. The other four are your opening act. You can go on without them, but they won't succeed without you."

Thinking about it now made the grin on her face stretch as far as it could across her round face.

"You seem happy," Zach offered, not looking up from his phone.

He doesn't even have to look at me to sense my mood. I freaking love him.

"I *am* happy," she agreed, leaning toward him.

He pulled his phone close to his chest for a second before clicking it off and shoving it in his pocket. Then, he turned to her and matched her smile. "I'm happy too."

As they crossed campus and headed back to their adjacent residence halls, she caught him staring at a group of girls near the small, domed structure.

"What are you looking at?" She tried to sound curious, not jealous and not at all paranoid.

"The thing right there," he responded smoothly, pointing at the open complex.

"The cupola?"

"I guess so," he answered, but didn't sound too sure of it.

"Didn't you listen to Shelby at all during our orientation? She was very thorough with her tour."

"HJ, I was busy networking—you know that." His tone was belittling and annoying … but she did know better.

He'd always been a social person, and after all the people who'd ridiculed him and his family back home for the way they were in the political spotlight, he deserved to be able to have genuine conversations with people who actually wanted to get to know him.

Just not with the girls.

"I know; I know." She brushed it off. Pointing to the gazebo-style architecture that lay almost directly in the center of campus, she informed him, "That's the cupola. Well, it's a replica of the original."

"What happened to the first one?"

"Okay, well, this campus used to be a boardin' school."

"It did?"

"You really didn't listen at *all?*"

He gave a hopeless shrug, and the sun seemed to glint off his eyes. *His eyes.* The bluest blue you'd ever seen.

"It was an all-boys boardin' school. I think it opened in, like, 1910 or 'round then …"

"Huh," he replied as he watched a group of guys with Greek letters printed across their shirts walk by.

She kept talking. "Well, the original cupola structure used to be on top of the administration building at the boardin' school, but there was this crazy hurricane one summer in … I think it was the '70s. Maybe the '80s? I don't know. Anyway, the thing was knocked off where it had been cemented to the roof."

He jolted around to look at her, those icy-blue eyes making her feel like she'd been swallowed up. Six years they'd been together, and she still got butterflies.

"Shit, are you serious?"

"Yes!"

"Damn. Now, I wish I had listened."

"See?" She gently nudged him with her bony elbow. "Anyway, it broke into pieces, and they had to get rid of it. But this was what made them change it into a private college. So, they decided that they should have some way of rememberin' the school, so the Board of Trustees for Olympia reached out to some of the boardin' school alumni that were still around and told them what they were plannin', and they donated enough money to make a replica."

"Huh, that's pretty cool."

"Yeah." She smiled as he agreed with her, silently thanking him for not ridiculing her storytelling. She knew she talked a lot, and he used to remind her constantly when they had been younger. Either he didn't care about it anymore or he'd just gotten used to it. She told herself it was the latter.

Then, she remembered she'd forgotten something—the one thing she remembered every time she walked past it. "But you know the thing with it, right? Like, the curse?"

His light eyebrows knit together in judgment and confusion, and he sounded already bored with what she hadn't yet informed him of. "What curse, Hanna June?"

"If you walk under it, you won't graduate in four years." She could feel how big her already-dominating eyes were as she warned him.

They had reached her dorm room now. She hoped her roommate wasn't there as she turned the key.

Empty.

"That's such bullshit." He dropped his backpack to the linoleum floor and sprawled out on her comforter.

"Zachary, don't you dare even think about walkin' under it!" She hated being serious with him because it usually ended up in an argument—with her apologizing—but this could affect their future.

Maybe it was a silly myth, maybe not, but there was absolutely nothing that was going to get in the way of their plan. They were going to graduate in four years and get married right after. They'd stay together as he went to flight school and she went on to get her graduate degree even if it meant doing all her classes online just so she could be with him. After they both graduated, their parents had promised to jointly buy them a house, and then they'd start a family. That had always been the plan, and so far, things had worked out. And she'd make sure they continued to.

"I wasn't, baby! I was just joking. Look, I'm sorry." He coaxed her down next to him. "I was just trying to have some fun. I didn't mean to get you all wound up. I know you've got a lot going on." His voice had turned suddenly, and it was now so soothing to her.

She toyed with the collar of his seersucker button-down. "I should be able to tell when you're jokin' by now. I'm sorry."

"It's okay."

God, I'm so lucky. I would be a total train wreck without him.

The whole thing had been their parents' idea. Right before Zach's little sister was born, it had come out that his father had had multiple affairs. He was in politics, so it wasn't a huge surprise. Still, they were coming up on an election year, and he wasn't showing as well in the polls as he had been projected to. So, a deal was formed between Richard's "people" and Hanna June's father, Duke. His father had recently passed, leaving their growing media conglomerate, Pruitt Media, in inexperienced hands. He'd made some risky financial decisions, and it just might have cost him the company if Richard's campaign manager hadn't proposed the exchange. Pruitt Media became Richard Alexander supporters and was rewarded handsomely for doing so, and in return, Pruitt Media received the backing it needed to turn their red into black and eventually take over most of the southeast.

In order to ensure these services continued in later years and to draw some good attention their way, the two men and their wives proposed the idea of a union between their children.

Right before her family had made the move from Jackson to Charlotte so her father could run the company better, their families had gone on a vacation together to Hilton Head Island, where they sat the two five-year-olds down and told them what the expectation was from them as they got older. HJ clearly remembered how they'd dressed up the arrangement when they explained it to her, saying that she was like a princess who was betrothed to her prince.

That night, the two of them lay on their backs, side by side, in a huge pop-up tent on the beach while their parents drank wine around a bonfire a few feet away.

Zach turned to her and said, "So, you know we gotta marry each other, right?"

A tiny smile crept across her face. "I know." Her accent was so thick back then. She had to work to dial it back after they moved to DC a few years after that.

He gave her a small nod while looking down at the tie-dye towel underneath him. "I'm really glad it's you."

At that, her smile faded, and an embarrassed sort of panic set in. "You are? Why?" She had paused in between the two sentences.

"You're the prettiest girl I've ever met. And you're really smart. You kind of remind me of a grown-up."

She did all she could to keep her adultlike demeanor he was now praising her for in check when she wanted to jump around, giddy with excitement and love.

"Thanks. I'm glad I get to marry you too. All the other boys are gross and mean."

"I'll never be mean to you," he reassured her before he leaned in closer and met her lips with his.

It had been an awkward, sweet first kiss the two of them shared at just five years old. Neither of them had been embarrassed though because they knew they would have plenty of time to get it right.

Now, she looked at him next to her. He was so handsome, and he could make her laugh. He knew her inside out, better than anyone else in the world. They'd been together practically their entire lives. There were girls out there who were considered lucky if they married their high school sweetheart. But she got to marry her kindergarten boyfriend, so what did that make her?

Girls wanted to be her—that was something she'd just gotten used to. Boys wanted her, but no one aside from him got to have her.

She had aced recruitment and was the first PNM to get a bid from Eta Rho Alpha, and somehow, on top of all the good things thrown her way, she also got to be the star of a reality TV show. How many girls got to go to school with the love of their life, have amazing sisters as a support group, do interviews in between classes, and have cameras follow them around?

Everything was so, so perfect.

Chapter 4

Solo interview with Zach.

Kronos: Zachary Alexander.

Zach: Dwayne Kronos.

Kronos: [*laughs*] Ready to get started?

Zach: That's why I'm here.

Kronos: [*nods slowly*] What do you think of your costars so far?

Zach: Amber seems chill. Kinda introverted but hot. [*pauses, then speaks rushed*] Obviously not hotter than HJ though. [*clears throat*] I don't really know about Dawn. She's a lot older than us.

Kronos: And what about the other young men?

Zach: [*awkward silence, shifts uncomfortably*] Kai is, like … he's cool, I guess. And Damon is … quiet.

Kronos: Do you feel uncomfortable, talking about them?

Zach: Yeah …

Kronos: Why is that?

Zach: 'Cause, ya know … they're my brothers. Well, half-brothers. We all have the same dad.

Kronos: Mmhmm. You don't have much of a relationship with them?

Zach: I mean, I knew *about* them, growing up, but I didn't actually know them. Used to hear my parents arguing about them sometimes.

Kronos: Do you think that put a strain on your childhood?

Zach: Nah. I mean, I don't think so. I had a pretty kick-ass childhood. Went on a lot of vacations, always had the newest things, got to do whatever the fuck I wanted. Oh shit, wait. *Shit.* I'm not allowed to curse, am I?

Kronos: [*chuckles*] We can just bleep you out.

Zach: Okay. Good, good.

Zach: I mean, I've had a great life so far. But, like, it was weird. I had two brothers that I never knew. And now, I'm forced to be around them all the time. Yeah, we have the same dad, but they're basically strangers, and I don't know if I should act the same way around them as I do with Grain Brain and Dawn or not.

Kronos: I'm sorry. Did you just refer to Miss Hargrove as Grain Brain?

Zach: Yeah.

Kronos: Can I ask why?

Zach: [*shrugs*] Everyone needs a nickname.

Kronos: And who came up with that one?

Zach: Me.

Kronos: [*nods, smiling*] That's perfect.

Zach: [*raises eyebrows at his reaction*]

Kronos: So, tell me, all feelings aside—what do you really think of Mr. Newport and Mr. Montclaire? Act as though you're not related and this program is the first time you've ever interacted with them.

Zach: [*pauses, thinking, looks directly into the camera skeptically*] I think Kai is kind of a wuss. Ya know, like, he's totally hung up on Amber, and it's so obvious. You can smell the desperation wafting off of him. And Damon is just stuck in his ninth-grade emo phase. Bro, wear a color other than fucking black. Talk to people other than Sutherland. There're a few thousand other kids here. And maybe smile once in a while. Like, shit, he always looks like he's about to commit murder.

Kronos: Interesting observations.

Zach: [*leans back in chair, puts hands up, as if to prove he's innocent*] That's my honest takeaway, all feelings aside.

Kronos: [*nodding*] Do you like being away at school?

Zach: [*pauses to think about it*] Yeah. But honestly, it's not *that* different.

Kronos: Can you explain what you mean by that?

Zach: Kinda like … well, I'm seeing a lot of people I went to school with, like, on Insta and Snap and shit, who have this, like, newfound freedom away at school. But to be honest, I've always had that. I drank with my parents at the dinner table, I smoked weed at house parties that I was allowed to throw, I fucked my girlfriend while they were home.

Zach: It's really not any different, except that, now, I have to do my own laundry.

Kronos: Do you think you had a more privileged life, growing up?

Zach: Oh, absolutely, like, no question about it. But, like, I wasn't a dick about it. Didn't go around, throwing it in people's faces. Like, I went to public school, ya know?

Kronos: [*nodding*] Mmhmm. So, if given the opportunity, would you move back to the DC area and go to school there?

Zach: [*leans back in his chair, puts his hands behind his head*] Hell no.

Kronos: Why do you say that?

Zach: [*pauses*] I wanted to be in a place where I could meet new people.

Kronos: Well, that could be anywhere outside of your hometown. Why did you choose Olympia College?

Zach: [*clears throat, leans forward, and rests elbows on knees*] So, uhh, part of the deal between our parents is that HJ and I had to go to the same college. We both knew that we wanted to study, but we both kinda had different ideas of what kind of college we wanted to go to. Like, she wanted to stay in the South, but I wanted to go at least four hours away. I was mainly looking at schools in New York City and LA—you know, bigger cities. Embry-Riddle was my first choice, but I didn't get in.

Zach: We both got in here, UCF, Clemson, and Baylor. But we chose Olympia because of the scholarship program. It's also the closest to the beach and to home though, so that was a plus. And then she made the dance team here, too, so it was kinda like *duh*.

Kronos: Most couples don't go to the same college. Why did you two have to?

Zach: It was part of the agreement.

Kronos: What agreement?

Zach: [*leaning forward, confused*] Kronos, you know about it.

Kronos: [*mimicking his gestures*] Yes, Mr. Alexander, I do, but the people who will be watching this do not. So, if you could elaborate …

Zach: [*clears throat, sits back up, slightly embarrassed but trying to hide it*] Oh, yeah, sure. Uh, so, basically, we're getting married. Our parents decided on it when we were, like, four or five. They told us about it, but ya know, we were kids, so it didn't really sink in until years later.

Zach: So, anyway, her family moved up from Charlotte to DC, so we could actually grow up together and spend time with each other. That was when we were … uh, I think we were twelve. She started going to school with me and … well, now, we're here.

Kronos: And do you think you made the right choice, coming to Olympia?

Zach: [*smirks*] I think if I had gone to another school, I wouldn't be on TV. So, you tell me.

Chapter 5

DAWN

IT'S SO MUCH LOUDER NOW, Dawn thought as she crossed the street with her Shetland sheepdog, Nora.

Classes had started a few days earlier, and her quiet hometown had once again turned into party central. Well, a very small, secluded party central.

She pushed open the door to Ground Floor and saw Damon seated at the back corner table, running a highlighter through lines of whatever book he'd decided to mark up today. Nora held her mouth open while Dawn folded up the leash, placed it in her mouth, and watched her pup trot on over to her obnoxiously tall friend. She watched him gently take it from her without tearing his gaze away from his novel. Dawn sauntered up to the counter to order a large black coffee and waited off to the side for her name to be called.

"Excuse me?"

Dawn turned around to see a young man—probably about her age, maybe older. Dawn knew from the cover design that he was holding the same textbook she used on Tuesday and Thursday mornings.

Dawn said nothing but raised her eyebrows in question.

"Hi, you—umm, you're in my City Planning course, right? With Delgado?"

She nodded slowly, chiming in, "Yeah, I think so." She honestly didn't recognize him, but classes had only just started, and it was a fairly big lecture hall.

"I sit, like, two rows behind you. I'm Derek." He stuck his hand out, and Dawn gently shook it. "I know we don't really know each other ..." he continued on.

Dawn knew where he was going with this, and the answer would be no—as always. But she lifted her eyebrows as an invitation for him to continue.

"Would you wanna go out sometime? Doesn't have to be anything big. We could just get coffee or something ..."

She looked him up and down. He definitely *was* cute in his shorts and pale-yellow shirt. But she had sworn off dating until she had a stable career. That was the thing college kids got so hung up on— finding the right person and the right friends instead of the right career path. Guys and girls would keep coming, but your dream job? That was something that required focus and dedication and good grades and perfect interviews and portfolios—all of which Dawn had plenty of. Her soul mate would be waiting for her once she did what she could to help as many people as she was able to.

Besides, if her career plan fell into place, she'd be helping out a lot more people who actually needed it rather than just having someone's hand to hold. That idea was much more appealing to her anyway. She had a very specific plan, and she would do everything to make sure it happened.

"I'm sorry, but I'm actually not available." She gestured to Damon at the back table, lost in his book.

Derek shifted from his right foot to his left, just as the barista called out Dawn's name for her order. She ripped off the tops of all six sugar packets in her hand in one fluid motion and dropped their contents in.

Derek raised his eyebrows as he watched her, waiting a beat before saying, "My bad. He's a lucky guy." He started to back away but turned back to Dawn and handed her a business card. "If things go south or if you change your mind, give me a call." He held his eye contact with her at the last part of his proposal before leaving the café.

Dawn shuffled back to the table.

"I hope you didn't tell that guy that I was your boyfriend," Damon said without looking up from his book.

Dawn sank down into her seat. "I did. Didn't think you'd have a problem with it. We've both done that before ..." Her thoughts trailed off.

"We have. With miserable prospects. *He* seemed like he's past his kegger days though. Why did you reject him?"

Dawn narrowed her eyes at him. "I have a plan, Damon. You know that." She glanced at the café door before adding, "No matter how cute and smart he is."

"Smart? Do you know him?" Damon slowly shut his book, his interest piqued.

"He's in my Advanced City Planning course. He's really good with numbers. Like, even Delgado was impressed with how fast he was computing some of the scenarios he randomly threw at us yesterday."

Dawn toyed with the card in her hands. She finally read it, "Derek Clemente, Junior Historic Preservation Planner, City of Olympia." *He works for the city? That could be helpful. Maybe I should call him ...*

"I think you should at least give him a chance." Damon saw her get lost in her thoughts. "I know you're not going to listen to me though. Hell, I wouldn't even listen to myself. But maybe ... think about it. Nobody *really* wants to be alone."

"I don't want to *be* alone, Damon. I just need to stay focused while I get myself where I want to be. And anyway, who are you to talk? You haven't dated anyone since, like, your senior year of high school."

"Dawn, we've gone over this. I don't have time."

"You'd probably loosen up a little if you got laid ..." She mumbled the words into her coffee, not wanting him to hear it, but also *wanting* him to hear it. He had said similar words to her not two weeks earlier.

He just narrowed his dark eyes at her across the table. "Dawn, that is not a conversation you and I are going to have again."

"Yeah, yeah, yeah. I know the speech." Dawn took a sip of her coffee. It was still not sweet enough for her. She walked back up to the counter to pluck three more packets from the plastic container.

Sometimes, he scared her. Which was actually pretty impressive, considering most people on campus easily made way for him when they saw his long legs headed in their direction. He was just one of those people who had this presence about him that screamed *terrifying.* Maybe even deadly.

Although, truth be told, Dawn knew Damon had killed people before. One autumn night last year, they had been at Damon's apartment, drinking together. They had only just met a few months prior, but they had immediately hit it off. Dawn had never made a friend so easily in her four years at Olympia, and she had a feeling Damon had gone through a similar thing during his undergrad in Connecticut.

That night, they had both done way too many vodka shots, and they ended up on the roof of the building. He was always so stoic and harsh, and the few times he did joke around, it was all sarcastic. She had never seen him loosen up the way he did, and she figured she likely never would again, so she might have encouraged it a little.

Stumbling around on the massive concrete slab nine stories above the tiny city of Olympia, he told her about his childhood and compared himself to Annie—how both of them had never really known either of their parents and gone on to get adopted by rich families from New York. He sang a verse or two from "Tomorrow"—terribly off-key—and then slumped down next to her, laughing.

Dawn remembered watching him look out toward the buildings in the distance as his smile slowly faded and said, "I had it worse than that redhead did though."

"What do you mean?" She gave a hopeful laugh, praying the conversation wouldn't turn south.

She was wrong.

"Annie was orphaned. Her parents just gave her up. Maybe they realized they couldn't take care of her, or maybe they just didn't want to. Doesn't really matter though. She never got to know them."

Then, he turned and looked at her, and for the first time in their friendship, his eyes were devoid of any color.

"I knew mine. And I loved them. And they loved me. And then someone took them from me. Right in front of me."

Dawn gulped down hard even though her mouth was completely dry. Up until that point, she had always known his parents had been killed—it had been national news at the time, and although she was little then, she had immediately placed him during their first day in their Intro to OC course.

She couldn't think of anything to say. How was anyone supposed to respond to something like that?

Lucky for her, he kept the conversation going. Well, maybe *lucky* wasn't the right word …

"I'm gonna find him, you know." He picked up the bottle of bourbon he had brought up to the roof. A gift from his uncle for getting into college, which he had been planning on saving until he graduated. So much for that. "I'm gonna find him, and I'm gonna kill him. I'm gonna make him wish he had killed me that night too."

Dawn's nerves kicked in at that moment. Feeling both nervous and uncomfortable at his calm demeanor and the information he had just shared, she stupidly asked, "How do you plan on getting away with murder?"

"Easily. I haven't been caught any of the other seventeen times I've done it."

He sloshed the brown liquid around in the bottle and took another swig before standing up and announcing he had to take a piss.

About five steps behind—somewhat because of his extremely long legs, but mostly because of what he had just told her—she followed him down a few flights of stairs and into his apartment. After exiting the bathroom, he announced that he was going to go to sleep and invited her to crash on the couch.

She hadn't.

The conversation was never brought up again, nor was anything else about that night, by either of them. Honestly, Dawn wasn't sure if he had still been drunk when he shared that. A small part of her hoped that he had been, but the larger, much more rational part— the pieces of her that could read people—told her that he had never said anything more truthful in his life.

Chapter 6

Kronos: So … can any of you guess why I grouped the three of you together?

Zach: Uh, we're all guys?

Damon: [*annoyed*] We all share a biological father.

Kronos: Correct, Mr. Montclaire. Same dad, different moms. [*turns to Zach*] But he lives with your family, correct, Mr. Alexander?

Zach: Yeah.

Kronos: Are you all close in age?

Zach: Damon is way older, but [*turns to Kai*] I think we're, like, a year and a half apart?

Kronos: Kai, does that sound correct?

Kai: [*stoned out of his mind*] I'm not gonna lie. I'm really high right now.

Kronos: [*amused*] Did you feel like you had to get high for this interview?

Kai: Uh, yeah.

Kronos: Why is that?

Kai: I mean, you told us we were going to be the first group interview, so it was kind of a no-brainer that the topic would be our dad. Why would I wanna sit here and talk about the guy who left me and my mom on our own and then went back to his family?

Kronos: So, it bothers you that you grew up without a dad?

Kai: I'm not a fucking robot.

Kronos: No, no, of course not. But you're just saying that you're upset by his actions?

Kai: Of course I'm upset by his actions. He's on a campaign tour around the state and meets my mom. They sleep together, she gets pregnant with me, he's on the other side of the state and tells her to figure it out. Then goes back to his wife and gets her pregnant a few months after I'm born and goes on to win his election. Bad people don't deserve good things, and good people don't deserve bad things.

Zach: My dad isn't a bad person, and—

Kai: He's *our* dad—all three of us. He didn't even want to claim Damon until he was, like, five, but by that time, he had fucked up so badly that a judge wouldn't even allow him to be in his life. And he never once paid child support. But did he ever do jail time? No, because he's above it, just like he's above everything else. Just like he's instilled in his son, who's grown up to be a preppy-ass bitch—

Zach: [*swings a punch, throwing Kai off his chair*]

Kai: [*gets up, nose bleeding*] What the fuck?

Zach: Don't call me that again. [*checks the collar of his shirt to see blood on it*]

Kai: [*swings a punch, knocks Zach to the ground*] Man, fuck you. [*rips off mic, leaves*]

Damon: I told you this was a bad idea, Kronos. [*gets up*]

Kronos: Not exactly the term *I* would use for how these two minutes played out.

Zach: Is anyone gonna help me up?

Damon: No. [*walks out behind Kai*]

Chapter 7

AMBER

Her plants were overtaking pretty much her entire balcony, so it was a good thing she lived alone.

Not that she liked to be alone, although she had to admit, it was better than living with strangers. If she had things her way though, she'd still be living at home with her father and sister.

Back at home, Amber had played a huge part in raising Fleur after her mom died. She had come from foster care, having been in really terrible living conditions and constantly bounced around since age four. Amber's mom had been a teacher and worked extremely hard to both reteach her everything she already knew, but also to get her caught up in school once her adoption went through. When she passed, Amber had seamlessly taken over all her responsibilities.

If it hadn't been for her phone buzzing in her pocket, she would've gotten lost in her own memories of holidays and family dinners.

It was Hanna June, texting her for the fourth time in a row. She was adamantly trying to organize a dinner party for the six of them to informally get to know each other "without all the cameras and weird pressure from Kronos," as she put it. She wanted to be the hostess but had nowhere to invite everyone over to since she was in a dorm.

As much as she didn't want to be a part of the whole program, she really could use a distraction.

Amber: Can you find out if Thursday is good for everyone?

HJ: Zach and I are good, and I'll find out from Dawn about her and Damon. Can you text Kai? I don't have his number

Amber: Yeah, I can text him

She did *not* want to text Kai.

She got so nervous every time they talked, whether it was in person or through a text. She even got jittery when she saw him on Facebook.

Did she like talking to him? Absolutely. But should she be talking to him? No.

Boys were nothing but a distraction. Amber's only job was to graduate in two years, so she could move back home.

She could get a job with her dad's company easily, and although some people hated the idea of going into their family business, she loved it. It was perfect. She would get to live at home so she could be there for Fleur, and most of the position her father had been pitching to her for the last two years was a remote job. There was the occasional trip somewhere out west to visit properties and meet with partners, but that would take care of the travel bug she had. She desperately wanted to visit South America and parts of Europe, but she knew that it just wasn't realistic.

If she stayed on track, she'd be graduating in four semesters and then moving back home—and that was the main goal.

Not boys and definitely not traveling.

He's a distraction, Amber, she told herself as she pulled up a new message with him. She never saved the old ones anymore. She had realized one day last spring that she would spend an ungodly amount of time staring at them, waiting for something new to pop up after giving him short answers and trying to end the conversation without actually stopping it.

God, I'm a pain.

Amber: Hey.

Kai: Hey

Amber: HJ wants the six of us to have a dinner party-like without the cameras. She asked me to text you. Are you free Thursday night?

Kai: Yeah, that sounds good

Amber: Okay, cool. I'll let her know.

Kai: Where is it gonna be?

Amber: My place.

Kai: Oh

Kai: Okay cool

Amber: Is that okay?

Kai: Yeah

Amber erased the message thread, put her phone in her room, and left it there.

Thursday night, Hanna June had taken over her kitchen. On her stove was the tallest pot Amber had ever seen, bubbling with pasta inside. There were two long loaves of rosemary and olive oil ciabatta bread toasting on the counter behind them.

Even though Amber had insisted she was rather capable in her own kitchen, Hanna June had only delegated her to making the largest salad Amber had ever assembled. *There's only six of us, not sixteen,* she thought as she chopped up cucumbers.

HJ had also brought over several bottles of wine, and Amber had taken the liberty of breaking open a cheap looking Pinot Grigio. She had emptied half of it when there was a knock on her door.

"That's probably Zach," Hanna June said as she left the kitchen.

Amber glared after her. *Glad she's comfortable answering my door,* she thought as she sipped her wine.

A moment later, Hanna June quietly returned with Kai in tow. Amber downed the rest of her wine and quickly refilled her glass.

Kai awkwardly gestured a flower in her direction. "I brought you a dahlia. I know poppies are your favorite, but they're not in season, so … here."

Amber's heart momentarily swelled inside her chest. She had told him once, a year ago, that they were her favorite, but she hadn't thought he had remembered.

She put her wine down and reached for the plant, murmuring, "Thanks," to him. He was tall—not nearly as tall as his older half-brother, but still fairly tall. And his eyes? Oh, they were the deepest blue Amber had ever seen on a human. She felt like if she fell into them, she simply wouldn't stop.

There was another knock on the door. Hanna June nearly dropped the wooden spoon before running to the door.

Kai watched her leave before turning to Amber. "She's answering your door?"

Amber shrugged and picked up her wine again.

Hanna June returned with another disappointed look on her face, followed by Dawn and a pissed off-looking Damon, who was balancing a coffee cake on his fingertips. Dawn set her massive bowl of fruit on the countertop and stood next to Hanna June to ask if she needed any help. Damon sat down quietly at the table and poured himself a glass of red wine.

A few quiet moments went by before Amber's front door flew open for a third and final time, and in Zach stumbled. "Hanna June!" he yelled as he moved through Amber's small living room and dining area and into her kitchen.

HJ stayed in front of the stove, angrily stirring her spaghetti.

That must be finished cooking by now, Amber grumbled to herself.

Zach came up right behind her and wrapped his arms around her waist. Her mouth stayed in a thin line, and she refused to look at him.

"Hanna Juuuune," he whined, thrusting his hips against hers. "June Buuuug. Baby, baby, listen. I know I'm late. I know. But listen. Shh, shh. Listen. I got here as fast as I could. I really—I really did. I love you. I couldn't wait to see you, and—look! Here you are, and oh my God, you look sooo hot. I missed you so much, and I'm here now. I love you, baby. I love you so much, HJ."

Most of his words were slurred, and Amber could smell the alcohol wafting off of him from three feet away. She could see Damon wrinkle his nose in disgust, assuming he was picking up the scent rolling off his youngest half-brother too.

Amber turned back to the couple in front of her stove to see him grinding against her. "In my kitchen? Seriously?"

Zach backed up from his girlfriend. "Sorry, sorry, Amber *Hargrove*. See? I remembered your last name. 'Cause that's how *Mr. Kronos* insists on referring to us all like. And let's see. Let's see. Okay … you're an enviro major, women's studies minor, which I'm pretty sure is supposed to be just for lesbians and you just don't give me *that vibe*. And you're, like, weirdly obsessed with your family. See? I remembered!" He looked back and forth between Amber and Hanna June, like a proud four-year-old.

HJ scrunched up her nose as she looked at her so-called beloved. "You're sloshed right now, so you don't even know that what you just said was *so* insulting. You owe Amber an apology." She poked at his chest with the end of the spoon.

"For what? I'm jus' speakin' the truth!"

"Actually"—Dawn stepped over and placed a gentle hand on Zach's back—"Hanna June is right. Amber might have taken the words you said in a different way than how you meant it."

Zach slowly looked up at her face as she politely explained while his girlfriend picked up a glass of wine and took a long sip from it.

"You should also remember that Amber has graciously invited us all into her home."

A beat passed before Zach's gaze moved above her hairline, and he said, "How do you get your hair to be so coily like that?"

Hanna June rolled her eyes and turned her back to them, finally draining the pasta before taking another long drink.

"I think you should apologize to Amber, Zach." Dawn tried one more time, walking him into the living room, a glass of water in her hand that Kai had silently filled for her to give to him.

Amber didn't care though. It was more annoying than anything at this point, and even if he did apologize, she knew that he wouldn't mean it.

Damon refilled her wineglass and then his own. He seemed to be drinking faster than she was.

Kai sat down in between them, his tumbler sloshing lightly with some sort of brown liquid. "Well, this is definitely more interesting than I thought it would be."

"Wish I didn't have to see him grinding against his girlfriend in my kitchen," Amber grumbled into her drink.

Kai turned to look back at HJ, who was quietly washing the pot she'd finished using as the rest of the food sat ready on the countertop. Her phone kept buzzing, as texts arrived. Amber figured it was her sorority sisters.

They could hear Dawn talking to Zach, having completely changed the topic now. "You know, I could totally be a weatherman," he was all but shouting from the couch.

"Wow, she's a saint. I could never willingly do that," Amber said, watching Dawn intently listen to what the drunk eighteen-year-old was saying.

"She's the best person." Damon finally spoke.

"And you're not together?" Kai questioned him. Amber had been wondering the same thing, but she definitely wasn't about to ask him. Damon was pretty intimidating with his black eyes and sharp features. His moves were all very stealth-like, as if he were ready to jump into action any second.

Damon let out an annoyed sigh. "We are not, never have been, and never will be."

Kai nodded silently, the look on his face indicating that he didn't have anything else to say on the topic.

Damon suddenly pulled his phone out of his pants pocket, glanced at the screen, and turned to Amber.

"Amber, I have to take this. Is there somewhere quiet I can go?"

"Oh, yeah, sure. Balcony is right off the living room, or you can use my room. It's the door all the way at the end of the hallway."

Chapter 8

DAMON

HE DIDN'T BOTHER TO FLICK the light on in Amber's bedroom. He could make out most of the shapes—the bed, nightstand, desk, dresser. A chair in the corner with a pile of clothes on it. Lights dangling around the border of each wall. Pictures collaged on the wall. Plants *everywhere*.

He had always liked plants but could never seem to keep any alive. Even cacti shriveled up at his sight.

He slid the bar on his phone to answer Paulina's call. "Yes?"

"Damon, darling, I'm sorry to disturb you, but there's a conversation the three of us need to have, and it just can't wait any longer."

He assumed David was sitting next to his mom, although he failed to indicate his presence.

"Is someone dying?"

"Dear God, no! This is about you—your education and your future!"

Damon rolled his eyes, thankful she couldn't see him. The woman had brought so many blessings into his life after he lost quite literally everything, but sometimes, she was just so overdramatic.

The sigh that slipped out of his mouth was louder than intended. "I honestly don't know what you're talking about. I'm doing everything I'm supposed to. I'm going to graduate magna cum laude in four months with my master's degree, and there's no reason why I shouldn't be accepted for my doctorate, *Mom*." She knew that he never called either of his parents by their title unless it was sarcastic.

"Sweetheart, we worry about you. We just …" She let out a big sigh that Damon could practically feel through the phone. "We worry you won't be happy with where your degree takes you."

He knew exactly what she meant, even without her saying it. Knowing she *couldn't* say anything and that, surely, a trip back home would be organized before they hung up.

"Well, if that turns out to be the case, then you and I—and David—know that I'll be welcomed back to the family business with open arms." He briefly wondered if they could sense his sarcasm but then realized he didn't actually care.

They all knew his standpoint on the situation, and even though the Montclaire family had been killing people for hire since the 1940s, he had made it a point early on to remind Paulina and David that he was only a part of their family because of some papers.

They had used that as fuel against him, as a child, saying that he should feel angry with the man who had taken his parents away from him in cold blood, right in front of his five-year-old eyes. He should use that anger and that hurt and channel it and someday hunt him down and take his own life.

And Damon planned to do all that. But he was going to do it on his terms—not because it was some fucked up multigenerational career that his adoptive parents had thrust into his unwilling hands.

The agreement they had landed on when he first got accepted to Olympia College was that he would complete the necessary degrees for his intended career and then return home for a year to work for the Montclaires before ultimately making the decision on whether to use his degree or become a paid assassin, like his non-biological uncle, his father, and his father before that.

But the fact that it was being brought up again when he was halfway done with his schooling, and by the tone in his mother's voice … well, he didn't think it meant anything good.

"Damon, dear, we have no problem paying for your education even if you don't end up using your degrees—you know that. Hell, you know my bachelor's in nursing sits on the wall in my office, just collecting dust!"

Except for all the times you've had to patch Ernesto back together when he came home from a job after things took an unlikely turn.

What does Paulina even need an office for?

Thank God David didn't follow in his father's footsteps. He's the clumsiest man I've ever met.

Shit, I'm gonna pass out.

He pulled a pepperoni stick out of his pocket and wondered when they were going to eat.

"But," she continued, "we're worried now that you'll never come around and find the time to settle down."

What the hell does that mean?

"What the hell does that mean?" He bit off a piece of pepperoni.

"Well, Damon, it means, we've added a stipulation to the access of your trust fund."

He put the pieces together all too fast. *No. She isn't being serious. This has to be a joke.*

"Paulina," he shoved out through gritted teeth.

She didn't let him say anything else. "We need you to get married."

"No."

"Not now! We know you're very focused with your schoolwork and … deciding. But you need to pick a bride. I can set up another gathering the next time you're home!"

"No." His answer came out of his mouth far too quickly.

Two years ago—just before he moved down to Olympia—Paulina had organized a party for Damon, which was basically several rounds of speed dating with a dozen of Manhattan's socialites. It was a disaster. Every girl all but threw herself at him. With their necklines too low and their makeup too heavy, they practically reeked of desperation. Two girls had even gotten into a brawl in the foyer bathroom and had to be escorted off the property.

"It's not up for discussion. We've already had the contract amended. You have until you're thirty to get married."

"Or what?" It came out posed more as a threat than he'd meant to, but he wasn't sorry.

He shoved the pepperoni back into his pocket, not caring to close it up even though he knew Spot would obsessively sniff his pants when he got back to his apartment.

"Or you'll be paying us back for your entire education, plus interest. Once you've paid back half of it, you'll have access to your trust."

"Paulina!"

"Don't you call me by my real name. I am your *mother*. I might not have brought you into this world, but you will not disrespect me again! You will be married by your thirtieth birthday, or you'll lose access to your trust. That includes your inheritance left by Lydia and Marco."

His blood boiled. He hated when they referred to his biological mother and his first stepfather by their real names. It was insulting to him, and to the few memories that he had of them.

"We'll see you in two weeks." His "dad" finally spoke up. "I just bought a plane ticket for you. We'll see you then."

Click.

He wanted to throw his phone. Or punch a hole in the wall. Something.

But he couldn't—that would draw too much attention.

Instead, he grabbed a small throw pillow off of Amber's unmade bed and squeezed it between his fists until his knuckles turned white. Then, he threw it on the floor. Then, he picked it up and did it two more times before he was finally aware of his heartbeat again.

But he still wasn't ready to go back out and see anyone.

He stalked back to the door and turned the light on. The room was immediately filled with color—rusty-orange floor-length curtains, a poofy mustard yellow comforter, green from all the plants, and paintings all over the walls among the multitude of photos.

That was what called to him—the captured moments of Amber's life. He preferred to find out details about people without talking to them about it. Maybe it was the few years of reading through files of people his uncle Ernesto had deemed "unnecessary to society," but whatever the case, it pulled him over to the mass of colorful pictures.

None of them were in frames, just taped to the wall in no order whatsoever, it seemed. There were only two taken in Olympia—one at her orientation with her bright green lanyard around her neck and the second with the random cow statue that stood on the east side of campus. The cow never made any sense to him—it wasn't their mascot, and there was no plaque or any indication on it, signifying its purpose there.

There was a young girl in the picture, too, with her hands on the cow's head, as if she were petting it. She didn't look anything like Amber, even the eyes. Both of theirs were green, but Amber's were brighter, happier even. This girl's eyes were so much darker.

Several of the pictures featured her.

This must be the sister she talks about. Or adoptive sister or whatever.

There was one Polaroid in particular that he couldn't stop looking at, and it was one that Amber wasn't even in. It was the girl again, but you could barely see her face. She had her back to the camera, her white dress completely open in the back. Damon could count her vertebrae. There was a mass of assembled flowers in front of her, all blurry dots of purple, yellow, and blue. She had her head turned toward the camera, but she wasn't smiling. Instead, the look on her face was one of wonder, as if she was questioning why anyone would ever take a picture of her.

Damon reached up and touched the glossy card stuck to the wall. He thought, just for a moment, about taking it. But that would do nothing but raise questions, and that definitely wasn't something he wanted to explain.

Instead, he pulled his phone back out, glad he hadn't thrown it earlier, and took a picture of it.

Then, he put his phone away, turned off the light, and walked back out to rejoin the others.

But mainly just to finish his wine.

Chapter 9

SOLO INTERVIEW WITH DAWN.

Kronos: Miss Sutherland, ready to begin?

Dawn: Yes, sir.

Kronos: You're the oldest member, correct?

Dawn: Yes, sir, I'm only a few months older than Damon, but there's several years in between us and the other four.

Kronos: Does that make it hard for you to connect with the rest of them?

Dawn: No, I don't think so. Not for me at least.

Kronos: Does that make you feel more motherly toward them?

Dawn: [*considers this for a moment*] I don't think so. Honestly, I feel as though Amber and Hanna June both take on a more matronly role, but in different ways. Amber is more comforting, from what I've seen so far, but HJ is more take charge of things. I think the others come to me when they want more of a teacher to talk to.

Kronos: Now, seeing as you're the oldest and clearly the most insightful on the show, do you mind sharing with us what your interpretation of the other five members is?

Dawn: I have no problem sharing, but please keep in mind that I'm still getting to know them. I've only known them a week and a half, and we haven't exactly hung out in an informal setting. My perceptions could be entirely wrong.

Kronos: We will keep that in mind.

Dawn: [*takes a deep breath*] Well, I think Kai needs a major boost of confidence. He's clearly pining for a girl who either isn't interested in him or is just oblivious. And it hurts to watch it.

Kronos: How can you tell he feels that way?

Dawn: He talked to me about it. Told me how they'd gone out before, and it unfortunately didn't go anywhere, but he really wanted it to, and he'd like to go out with her again. He asked me how he should go about asking her out and what he could do to not blow it this time.

Dawn: He's very anxious about it, about her. But even if he hadn't opened up to me about the situation, it's painfully obvious. You know love when you see it, and what's worse is that you can easily pick up on one-sided love too.

Kronos: He just opened up to you? That probably made you feel good.

Dawn: He honestly just seemed like he needed someone to talk to.

Kronos: Now, what do you think about Miss Hargrove?

Dawn: Amber is hyper-focused on her family. Which is great—don't get me wrong. But she's twenty years old. She shouldn't be playing the role of mom, wife, sister, head of the household, cook, maid, bill payer, *and* student—that's just unfair to her. It's sad because I think she stepped in to help out after she lost her mother, which was incredibly selfless on her part. But I think it's become expected of her now, and it shouldn't be. She's so smart, and she truly *loves* what she's studying. She should be able to focus all of her energy on her desired field and throw herself into her future career path, but she can't. Or rather, she feels like she can't.

Dawn: Hanna June is a whole other story, in my opinion. I think she loves what she's studying, but I think that's only because she's been conditioned to love it. I've only talked with her one-on-one a handful of times, but this poor girl's entire life has been planned out for her. From what she says and does, to who she dates and eventually marries, to what she's going to do with her life. I feel like she doesn't actually know who she is … and that's so sad.

Kronos: What about her significant other?

Dawn: [*takes a deep breath*] Zachary. He's, um … he's something. Overly confident, in my opinion. I don't really feel like I can trust him … I think he was handed a lot in life, very early, and will probably be one of those people who just glides through and doesn't really think about anyone else.

Kronos: [*nods slowly, eyes narrowing slightly*] And lastly, tell me about your friend Mr. Montclaire?

Dawn: [*smiles*] Damon's my best friend. Which a lot of people think is very strange and I can definitely understand that. We're very different, but that's why I like hanging out with him. From the moment we met, we just clicked—he was easy to talk to, never any awkward silences or anything. We have a lot in common, but also don't agree on everything—which works out because we both like to learn and analyze things from different points of view. I don't think I could have that same type of relationship with Zach or even Hanna June.

Kronos: [*nods, silent for a minute*] I like all your opinions about your costars. Very thoughtful.

Dawn: [*smiles*] Well, thank you.

Kronos: Now, you and I have spoken informally about what your career plans are, but I honestly find them quite interesting. A real game changer in the way our world functions. Would you mind sharing them?

Dawn: Oh, not at all! Well, I noticed a few years ago that a lot of malls are going out of business and that many things are available online now. You can even order your groceries online and just drive up to the store, and the employees will put them in your car for you! How amazing is that?

Dawn: Anyway, I noticed that a lot of these really large buildings are becoming vacant. But I also noticed, at least around here, that more and more apartment buildings are going up … and yet there's still a serious homelessness issue.

Dawn: So, I got to thinking, what if we could repurpose those empty malls to be affordable apartments?

Kronos: That would be quite an excellent plan, but how would homeless people afford them?

Dawn: See, that's the thing—they can't. Most people don't make enough money, many people are addicts of some sort, and so many of these individuals have mental health issues, and when they hit a wall, they get stuck on this idea that they simply cannot get up and turn things around. Some know they need help, but might not know how to go about getting it while others don't think there's anything wrong.

Dawn: So, then the question I started to ask myself became, "How do we get these people in here in order to help them? What can we give them that they can't say no to?"

Kronos: And did you come up with anything?

Dawn: [*proud smile*] I did—their lives. If I can find a way to give these people back their lives—many of who think they've lost everything and there's no turning back, which can sometimes be the reason they keep going; they don't see a point in trying to fix things—if I can figure out a way to get them back up to the top, get them clean and healthy and feeling good about themselves, then how can they say no to that?

Kronos: And did you devise a plan to make that accessible to them?

Dawn: It's still in the works, but I think I've got a pretty clear path of where I'm going with this.

Kronos: And what might that be?

Dawn: [*stifled laugh*] Actually, I don't think I want to share too much more—don't want anyone to take my idea, you know?

Kronos: [*hands up defensively*] I definitely understand that. Don't want to share too much. We can change the subject. Tell me, Miss Sutherland, do you like going to school in your hometown?

Dawn: I do. I love it. I had to live on campus my freshman and sophomore year, and then I was an RA for the last two years of my undergrad. And for my master's, I moved back home, which is only twenty minutes away, and I just drive to campus when I have class. And now, for filming! [*laughs*]

Kronos: And how do you like the filming, the whole idea of being on TV?

Dawn: It's definitely … not my favorite thing. [*laughs*] It's very weird. Like, it still doesn't feel like it's actually going to happen. There're two cameras pointed at me right now, [*gestures to cameras*] but it doesn't feel real! It's exciting though. And it's helping to pay for my schooling, so I can't complain.

Kronos: Would you recommend Olympia College to other incoming students?

Dawn: Absolutely. I mean, I'm a little biased because I've lived here my whole life, [*laughs*] but, yes, without a doubt. There are more students here than any other private school in the state, which is why we have the better sports teams, I think. Class sizes are still pretty small though, even lecture halls. There are *so* many majors to choose from. Downtown is literally right next to campus, which is a big deal to most college kids. The beach is about an hour drive, same for Charleston, depending on what you're looking to go do. Columbia is only thirty minutes away. Honestly, I didn't apply to any other schools for my undergrad or my graduate degrees. I knew Olympia was where I was meant to be.

Kronos: [*nods, smiling*] Perfect.

Chapter 10

KAI

"I DON'T WANT TO DO THIS."

"Well, I don't want to either, but it's probably a good idea. Just so, you know, you don't end up punching him again. On national television."

Amber was standing barefoot in his tiny kitchen at the front of his RV. The look on her face said that, she, too was reluctant to meet up with them. He knew it definitely hadn't been her idea—to have them "talk it out without the cameras"—but she had agreed with Hanna June about getting them to do it in the first place, and evidently, it had been her job to get him to come. While he wanted to be mad at her for playing a role in it regardless, it was honestly hard for him to be upset with her.

They walked down College Road, side by side, Amber's kimono flowing out behind her. They sauntered through the crosswalk among the other students on their way to midday classes.

I'm so glad I picked my classes to only be on Tuesdays and Thursdays.

Sullivan Street didn't have a road sign, which had always bothered Kai. It was primarily used by the college kids who lived in the apartments off of it, on their way to the bar at the corner, but he still figured it needed a proper street sign.

He slowed his pace down just slightly so he could look at her without her noticing. The sun illuminated the brown highlights in her red hair, and he could smell the floral scent rolling off of her. Her lips had been slightly chapped when they kissed. He wondered what they felt like now. He wondered how many people she had kissed since him. Maybe none ...

Shit, I need to change the subject.

"No one's even seen it yet. They said the pilot won't air for another month. Maybe they'll edit it out," he stupidly suggested. He knew damn well Kronos wouldn't let the first moment of action *not* air.

"Kai, you're smart, so don't act stupid. There's no way they're going to get rid of that. It'll probably be one of the clips they show in the commercial for the show."

She was right. There was no sense in arguing back, so they walked another block in silence before she piped up.

"Just do me a favor." She interrupted his daydream as she turned to meet his gaze. She had the prettiest green eyes he'd ever seen. Even if they were minorly bloodshot.

Wait, bloodshot?

As he turned his head toward her just a little, she snapped hers back to focus on her feet. He straightened his form but kept his eyes on her.

"What's that?" Maybe she'd look at him at some point during her request.

"Be nice please. I know he's basically a complete asshole, so just please play the role of the mature, older brother."

"I thought that was Damon's job."

"Older, yes. But maturer? I don't think so. He's just antisocial. I honestly don't know why he's in the program because his family has a ton of money—he doesn't need a scholarship. Did you know he went to an Ivy for his bachelor's degree?"

"Of course he did."

"Look, the six of us are all going to be together for however long this goes on for. It's going to be a lot easier if you two can be in the same room without one of you physically assaulting the other ..." She turned to look at him as she spoke the last three words.

And her eyes were definitely bloodshot.

"Are you okay, Am?"

"Yeah."

His brow furrowed at her short—and clearly false—response. "You sure?"

"*Yes.* Why?"

"'Cause your eyes are bloodshot."

For a moment, her green irises widened just about as far as they could before she snapped her head back forward, focusing on the sidewalk in front of her.

Leaning down slightly, he lowered his voice. "Amber?"

"I was just crying. It's fine."

"Amber, if you were crying, then something is obviously not okay."

"No, it's fine. I promise. Look, I really don't want to talk about it."

"Oh, okay."

Kai didn't know what else to do, so he stuffed his hands into his pockets, and they completed their walk to Bev's Taproom. Just as he was about to pull the door open, he felt an arm on his elbow pulling him back.

She pulled him close to her—*really close.* A group of girls giggled as they walked inside past them. Neither of them paid them any mind though.

"Kai, just … like …"

Their lips were centimeters from each other. He could taste her breath. She reached up and fixed the collar on his shirt. She had made him swap out of something other than his normal old T-shirt, settling on a salmon-colored button-down.

"I like doing this with you. The show, I mean. I just … I like spending time with you. Even if there're usually cameras watching us."

"Yeah, I really like getting to spend time with you too. Even if there *are* cameras around."

"But just, you know, I like you better without your face being slightly messed up."

He couldn't hold in the smile that her words caused, and the feeling of her hands almost against his skin made it just so much better.

"So"—her hands drifted down to his chest for just a second before she pulled them away and held them at her sides—"I really need you to go in there and make nice … *please.*"

Her eyes dropped to his chest as he gazed down at her. "I can do that."

"Okay, good." She peered up at him—not that there was much of a height difference between them, just four inches. "Come on. Let's go inside."

The four of them all sat at a booth in the center of the restaurant. Some people looked at them, but most paid them no attention at all.

What if this thing does take off? What if people watch the show, and, like, it goes on for a few years? What if I have to move my classes online? I don't think I could do that. I can barely do school now.

Will I be able to go to Panthers games with Uncle Kris?

Will I be able to go home to see Mom?

Shit.

The tone of Zach's voice broke him out of his semi-spiral. "Why are we here?"

God, he's so fucking whiny.

"Y'all need to talk to each other about your daddy issues." HJ leaned over closer to him.

"I don't have *daddy issues* because he was never *my daddy*."

"And that's part of your issues—you didn't have a father figure 'round, growin' up," she offered.

Kai's head hurt with how hard he rolled his eyes, just before he caught a glimpse of Amber glaring at him. The white had returned to her eyes after she downed a glass and a half of water before Zach and HJ showed up.

I told her I'd stop fighting with the blond brat across the table.

Swallowing, he looked at this easily qualified grade-A asshole—unfortunately also his half-brother—across the table from him. He stared into his eyes—the same eyes he had. The same eyes that made people do a double take when they first saw him. The same eyes that had always made him extra "different." They made more sense on him, genetically. But he also knew that Hanna June didn't get trapped in Zach's eyes the way Amber got sucked into his.

And the look on Amber's face when that happened … that made the sideways glances worth it.

"I hate you."

Zach's eyebrows knit themselves together. "What?"

"*I hate you.*"

The silence that flowed between them after that was heavy and hung there in the air. The boys kept their eyes on each other while both girls seemed to try and drill holes into the table with their stares.

"Okay …" HJ started. "That's a good start …"

"Kai, why do you hate Zach?" Amber gently touched his arm.

"Because he got the dad. He got the dad and the huge house in the city and the little brother and sister and the SAT tutors and the vacation at exotic resorts and ski lodges, and I got … I—I got the struggling-to-pay-bills mom who never wanted to go to court and demand child support the way she should've because she didn't want the press to get ahold of the DC politician with *another* illegitimate kid and have my face in the papers even though I have to be on TV now in order for me to go to school so I don't end up struggling through life like she did."

"Shit," came out in a whisper under Amber's breath.

Zach leaned forward, his chest against the edge of the table between them. "How the hell is that any of my fault?"

"It's not! But, like, you go parading around all the shit you have—the shit you have *because* you got the dad, and I didn't. And that's what pisses me off—that you don't care that me and my mom have struggled our entire lives. You don't care that you get to go out of the country four times a year, and I've never been off the East Coast. The only thing I've got on you is that I've been up and down the Outer Banks more times than you ever will … to clean yachts for people like you. You don't care that I *have* to be in this program in order to be able to afford to go to school because I can't even get approved for a loan. You're gonna be on TV, which is all you care about, which is such bullshit because, like, you're already at the top of the food chain and then you just get more. That's bullshit. It's not fucking fair."

Again, no one spoke for quite a while. The waitress came and left after dropping off a big plate of wings. Nobody ate. Zach seemed to be lost in thought, focused on the celery at the edge of the plate. Hanna June played with the ice in her water, using her straw. Amber cracked her knuckles under the table.

"What would make it fair?" Zach was looking at him again.

"What?"

He flipped his phone over, glanced at it quickly, and then flipped it back facedown. Hanna June watched every movement and sat up a little straighter.

"You said it was unfair, and ... I kind of agree. So, what would make it fair?"

Shit. I don't know.

Zach reached forward and dropped three wings onto his plate, reached across HJ to grab the ranch from the center of the table where their server had placed it, and poured some out onto his plate.

"I don't know ... I need—" He had to stop to clear his throat. "I need to think about that."

"Let me know," he answered with a mouthful of honey barbeque chicken.

Hanna June switched between crunching on a stalk of celery and a carrot, keeping her eyes on her boyfriend. Amber grabbed four wings and drizzled ranch all over them. Kai wasn't very hungry.

Twenty minutes later, their waitress dropped off the check.

"I got it," Zach mumbled while folding a piece of gum into his mouth.

Seeing him pick up the check without a worry in the world was what sparked the idea in Kai's head.

Kai spoke up as Zach struggled to add the tip to the total. "Make him pay."

All three of them turned to look at him.

"What?" Zach wiggled the pen back and forth.

"Make him pay back all the child support money he owed my mom over the years. Keep it quiet, and tell him that if he doesn't do it, I'll talk about it on the show. Make it as public as I can."

"You serious?"

"Very. And I'm pretty sure ... isn't—yeah, isn't this an election year?"

Zach's thin mouth shut in a straight line, and he gave his half-brother a short nod. "I'll talk to him."

Chapter 11

Kronos: So, the two of you are much older than the other four participants. Is that strange for you?

Dawn: Not really. Some of them, I can tell there's an age difference, but others, not so much.

Kronos: What about you, Damon?

Damon: [*blank stare*] I didn't know I was supposed to feel something about the people who are younger than me.

Dawn: [*hits him on the knee*] Stop it.

Damon: [*rolls his eyes*]

Kronos: You two know each other outside of the program?

Dawn: Oh, yeah, we've been friends since we started grad school.

Kronos: You two didn't both go to Olympia for your undergrad?

Damon: [*watching his foot* bounce] You know we didn't.

Dawn: I did. Did my bachelor's degree here, I'm finishing my master's, and I'll hopefully get into the doctoral program online here too.

Kronos: What about you, Mr. Montclaire? Where did you attend for your undergraduate degree?

Damon: Yale.

Kronos: Wow, an Ivy League. That's impressive.

Damon: [*stares at Kronos*]

Kronos: Okay! So, how did you two meet at Olympia?

Dawn: We got paired up in a university intro class … oh shoot. What was the name of it?

Damon: Introduction to Olympia College.

Dawn: Yes, that was it! It was us and this other girl who honestly looked like she was twelve. But we just realized we worked well together, so we became study buddies, just someone to have to kind of keep us focused and on track, and it just morphed into this friendship we have now.

Kronos: Now, this friendship seems entirely genuine, like it's not something that either of you really has to work hard at. Has it always been this natural for you two?

Dawn: I think so. We just clicked right away.

Kronos: Mr. Montclaire, do you agree? You just clicked?

Damon: [*stares at Kronos, then at Dawn*] Easiest friend I've ever made.

Dawn: Well, you don't have that many friends …

Damon: [*glares at her*]

Kronos: So, just give me a little insight into how this works because, Miss Sutherland, you're so kind and warm, and, no offense, Mr. Montclaire, but you're very closed off. Scary even has been the word to describe you.

Dawn: I think the fact that we're complete opposites is what makes it work.

Kronos: So, what is it that you guys do when you hang out?

Dawn: Oh, we do lots of things. We meet at the dog park pretty much every day. We go to the coffee shop, the library, that '80s store uptown that sells all those vintage tees and records. We do a lot of things. Damon doesn't always enjoy them, but he lets me drag him all over.

Damon: Hmm.

Kronos: It sounds to me like you guys are dating.

Damon: Kronos …

Dawn: No, no. Definitely not dating.

Kronos: Why not?

Damon: Because we're not.

Kronos: Has it ever been a topic of discussion between you two?

Damon: No.

Dawn: We're just better off as friends. It honestly isn't even something that we've ever considered.

Kronos: Why not though?

Damon: We just haven't.

Dawn: We would never work together. We are friends, we always have been, and that's all we ever plan to be.

Kronos: Okay, okay. Say no more. So, do you plan to stay in each other's lives once you graduate and move on and your futures develop?

Damon: [*leans over and loudly whispers to Dawn*] Just say yes, so this can be over.

Dawn: [*gently hits him on his pec with the back of her hand*] Yes, we will remain friends.

Chapter 12

ZACH

As he left the ZUS house, Zach proceeded to text in the group chat with his parents and HJ.

> **Zach: You're currently texting with the newest brother of Zeta Upsilon Sigma!**
>
> **Dad: That's my boy!**
>
> **HJ: OMG yay!!! So so proud of you baby!!!**
>
> **Mom: So proud of you, sweetheart. We can't wait to come down for Parents' Weekend to see you two!**

Not a minute after his mother's text came in, Hanna June was calling him.

Zach picked up to hear her over-excited, high-pitched squealing. "Zachary Drake Alexander, I am SO proud of you! I knew you'd get a bid; I just knew it. You were silly to try and get a bid from *every* frat as a backup. I just knew Zeta Sig would want you. How could they not?!"

"Thanks, baby."

"And this is perfect 'cause, now, we can go to each other's formals and parties together! By the way, Eta Rho is having a party on Friday, and the girls really want me to come. They said I'm one of the three freshmen that they want to move into the house next year because, you know, they don't have enough rooms to have all the girls live on Greek Row, so they have to be very picky-choosy about who they allow to live in the house ..."

Hanna June went on while Zach felt a text come in.

Unknown Number: Hey, this is Tori, I'm a Kappa- heard you just got a bid to Zeta Sig!

Zach: You heard right

Unknown Number: We should hang out sometime

Zach: I'm free now?

Unknown Number: Perfect, what dorm?

Zach: Dodona, I'll wait for you at the back door

Zach: the one that faces 5th st

He wasn't typically a double texter, but he had to make sure she didn't go to the main entrance. He picked the phone back up to his ear.

"... I'm just so excited. This is all working out so, so perfectly. It's literally exactly like what we talked about—like, everythin' is goin' accordin' to plan!"

"I'm so excited too, babe. Listen, I gotta get going." He crossed the mall, his residence hall in front of him now. "I'll see you later though, okay?"

"Okay." Her reply was unenthusiastic. The tone she had just had in her voice was gone, replaced with obvious disappointment. "I just kinda wanted to celebrate with you."

"I know, but I gotta keep up with my grades if we're gonna stay in school, right?"

"Yeah, you're right," she sighed.

"I know." He stepped onto the little path that connected the walkways on campus to the sidewalk along Fifth Street, taking long strides. It really bothered him that the road had two names. "Let me work on this paper for a little bit, and we can go out to eat at that new Mexican place downtown, okay?"

"Okay. I'll see you in a little while. I love you so much."

"I love you more." He hung up the phone as he saw a tall girl—maybe almost as tall as him—with curly, long black hair, leaning against the railing. Her shorts were so short that they might as well have been denim underwear.

"Hey," she greeted him as she pushed her sunglasses up onto the top of her head.

"Hey." Zach gave her *the nod* as he fished out his key fob.

"You're even cuter in person. Ashlyn showed me your picture. The guy she usually hangs out with is a Zeta Sig also."

The door unlocked with a buzz, and Zach held it open for her. As she strode past him, he caught a whiff of strawberries. "Thank God for Ashlyn." It came out dry and a little raspy, but he didn't care.

He followed her in, and they walked side by side down the hall.

"You know," she began the conversation, "you're pretty lucky. Freshmen don't usually get central housing dorms. They usually stick them down at West End. Which isn't bad—it's near downtown."

"I like being in the middle of campus." He looked over at her. "Easy access to everything."

They stared at each other for a moment too long, and he glanced down at her mouth before looking away at the perfect time.

"I'm right here." He unlocked his dorm door and, once again, held it open for her.

She pranced past him, glanced around, and perched on the middle of his bed. "So … how do you like—"

"I really don't care for small talk." He kicked off his shoes and started unbuckling his belt.

"Oh, thank God," she answered and pulled her shirt over her head.

Zach took two steps toward her, guided her down onto his bed, and started removing her shorts.

Not ten minutes later, they were both putting their clothes back on.

It was a funny thing; before sex, both people were typically eager to get off each other's clothes, but afterward, neither person helped the other get redressed.

Zach was buttoning up his shirt and was about to grab his deodorant when she broke the silence.

"Your girlfriend is an Eta Rho, right?"

Zach froze. He nearly dropped the plastic container in his hand and just stared at the girl in front of him.

She obviously knew, so what was the point in lying to her? "Yeah."

She nodded. "I saw her at Bid Day. She's pretty."

"Yeah"—he swallowed—"she is."

She shimmied back into her shorts, slid her shoes back on, and headed for the door. "I'll see you around. Don't lose my number." And with that, she was gone.

Zach had half a mind to chase after her. To catch up with her and plead with her to not tell HJ or any of her sorority sisters. Convince her that this was a onetime thing and he didn't do things like this. Tell her it was a mistake and that he'd never do it again.

But all of that would have been a lie.

It hadn't been a onetime thing in years. He did stuff like this all the time. It wasn't a mistake. It was a conscious decision he made. And he knew he'd do it again.

Hanna June knew he cheated on her. He'd never admitted it before, and he never would, but he knew that she knew what he did.

The thing was that it didn't matter—she couldn't break up with him, and he couldn't leave her. They were stuck together for the rest of their lives. Maybe, one day, he'd settle down.

Not likely.

Chapter 13

AMBER

Fleur: can u help with my essay when u come home this wknd?

Amber: Sure, what's it on?

Fleur: romeo and juliet... They're both really fucking dumb

Amber: Fleur!!

Fleur: sorry, but it's true! Like both of them just need to calm down

Amber: Yeah, okay maybe you're right... It's still the greatest love story of all time, though.

Fleur: incorrect, that would be twilight lmao

Amber loved the sisterly conversation she got to have with Fleur. They didn't happen often, but when they did, it was like she got a serotonin high.

Amber: How's dad?

Fleur's answer didn't come for almost an hour. Amber was about to call her when the text delivery finally lit up her phone screen.

Fleur: idk he's been gone since tues morn

Amber's heartbeat sped up. *He's been gone for three days? Where the hell was he? Why hadn't he contacted her?*

Amber: Do you know where he is? Or why he left?

Only five minutes passed this time, but Amber felt like it had been days.

Fleur: he said he went back to kansas for work, didn't say when he'd be back tho

Amber: What have you been eating?

Fleur: am calm down, you're acting like juliet, jumping the gun lol

Amber: Fleur, please tell me what you've been eating.

Fleur: i can hear your tone through the phone omg uh okay i had the rest of the chicken you made on tues, i made a pb and j on wed, and then i found a panera gift card with like twelve bucks on it at school, so i just used that for dinner tonight

Amber: Breakfast too

Fleur: we have cereal…

Amber: We do?

Fleur: you know how dad owns a mass ag company?

Fleur: do I need to explain to you the agreement he has with the milling company or…?

Amber: Oh, that's right. You still get free lunch at school?

Fleur: omg yes amber, if you'd like me to weigh in next time you're home just lmk

Feeling slightly better that Fleur had at least been eating regularly, she left the conversation with her sister and started another one.

Amber: Hi dad

He answered surprisingly fast, calming her nerves more.

Dad: Hey baby girl

Amber: How are things going?

Dad: Oh just fine. How are you?

Amber: Well, I'm not great. Fleur told me you haven't been home since Tuesday night?

She threw her phone down on her bedspread and dragged her hands through her hair, pulling several loose strands out. She hated being away from home—and it was only an hour and a half. She knew plenty of people who'd gone time zones away from their families. That seemed like such a nice dream to have … for other people though. Amber hadn't been dealt those cards in life.

Dad: I had to have a few meetings with corporate out here. I'm supposed to be flying back home tomorrow afternoon. I'm sorry I didn't tell you, things have been crazy at work.

Amber: Trust me, I understand crazy schedules. But dad… you can't leave Fleur alone.

Dad: Sure I can, she's very capable.

Amber: Dad, she's 15

Dad: She's fine Am

Amber: Okay… goodnight

Dad: Goodnight sweetheart

Amber threw her phone down again, grabbed her pillow, and screamed into it. Not too loudly though—she didn't want to disturb her neighbor or, worse, have anyone ask questions.

After placing the pillow back in its spot on the center of her bed, she grabbed her keys from her nightstand and walked over to her closet, lugging the fireproof safe out. Sitting on the floor, she unlocked it and lifted up the paper covering the old Altoids tin.

Her shadow stretched across her room, illuminated by the four different woodsy-scented candles she'd lit before settling down to try and study for her Mass Production on Agriculture exam tomorrow, but ultimately being distracted by her nightly check-in with Fleur.

She began her process as her mind started to wander.

Why didn't she tell me last night that he'd left? Or even the night before? This wouldn't have happened if I was there.

Maybe I should set up cameras … that way, I'll always know if he just leaves. Or if she has people over. Not that she would ever do that … not that she has friends to invite over …

Good thing I've been doing this for so long that I don't need to pay attention to it anymore. Seth Rogen would be proud.

Oh God, wait, no. No. Do not admit you're a stoner. You can't be a stoner. People who smoke weed are lazy and unmotivated and don't amount to anything …

Except, no, that's not true. Because, like, look at all the shit I do. 'Cause, like, it's a lot. I manage a household from, like, one hundred miles away. I help a teenager with her schoolwork literally all the time. I'm attempting to keep a grown man as sane as possible. And I'm a year and a half away from graduating college. Oh, and I'm on TV now, apparently.

Which still doesn't feel like it's happening …

OMG, wait, they say the camera adds ten pounds … shit, I'm gonna be hungry after this. Eh, I'll just order Cookie Dude or something.

Holy shit, this is, like, the prettiest joint I've ever rolled. Wow, I am so good at multitasking. Damn right Seth Rogen would be proud.

Holy shit, this is, like, the prettiest joint I've ever rolled. Wow, I am so good at multitasking. Damn right Seth Rogen would be proud.

Chapter 14

SOLO INTERVIEW WITH HANNA JUNE.

Kronos: Miss Hanna June Pruitt, you ready to get started?

HJ: [*smirks*] I was born ready.

Kronos: Oh, I know you were. So, you and Zachary have been together for how long?

HJ: We've been officially a couple for about six years, but we've been, like, set up or betrothed or whatever y'all wanna call it since we were almost five. So, thirteen years ago.

Kronos: That's quite a long time to be with just one person.

HJ: You know, I think about that a lot, and maybe it would bother most people—you know, not being able to get to know other people—but I love it. It works for us.

Kronos: You two have never entertained the idea of possibly taking a break and exploring the world of dating?

HJ: Oh good Lord, no! [*laughs*] We could never do that. First of all, it would infuriate our parents. And it would be breaking a legal contract—on their part, of course, since we weren't old enough to sign any legal documents at the time. We could barely write our own names! [*laughs*] It would just turn into a complete disaster. And second, neither of us wants to do that.

Kronos: [*slightly amused look on his face*] Is that right?

HJ: [*nodding*] We're both very content with our relationship.

Kronos: So, the idea of being single temporarily and just kind of figuring out who you are as individuals isn't in the cards either?

HJ: I don't think our parents would like that either. And I know I wouldn't.

Kronos: Hmm. Okay, so tell me, what's your favorite thing about Olympia College?

HJ: Hmm. [*pauses to think*] Honestly, I like a lot about it. The campus is so nice. I love how close it is to downtown. So far, I like almost all my professors. My sorority sisters are an absolute dream come true! [*pauses again*] No, I can't decide! [*laughs*] I love everything about my school.

Kronos: How about this question instead: what's your favorite thing about your costars?

HJ: [*eyes widen, pauses*] Um, hmm … well, obviously, my favorite thing about Zach is everything. [*laughs*]

HJ: But, umm … I guess I love how easy it is to talk to Dawn. I wasn't really sure about her at first, and I think she felt the same way about me, but we're definitely warmin' up to each other.

HJ: Kai seems pretty nice … but I'm pretty sure he only talks to me when he's high. Every other time I see him, he just seems really sad. And I also don't know how Zach feels about me talking to him or Damon, so I honestly don't really like talkin' to 'em. That's how I know Kai is high though——I feel like he seeks me out, like he *needs* someone to talk to. And then he's close enough that I can see his eyes are completely bloodshot, and I get a contact high just from being next to him.

Kronos: And your favorite thing about Mr. Montclaire?

HJ: [*takes a deep breath, seems frustrated*] I don't know. I can't really figure him out. Part of me wants to be scared of him, but another part of me wants to tell him to cut the tortured emo crap and just be real. Don't get me wrong. I know he's been through a lot, obviously—I think the whole country knows about his story. But still …

Kronos: And Miss Hargrove?

HJ: [*tight-lipped, opens mouth wide, as if to say something, shuts it quickly*] I don't really know about her.

Kronos: [*pauses*] Can you elaborate?

HJ: [*long pause*] I can't figure her out either. She seems like she'd be a complete stoner, but I don't think she actually is. She also is *way* too involved in her family. I mean, I know she's got a rather complicated situation goin' on as well, and I'm honestly not even sure about the details of that … but I feel like she spends way too much time doin' things that her daddy is perfectly capable of doin'. That shouldn't be her responsibility.

Kronos: Interesting.

HJ: And she's an enviro major … that seems incredibly boring.

Kronos: Okay …

HJ: And then … every now and then, she looks funny at Zach, and I'm pretty sure it's the same look that she gives Kai sometimes, and I *know* something happened between them last year. So, ya know, it just makes me wonder if she's thinkin' about hookin' up with my future husband or not. Which makes me not particularly like her in those moments.

Kronos: That all makes complete sense.

HJ: It does, doesn't it?! [*nervous laugh*] I'm glad you don't think I'm crazy!

Kronos: No, not at all. I think your feelings toward the possibility of Mr. Alexander being on someone else's radar are completely warranted.

HJ: Not that he'd ever consider it!

Kronos: No, no. Of course not.

HJ: [*glances at floor, bites lip for a millisecond before looking back up at the camera with a huge smile*]

Chapter 15

GROUP INTERVIEW WITH ALL THE GIRLS.

Kronos: We did an interview last week with all the young men, so I think it's only fair to conduct one with all the young women.

Dawn: I think that's a great idea!

Kronos: And, you know, I just want to add, you ladies are much more suited for television. The boys, not so much.

HJ: Well, Zach probably gives great prompt answers durin' his interviews.

Kronos: He does, but I think the audience is going to want to watch you all more. That's how the social media accounts are looking anyway.

Amber: Wait … there's already people following the show and the pilot episode doesn't even air for another week?

Kronos: Oh, yes, Miss Hargrove. We've got one hundred fourteen thousand likes on Facebook, eighty-one thousand followers on Instagram, and twenty-six thousand on Twitter.

Amber: *[eyes get huge, slowly sits back in chair, looks like she might hurl]*

HJ: [*excited squeal*] Oh my God! [*turns to Amber and Dawn*] Y'all, this is amazing! There's already so many new people who have followed me and Zach on our socials. Soon, we're going to have fan bases, and they'll make ship names for us—but would they use my initials or my whole name? Or just one of my names? I hope they use June instead of Hanna because I honestly prefer that name. Ha. Ain't that strange? Do y'all have middle names?

Kronos: [*leans forward as he cuts her off*] Miss—Miss Pruitt, we need to start filming.

HJ: Oh! [*sits up straight in her chair, smooths out hair, places hands in her lap*] Okay, I'm ready.

Kronos: [*signals to start rolling*] So, ladies, is this the first time you've all spent time together, just the three of you?

Dawn: It is.

Kronos: Okay, good. We wanted to do a group interview with just the girls. The boys are related, so they know each other, and you've all kind of got your pair, so to speak, that you know, so we wanted to get just you all.

Amber: Sorry, what do you mean, our pair?

Dawn: I think he means the person we knew when we first started the program—HJ had Zach, I had Damon, and you had Kai.

Amber: [*pauses*] Oh.

HJ: You're right though. We're the only ones who aren't connected in any sorta way. So, we really [*turns to Dawn and Amber*] don't know anything 'bout each other.

Kronos: Well, Miss Pruitt, what's something you'd like to know about Miss Hargrove and Miss Sutherland?

HJ: [*long pause*] Uhh … gee, I'm not really sure. Can you circle back to me?

Kronos: [*chuckles*] No problem. Amber, you have a question you'd like to ask Miss Pruitt and Miss Sutherland?

Amber: Is this supposed to be, like, a deep, thoughtful question or a pointless filler question?

Kronos: Whatever you'd like.

Amber: Okay … guilty pleasure TV show?

HJ: Easy. *The Hills*. Or *90210*.

Dawn: I've been watching a lot of *The Andy Griffith Show* lately.

HJ: [*turns to look at her skeptically*] Isn't that, like, an old show?

Dawn: Mmhmm, it's from the '60s.

HJ: Wasn't TV in black and white back then?

Dawn: Sure was.

HJ: And you like watchin' stuff like that?

Dawn: Oh yeah, definitely. All the ideas were new and original back then. Nowadays, everything is just copied and twisted a little bit.

HJ: Huh …

Kronos: What about you, Miss Hargrove?

Amber: [*confused*] What about me?

Kronos: You have to answer your own question too.

Amber: Oh. Um, I still watch *Full House*, like, every night.

HJ: Nick at Nite?

Amber: [*small nod*] Yeah.

HJ: [*smiles back*]

Kronos: Miss Pruitt, have you thought of a question to ask?

HJ: [*pondering*] Well, I feel like I should ask a big question to counteract Amber's easy one.

Amber: [*turns slightly red, toys with hands in her lap*]

Kronos: Only if you want to.

HJ: [*takes a breath, thinking*] I guess, like … what's the biggest goal you have for your life?

Dawn: Well, I shared this with Kronos last week, but I have a very detailed business plan in the works … [*thinks of how to summarize it*] Basically, I want to help people—especially people who feel like they've hit rock bottom—recognize and live up to their full potential.

HJ: Wow. That sounds amazing. [*turns to Amber*] Amber?

Amber: I think I'd really like to move back to the Midwest, probably Kansas or Nebraska. Have my family split time between there and—

HJ: No.

Amber: [*deer in headlights*] What?

HJ: I asked about you. Not your family. *You.*

Amber: Um, I don't really … like, I'm not … I haven't thought—

HJ: Think 'bout your family plans. Or a career goal. Or do you want to travel? You seem like someone who'd backpack around Europe. C'mon, Am. Think.

Kronos: [*leans back, folds hands, and watches the interaction proudly*]

Am: [*mimicking her*] Am?

HJ: [*confused for a second*] Yeah … it's a nickname for you.

Amber: I didn't know we were in a nickname kind of place.

HJ: [*rolls eyes*] Well, Zach refers to you as Grain Brain, but I don't really want to call you that, so I tried something different. [*slightly bitchy*] Is that okay?

Amber: [*tentative nod*] Yeah, I like Am better. Thanks.

HJ: [*small nod*] So, what's your biggest goal?

Amber: [*long pause*] I just want to be happy.

HJ: [*sad smile*]

Dawn: [*nods gently*]

Amber: I, uh, I'd really like to be head of agriculture out in the Midwest. After I take over my daddy's company …

Dawn: [*eyes light up*]

HJ: See, those are both *great* goals.

Amber: [*crooked smile*] Thanks.

Kronos: HJ, your turn.

HJ: [*turns directly toward the camera but keeps eye contact with Kronos*] You should know this by now. I want to be married to Zach and have a bunch of kids. Be a really great mom and wife.

Kronos: Okay, Dawn, your turn to ask.

Dawn: [*smiles*] Hanna June kind of took my question. But that's okay. I have a backup. What's your biggest pet peeve?

HJ: Oh, that's easy. People who grind their teeth and bite on their pens.

Dawn: So, teeth-related …

HJ: Yeah … it's the noise. It's worse than nails on a chalkboard for me.

Dawn: Huh. Amber?

Amber: [*lost in thought*] I … don't … know … [*to Kronos*] Sorry, I'm not good at coming up with these things off the top of my head.

Kronos: No, no, that's all right, Miss Hargrove. No pressure. [*to Dawn*] What about you, Miss Sutherland?

Dawn: Unkind people. Judgmental, noninclusive, and hypocritical. They're just the worst.

Amber: [*still lost in thought*] I guess I don't like secrets. People with ulterior motives. Not telling the whole truth. Things in that vein.

Kronos: [*nodding skeptically*] Good to know, Miss Hargrove.

Chapter 16

DAWN

HANNA JUNE WAS THE SHORTEST out of the three of them, but, *wow*, did she walk fast. Luckily, Dawn had a good five inches on her, so catching up to her wasn't too much of a struggle.

"Hanna June!" She didn't want to raise her voice because of all the people around, but that blonde ponytail just kept swishing its way away from her.

She stopped and turned around with a confused look on her face. "Dawn? Did you need something?"

"Yeah, actually. See, Amber and I …" She gestured behind her, but Amber wasn't there.

Again, she scanned the crowd on the grassy mall. There were several small groups of people hanging out—some had hammocks, some were sitting on blankets, and others were just lying in the grass.

"Where did …" Her voice was quiet because she knew that if she spoke her question out loud, there still wouldn't be an answer.

A moment of silence passed before HJ pointed back toward the Student Center. "That's her, right?"

Sure enough, Amber was fast walking toward them, head down, floral maxi dress flowing around her as she shuffled around the undergrads scattered among the walkways.

As she caught up to them, she mumbled, "Hey, sorry."

"What are you apologizing for?" Dawn questioned her.

"You guys were waiting for me."

"So?"

"I just … I felt bad that you had to wait."

HJ rolled her eyes so hard that it hurt Dawn's head.

"Don't feel bad that we chose to wait for you." Dawn faced HJ again. "Right after you left the interview just now, Amber said that she didn't feel like we knew each other any better, and honestly, I agree. So, I was thinking, since this show is kind of a major part of our lives, it seems like we probably *should* get to know each other better. I don't want us getting along to be an act, you know?"

"Okay, so what do you want us to do? Hold hands and tell each other our deepest, darkest secrets?" Judging by Hanna June's tone and her crossed arms, Dawn felt like she probably wasn't in a very *let's be best friends* place right now.

"It doesn't have to be like those terrible icebreakers they do during syllabus week or something. It can be completely casual, just the three of us hanging out."

HJ eyed her up and down slowly, glanced over at Amber, who was pulling apart the dead ends of her hair, and then back to Dawn.

"No cameras?"

"No cameras. I feel like that makes everything weird."

"Hmph," was the noise that came from HJ's throat, but she was nodding at the same time, so Dawn took that as a good sign.

Amber leaned forward. "It wouldn't be right now, obviously. But maybe we can plan for sometime this weekend?"

Hanna June pursed her lips and shifted her gaze from her tall costar to the redhead next to her. "Yeah … sure. That would be fine."

Saturday afternoon, Hanna June nearly swung the door off the hinges as she entered Amber's apartment. "I brought tequila!"

"Tacos are gonna be another few minutes," Amber replied while dropping some shredded cheese into a bowl.

"Perfect. That means I can start making drinks!"

"Just not too strong, okay? I don't need to be drunk when I have dinner with my parents later," Dawn piped up.

Hanna June cringed as she took a swig right out of the bottle. "Do you really like living with your parents? I can't imagine moving back home."

"Honestly, I didn't like it at first."

"Then, why'd you do it?"

"I had to. You can't be an RA in a grad program, and I couldn't afford to live on campus. I didn't really have much of a choice."

"Hmm." HJ took another swig, and her face screwed up. "Is that why you're in the program? Like, a money thing?"

"Yeah." She let out a laugh. "I don't really want to be on TV. But Kronos said that we only have to be signed on for two seasons, and then we're free to go if we want to."

This time, Hanna June's face screwed up, and it wasn't caused by alcohol. "What do you mean, you don't want to be on TV?"

Dawn's wide shoulders shrugged up and down. "I don't know. It's just not something that's really ever appealed to me. I don't feel the need for everyone to know my name."

The scoff that came out of Hanna June's mouth wasn't concealed.

Well, at least she's feeling more comfortable around us.

The blonde picked up her phone that hadn't stopped going off since she had gotten there, put it back down without doing anything, and passed an ornately decorated cup to Amber. "What about you, *Am*? Do you want to be on TV?"

Amber pushed the taco meat around in the skillet for a few seconds before answering, "I just want to do whatever is best for my family."

"*Ughhh*, no!"

Amber jumped and fumbled with the spatula for a moment after hearing the distressed and, frankly, annoyed, noise that had come out of Hanna June. "What? What's wrong?"

"You need to stop sayin' shit like that. We all get it; you're weirdly obsessed with your family, but, like, you need to chill!"

"They're my family!"

"Yes, and you're the daughter. There's no reason why *you* have to take care of everyone else. That is not your job."

They were in each other's faces by now. Dawn didn't think that either of them was going to get physical, but she also didn't like how worked up they each were.

"Look, my mom is gone, and I know you don't know what that's like, but someone else had to step in and—"

HJ cut her off. Again. "We know; we *know*. But if you need to be with them all the time that badly, then why are you here?"

This time, Amber just about screamed in Hanna June's little face. She had the plastic spatula waving around in the air, with drips of taco seasoning plopping down onto the counter. "Because I *have* to be!" You could see the saliva fly out of her mouth, and her face was almost the same color as her hair.

Dawn took that as her cue to extinguish the fire before HJ got pissy that Amber had inadvertently spit on her. She gently placed a hand on her shoulder and slightly tugged to get her to take a step back.

Amber's ragged breathing was returning to normal, and it almost looked as though Hanna June was shrinking inside herself, taking another long swig from the bottle as she leaned against the counter.

Dawn turned off the burner for the well-done meat and pulled up a chair for Amber, who gracefully stumbled back into it, her ivory dress flailing out around her. Dawn got a glass of water from the pitcher on the table, swiped the drink Hanna June had made for her, and placed them both in front of her. Amber reached for the alcohol.

She raised her own glass up, catching an extremely strong whiff of tequila before it even touched her lips. She shot HJ an annoyed look, but she just shrugged her shoulders at her and turned back to Amber, who had gulped down half the contents of her glass.

"What do you mean, you have to be?"

She put down the glass but didn't answer Hanna June.

"Is it a financial thing? Like my situation?" Dawn tried.

Still, she didn't answer. Instead, she downed the remainder of the contents in her glass, got up, and finished dishing the toppings into bowls.

Dawn and Hanna June watched her for a few seconds before Dawn took it upon herself to make the transition. No one had walked out, so they really couldn't be that mad.

Dawn picked up the bowls of cheese, lettuce, sour cream, and salsa, bringing them all over to the table, while Hanna June mixed together her next round of drinks, splashing together tequila and a dark soda.

When everything was ready, the three of them sat at the table, but nobody ate. Amber was tracing the flower design along the edge of the table with her fingertip while HJ and Dawn went back and forth between watching her and glancing at each other.

"This is pretty awkward …" Hanna June broke the silence.

Amber grabbed at her drink again, took a long sip, and started to speak as she set it back down. "My dad has some deal with Kronos."

Dawn could feel her dark eyebrows close in toward each other in confusion.

Hanna June leaned forward, keeping her wide eyes on the hostess, still ignoring her incoming texts. "What do you mean?"

"Like how your parents and Zach's parents have a deal? Same thing that my dad and Kronos have. He helped my dad out a few years ago, and in return, I have to be in the program or on the show or whatever."

"So … is that how you got into the program? Because Kronos knew you?" Dawn wanted to know more, so she could understand better, but she also didn't want to push her friend—were they actually friends? Dawn liked to think they were friends; they were definitely closer than her and Hanna June—to a point where she was uncomfortable.

She was shaking her head, making her long braid sway back and forth between her shoulders. "No. I mean … I don't know. I didn't meet him until after the contract was signed, but he knew about me when he bailed my dad out, so I just figured he was an investor or someone who worked with or for him."

"Wait." HJ spoke. At least she hadn't interrupted her again. "Bailed out, as in jail? Jeez, what did your dad do?"

The next second, Amber's green eyes flicked up to meet Hanna June's big brown ones, and then HJ was apologizing. "I'm so sorry. You don't have to tell us, obviously, because—"

"He drove into a pizzeria."

Silence sank in between the three of them. Amber suddenly didn't seem bothered by it though. While Dawn and HJ both picked up their jaws off the floor, she started assembling a taco for herself. As she dolloped some sour cream on top of a mountain of cheese, Dawn tried to follow her lead and move on as normally as possible.

After swallowing her first crunchy bite, she told them the story. "It was a few months after my mom passed away. At this point, the flowers and muffins had stopped coming, and everyone we knew just kind of … picked up and moved on with their lives. My sister and I were back in school, and my dad had gone back to traveling for work. His company was growing like crazy, so he was really busy. He'd be gone for a few days at a time, not always telling us where he was going or how long he'd be gone for. Well, there was this one night when we thought he was in Oklahoma for work. Turned out, he'd actually gone to Vegas, gotten shit-faced drunk, gambled away all our college money, and then he drove his rental car into a pizzeria on the Strip."

"Oh Mylanta."

"Jeez, Amber. That's horrible."

"Yeah. Well, I mean, I had no idea about any of it until after. Kronos is actually the one who told me. I still don't think my dad knows that I know the actual story. See, somehow, Kronos knew about what had happened, and *he* bailed my dad out. Then, he offered my dad the money for the damages to the pizzeria and to keep the story out of the press, if I would join this scholarship program he was working on putting together. I was just starting high school, so college was still a few years away. But the stipulations were that I *had* to go to Olympia College and I had to be signed on for the program for at least three seasons. And he said that there's a chance my sister might be able to get into the program too."

"Huh …"

Amber turned to face Dawn. "What?"

"That's just interesting … that you have to be in it for at least three seasons. I only have to be in the program for two, if I want."

Her friend—Dawn had decided that people didn't tell super-personal stuff like that to other people if they weren't friends—cocked her head at her. "Oh yeah, you did say that. That *is* weird."

"He didn't say anything like that to me. Or to Zach," Hanna June offered up. She looked a little worried.

"Well, that's probably because both of you actually want to be on TV. Neither of you required that much convincing, I'm assuming. Right?" Dawn spoke candidly as she explained her thoughts on the matter.

And by the look of sudden realization on Hanna June's face, she was right. "So, wait, you really don't want to be on TV?"

A slight look of disgust covered Amber's face. "No. I am perfectly fine with you being the female lead." She tried to laugh.

The taco assembling continued, and the tensions wafted away as both guests gave their apologies to Amber for her father's behavior that had ultimately led her here.

The conversation continued in between chews.

"So, you said you met him after the contract was signed?"

"Mmhmm, I think, like, two or three months after my dad's … episode."

"Wait, so you didn't meet him for the first time when we started the program either?"

The chewing slowed as both Dawn and Amber looked at HJ. "No, he came to my house a few times and talked with me and my sister. Mostly me. Just about Olympia, and, like, he wanted to know what kinds of things I liked to do. Nothing weird. What do you mean, either?"

"Umm, well, Zach and I kinda met with him, like, a year ago. Before we even applied to Olympia—that's how we found out 'bout the school. My counselor hadn't even ever heard of it."

Amber wiped some salsa from the corner of her mouth before anxiously answering her. "That's so weird. Neither had mine!"

"It's a fairly new school, compared to other colleges and universities," Dawn offered.

Having grown up in the city, she felt like she knew more about it than most of the students who went here. Olympia College was one of the largest private schools in South Carolina, but that number was still tiny when you compared it to the public universities. It was also the newest brick-and-mortar institution in the state, maybe even in the country. They didn't have a huge, domineering sports team— or the fan base to match it for that matter. The school was pretty much off the radar for everyone who didn't live in the surrounding counties.

"So, you didn't meet Kronos before it started, Dawn?"

"No, I did. But I was already a student here. I had talked to my advisor about getting additional funding for my master's program a month or two before undergrad commencement. A week or two after that, she called me back in for a meeting. Kronos was sitting in the office, too, and that was when he told me about the program."

"Huh." Amber stared in her direction, but she seemed lost in thought.

Hanna June stared down at the pile of food that had fallen out of the back of her taco. "Hmm, I wonder 'bout the boys …"

"Kai needed the money—I know that." Amber pointed a finger in Dawn's direction. "It was similar to your situation."

"Okay, that makes sense … but what about Damon?" Hanna June looked like she'd gone into full detective mode, trying to piece together the whole story. "His family has more money than Zach's does. And that's sayin' somethin'."

Both girls turned to look at Dawn.

"What?"

HJ was leaning across the table at this point, practically drooling for information. "What do you mean, what? You two are best friends. Out of not just the three of us"—she motioned to the little circle they were seated in—"but also out of everyone at the school, you'd be the one to know why he's in the program!"

Dawn paused for a moment as the realization set in that she actually didn't have an answer. "I don't know. It's not something we've ever talked about."

"Did he really go to an Ivy League?" Amber started drinking again.

"Yeah, he went to Yale for his bachelor's."

"See, *that* doesn't make sense!" HJ smacked the edge of the table. She'd started drinking again, too, but she was still in Sherlock mode. "Why would a New York trust fund baby leave an Ivy to come down here, in the middle of nowhere, to go to school?"

"Well, he hates being the center of attention …" Dawn tried to extend her calming aura over to HJ because this girl was about to be out of her chair in a minute with how amped up she was.

"But why *here*?"

"I don't … know …"

Chapter 17

ALL SIX MEMBERS WERE CALLED to do a group interview.

Kronos: All right, we've been filming for two weeks now. What do you think about it?

Dawn: It's been a very strange experience.

Kronos: Strange how, Miss Sutherland?

Dawn: Well, I can't speak for everyone, obviously, but I feel as though it hasn't been entirely … forced? We've only hung out once outside of this, and while I wouldn't necessarily call it successful, it wasn't awkward—despite most of us not really knowing each other.

Zach: Well … none of us came into this alone. So, I think that makes it easier.

Kronos: What do you mean by that, Mr. Alexander?

Zach: Like me and HJ came together. Amber and Kai aren't really, like, friends, necessarily, but they're not total strangers. And Dawn and Damon have been friends for a year. So, I think that helps, you know, having at least one person in your corner.

Kai: Yeah, actually, I'm with Zach on that one.

Damon: Me as well.

Kronos: [*smiling*] Wow, the brothers agree on something!

Damon: We are not brothers.

Kai: Yeah, don't say that.

Kronos: All right, all right. Changing the subject.

Kronos: The footage we're really looking for here is going to be very basic, very easy for you all. We're going to call it a speed round. I'm going to ask a whole bunch of simple, random questions. We're going to go around in a circle, and you're going to give me your answer. Just short phrases, even one-worded answers—I know there are several of you who like those. Just little bits, so the audience can get to know you better.

Kronos: These are going to be put into intro videos to be posted on the show's Instagram account probably next week, before episode two premieres. This way, viewers already have an idea of who you are, but it gives them just a little something personal about you to try and connect to.

Kronos: Are you all ready?

HJ: Yes, sir.

Zach: Let's do it!

Kronos: Great. Here we go. [*cameras begin rolling*] Start off with you, Kai. Favorite color?

Kai: Um … blue.

Kronos: Quick side question: are you high?

Kai: Very.

Kronos: Great. Moving on. Dawn, you're next.

Dawn: Orange.

HJ: Pink!

Zach: I don't know. Gold? Maybe blue?

Amber: Probably green …

Damon: [*sighs, annoyed headshake*] Black.

Kronos: Great. If you could have backstage passes to any concert for any singer, band, or group, alive or dead, who would it be?

Kai: Bob Marley.

Dawn: Definitely Prince.

HJ: Carrie Underwood. Or maybe Ariana Grande. No, wait. Shania!

Zach: Kanye, even though I've seen him six times.

Amber: Oh, I'd love to see Fleetwood Mac …

Damon: [*long pause*] The Beatles.

Kronos: Excellent. Last question. If you could trade lives with anyone, who would it be?

Kai: Jimmy Buffett. That guy has it made.

Dawn: Dolly Parton, but just for her philanthropy! I couldn't handle the boobs.

HJ: Easy. Princess Kate.

Zach: Any of those guys who make a living on Instagram or social media.

Amber: I don't know … Joanna Gaines?

Damon: My dog.

Chapter 18

ZACH

Kronos had called all six of them to meet at six in the morning, on a Saturday, wearing all white. So, naturally, Zach was hungover.

He'd gone out with a bunch of his new brothers last night to a few of the bars downtown. Honestly, he didn't remember most of it.

One of the guys in his frat had reminded him to text Hanna June when he got back to his dorm though, and he managed to do it without any spelling mistakes—right before one of the Theta sisters knocked on his door.

He'd set his alarms before he met up with his brothers though because he knew if he was late this morning, not only would HJ be mad at him, but so would everyone else—especially Kronos. And that man was not someone he wanted to be upset with him—Kronos was making him a *star*, for Chrissake.

He practically pushed what's-her-name out of his bed, handed her shoes to her, and gave her instructions to get to the back door when he saw the texts from his dad running down the length of his phone screen.

If he'd had time to read through them, he definitely would have—except he didn't. He had to get dressed before HJ saw the hickeys all over his chest.

Plus, his dad probably just wanted to yell at him for using his credit card last night. Not that he was going to do anything. He had never frozen the account on him or depleted his funds, so what did it matter?

Two quick knocks and one short one rapped on the door. He swung it open as he slid his belt into the loops. She had on a short white dress that she'd worn for Bid Day.

God, she's pretty.

"You ready to go?" Her huge dark brown eyes blinked at him.

He pulled her in and kissed her—really hard. He *had* missed her last night. And truthfully, he was going to ask her to come over last night, but she was already asleep when he got back. And she didn't want him drinking the night before, so he knew she'd just be upset that he was completely shit-faced drunk. And then the Theta sisters had walked in and said they were *obligated* to pay for a round for the newest brothers of Zeta Sig …

Huh. Guess I do remember some of it.

He pulled away from her, and she took a step back, trying to regain balance in her wedges, and giving him a dizzying smile.

"Oh, wait." Her train of thought changed as she reached up, adjusting the collar on his shirt.

Shit. HJ, please, I am begging you, do not unbutton anything …

"Collar's a little cattywampus," she mumbled as she folded it down correctly.

He kept his eyes on her but disguised his paranoia as lovingly as he could. "Thanks, baby girl."

"You're welcome, handsome man," she replied, pecking a kiss on his cheek.

He grabbed her butt and pulled her inside.

"Zachary!" she squealed.

"Come on. We can be a few minutes late," he said in between kisses on her neck.

"Actually, we cannot, *Mr. Alexander.*" She said his name in her best Kronos impression, which, admittedly, wasn't good at all. "Kronos texted me last night and said to make sure that *both of his stars* were on time for the shoot this morning."

One of his blond eyebrows arched. "He called us his stars again?"

"Mmhmm, yes, sir, he did. That's why I didn't want you drinkin' too much last night."

"Okay, if you're allowed to go out with your sisters, I'm allowed to go out with my brothers. There can't be a double standard!"

"No, no, baby, there isn't. I was just saying that maybe on the days where we have to do stuff for the show, just make it, like, an early night."

"I should be allowed to go out with my friends whenever I want to, Hanna June."

She took a step back from him, dropping her hands to her sides. "Zachary, that's not at all what I'm saying!"

"Okay. Then, what are you saying?"

I bet that Theta girl doesn't talk back to her boyfriend.

"Have you been listening to me? I'm saying that the frat isn't going to make you famous, so maybe put the show above your fraternity. Jesus," she tried to explain before she turned around and walked out.

Thirty minutes later, before the sun even came up, the six of them stood on the steps of the city library. Damon, Dawn, and Amber sipped at their coffees while Kai stood too close to the redhead.

This time last week, I was just getting back to Dodona. Why the hell do the dorms all have weird names? And why are we shooting this at the library?

It disappointed Zach how little this was actually shaping up to look like the photo shoots you saw in movies. There was no upbeat music pumping around them, no fans blowing in their direction, and no photographer with an exotic accent.

Kronos strolled over to Zach. He wasn't in his usual suit. Instead, the massive bald man had on an Olympia football T-shirt and some khaki shorts.

"How ya doing this morning?" He gave him a slap on the back.

"I'm really freaking tired right now, Kronos."

"You mean, hungover?"

Zach jolted his head to look at him so fast that it made him nauseous. He could feel how big his eyes grew at what Kronos had said, but he didn't care. He genuinely thought he was about to be in trouble. Apparently, he'd made a point to tell HJ to make sure he *didn't* have a late night out drinking, and yet here he was.

Fuck.

Well, I can't lie to him. He knows anyway.

"Yes, sir."

Kronos's ultra-white teeth shone in a smile at him as he laughed. "Been there. No worries."

"You're not mad at me?"

"Well, see, at your age, I would've done the same thing. I figured it was worth a shot, getting Miss Pruitt to try and talk some sense into you ... but then again, I also know that ... well, you don't always do things to appease her."

As he looked around to locate her, his head suddenly felt like it was full of rocks—heavy and dense. He pinched his eyes shut, but when he opened them, she was right there. Only a few feet away, talking to Rhianne. He could hear her drawl from where he was standing.

"You take anything for it?"

He snapped his attention back to Kronos. "Sir?"

"The hangover?" He gestured to where Zach's mop of blond hair sat atop his head. "Did you take anything for it?"

"Oh, no, sir. I didn't have time to."

Kronos nodded and then leaned in toward Zach. "I have something that might help."

But Zach still watched HJ. *Why am I such a dick to her sometimes?*

"Oh, yeah, I have some Pedialyte in my room."

A laugh erupted from Kronos, one that startled Zach and caused some of the production staff to turn and look. Kai had been taking solo photos but craned his neck away from the camera when he heard the sound.

Not meaning to have caused the attention he did, Kronos shut it down, waved his hand to signal to the others to continue, and lowered his voice when he told Zach, "Come with me."

Did Zach want to follow this large man into the changing tent? Absolutely not. Did he anyway? Obviously.

"Zip that behind you," Kronos instructed him, pointing to the flimsy canvas, as he quickly sauntered over to a wine cooler.

Following his instructions, he pulled the zipper all the way down to the edge and wondered what the hell was so much better than Pedialyte that it had to be this big of a secret.

Kronos slowly opened a metal cup as Zach approached him. He tilted the canister at an angle to pour some of the contents into the cap for Zach. And what came out was ... well, not what he'd expected.

Thick brownish-yellow liquid dripped out slowly. It looked sticky and hard to swallow. Kronos filled the cap less than halfway full.

"Bottoms up." He smiled at his so-called star.

Not bothering to hide the look of utter disgust, he raised the small metal top to his face.

It definitely *smelled* good. It couldn't be too bad then, right?

The taste was not at all what he'd thought it would be like—so sweet that he thought it might just rot his teeth at the first sip. And it *was* thick, but it went down easily, not at all like molasses.

Zach felt happy, giddy even. He thought about the argument between him and his girlfriend earlier and realized how dumb it was. He needed to apologize to her, to tell her how incredibly sorry he was for not listening to her helpful— and truthfully correct—advice last night. He wanted to tell her that he'd been an idiot, only thinking about himself and failing to see that what she was saying was true— the show was much more important than his fraternity. It made sense that he should make it his priority. He had to apologize to her.

He also felt strong—no, invincible—like there was liquid gold running through his veins. He felt more important than he ever had before—and let's face it; Zach had a massive ego, so that was pretty hard to beat.

The two of them retreated to the front of the tent, where Kronos unzipped the makeshift door and held it open for his leading male.

Stepping back out, he took in the scene in front of him. It looked similar to how it had just minutes before he drank the sugary substance—whatever it was—but everything seemed ... better now. The people had a glow to them, and Zach felt more protective over them. The crew members worked so hard to make this show the way Kronos intended. His costars had all agreed to do what they could to make it happen even though he knew they didn't all necessarily want to. But he *did* want to, and so did Hanna June. Kronos had made them his front-runners. Why? He wasn't exactly sure, but he definitely was grateful.

He marched right up to where HJ was standing at the top of the stone steps in front of the locked double doors and grabbed her around the waist.

He was about to apologize for his behavior earlier when he felt his phone start to buzz.

Who the hell is calling me this early?

He slid it out of his shorts pocket halfway to check the name. *Dad.*

Shit.

"Baby, I gotta take this. It's my dad. But I wanna talk to you when I'm done, okay?" He turned to the bald man in charge. "Kronos, I need to take this!"

The wave Kronos gave him indicated that it wasn't a problem, whatever he needed.

He hurriedly went back down the steps as he slid the bar on his phone to answer. "Hello?"

"Zachary, first of all, why haven't you texted me back? Second of all, you little shit. Who do you think you are, talking to me that way?"

What the fuck?

"What are you talking about?"

"Don't talk back to me like that! You think you can demand money from me the way you did, and it would just happen? Let me tell you something, son. I am so sick of this privileged brat you've turned into, and if you think—"

"Dad, Dad, Dad, hang on a second. Just one minute, okay?" He muted the phone call and pulled up the text to his father from the previous night.

Zach: Alright dadd listen

Zach: dont u think its aboot time you payed th money you owe

Zach: cause like they rlly need it like reaLLY bad

Zach: tbh u should of paid it a looong time ago

Zach: Like befor I was born

Zach: honesTLY its' pretty shitty that you never did

Zach: I shouldnt have to be the one to tell you to do it

Zach: you should of don it on ur own

Zach: you owe it to them dont you think

Zach: come on be a fucking man

Oops. At least most of my spelling was right. I think.

"Okay, Dad? Dad?"

Hanna June walked over toward him with a concerned look on her face. She could probably hear Richard's harsh, demanding tone from the craft services table.

"What the hell was that, son? How *dare* you-"

HJ handed him a napkin with what looked like a very small honey wafer on it. He shook his head at her, hoping she would telepathically pick up on his question: *What is it?*

Being together since they had been children seemed to have its advantages because she knew what he was asking, but she didn't have an answer, as she, too, shook her head but gestured over to Kronos, who was watching their interaction. He raised his own wafer in their direction, like a toast.

A weird honey-flavored toast at a quarter after six in the morning …

He took a bite.

Holy shit.

This might just taste better than that drink. Still don't know what that was … but, holy shit, this is good.

He toasted back to Kronos as Richard continued yelling in his ear.

"Are you even listening to me, son? If you're not gonna talk, don't answer the fucking phone!"

"Dad, I'm here. Look, I am sorry about the texts I sent you last night. I've been wanting to talk to you about that, and I guess my subconscious thought that last night would be a good time to bring it up. It wasn't, and I know that, and I'm sorry."

Hanna June tilted her head curiously at him as he apologized to his father.

His dad was silent on the other end.

Zach felt completely calm as he explained to his father that he felt as though his dad should pay back the child support money he owed to Kai's mother over the years, that it was just the right thing to do. Although her son was of legal age now, she had done him a favor by keeping the battle out of the court system.

He was about to tell his dad that if he didn't cooperate, Kai was prepared to share on the show that he'd never aided in any way to raising his "bastard son," even financially—which the country would know wouldn't have been a problem for him—when Kai snatched the phone out of Zach's hand.

"Listen to me. Are you listening?"

"Kai?" Zach could hear his father sputtering in surprise through the tiny end of his iPhone. His belligerent asshole tone had quickly shifted to cornered absentee father.

How did he know I was talking about him?

"Do you know what it's like to have to heat up pots of water just to shower? To eat dry pancake mix because there's no food in the house and your mom is out working her third job, which she *needs*, just to keep the lights on? Did you know that her credit score was so low for, like, seven years, that it didn't even register on any credit reports?"

There didn't seem to be any response on the other end, but he assumed it wasn't because he couldn't hear. He imagined his father's brain might have short-circuited.

And Kai just kept going. "No, you didn't know any of that. I bet you haven't spoken to my mom since before I was born, just like Damon's mom. And the chance for you to fix that is completely gone, so why don't you consider trying to salvage whatever you possibly can out of this relationship?"

"Are you trying to intimidate me?" Zach could hear Richard's voice bellowing through the phone.

Kai didn't bother to answer his question. "And you can start by paying my mom back the money she was owed twenty years ago."

"What if I don't?"

"I'll tell the world about how you ditched my mom and went back to your wife. And considering your past affairs, I don't think anyone will have a hard time believing me." Then, he hung up the phone and pushed it back into Zach's hand.

"Come on. Let's go. We have T-minus four minutes before the sun comes up, and none of you are in position!" Rhianne had somehow acquired a megaphone along with her espresso.

Zach's head felt like it was going to explode, and his mouth was the driest it had ever been. But after he took another bite of the strange little toast square, the pain slightly decreased.

Jägerbombs the night before a six a.m. call for a photo shoot? Not the best idea.

"That was kind of impressive, the way you talked to your dad." Hanna June slipped her finger in between his as they ascended the steps to the library together to the top.

Zach squinted so he could see the sun coming up over the river. *Having blue eyes sucks. Fucking light sensitivity.*

"Thanks."

They stood right in the middle of the massive columns as she tilted her head and looked at him sadly. "That just ... really wasn't okay. The way he screamed at you. Belittled you. Parents should never do—"

"HJ, babe, look, I really don't want to talk about it."

He looked down at her. *God, she's so pretty.* Her skin was still tan from their dual-family vacation to St. Lucia before their classes started, and her short blonde hair was tucked behind her ears. He took a step closer to her and kissed her. Like, *really* kissed her.

Leaning into her, he felt her lips soften against his, and he was reminded of how much she really loved him, despite all his screwups. All of his constant, purposeful screwups.

He could see the flashes from the cameras going off behind his closed eyelids as he pulled her closer, leaning over her frame.

He pulled away just enough to whisper, "I love you." He held her gaze and felt himself fall into her endless, dark brown eyes. Although they were dark in color, they seemed to glow, the same way everything seemed to have that yellowy aura after leaving the changing tent.

"I love you too."

"Good God, that was *fantastic!*" Rhianne was beaming from the sidewalk. She turned to the other four, who were standing next to her. "Thanks for waiting, you guys. Go on up exactly how I told you to. Zach and HJ, you two stay right where you are!"

Kai looked like he was trying very hard to keep from rolling his eyes, while Dawn had a pleasant smile on her face.

A few of Rhianne's assistants adjusted them and told them to move their heads in certain directions until Kronos approved of how it looked through the camera lens in front of him.

The first picture of all six of them featured all the males on the left and females on the right. Damon and Dawn sat on the bottom step, Kai and Amber above them, and Zach and Hanna June right at the top.

Chapter 19

DAWN

"DON'T YOU THINK THIS IS a dumb idea?"

Dawn laughed. "Of course it's a dumb idea. But it's a dumb idea that prevents me from taking out any more student loans than I already have. Not all of our dads are mayors."

Damon scoffed. "He's not my dad."

Dawn's shoulders sank. She felt horrible every time she mistakenly said the wrong title in regard to his family situation. It was confusing for anyone who didn't know.

Dawn had met Damon shortly after the whole bachelor speed-dating setup Paulina had arranged for him to find *the one*. The whole thing had been a complete disaster, as anyone could see from the clips of it that had ended up on social media at the time.

What she *had* been there for was when his biological father was reelected mayor of DC, where he publicly spoke about his three sons. There was, of course, the golden boy, Zachary, who was standing next to him; Kai, his bastard son—yes, he referred to his own child that way on live television; and lastly, Damon, the child he was never allowed to see again.

Dawn turned away from the TV that displayed the address to look up at her friend at that moment—she was tall, but he was much, much taller. "He's not allowed to see you?"

Damon didn't blink. "Court order."

Dawn learned that Damon's biological mother, a beautiful young woman named Lydia, had been interning in DC for the summer before returning to New York to finish her degree and worked closely with Damon's biological father, Richard. The night before her internship ended, they had a going-away/thank-you party for her and the other few interns. Rich confessed his feelings for her and told her he was sorry for waiting until the last minute, but he just had to make sure she knew how he felt.

A month later, she found out she was pregnant, and when she'd tried to tell him, he denied they had ever even slept together and said there was no way the baby could be his.

After Damon was born, she demanded a paternity test, which he refused. She tried to get child support, but he was climbing up the political hierarchy at that point and had people just offering her money to keep quiet. She didn't want money; she wanted a father for her baby boy.

Around the time Damon was one, Lydia met Marco Masterson, a lawyer in Manhattan. They fell in love, and without question, he stepped into the father role for Damon. They got married a few years later and had the adoption papers processed so that Damon was legally Marco's child.

However, just before Lydia had gotten married, Richard had contacted her again and apologized. He said that Damon was his child and that he wanted to be a part of his life. Lydia brought the case back in front of a judge, who agreed with her—Richard had had his chance, and he hadn't even wanted to claim the child—saying that if Lydia wanted nothing to do with him ever again, she wouldn't blame her and would gladly sign those papers for her to make it a legally binding contract. Which was exactly what was done.

The contract had to be honored, no matter what, so even after Lydia and Marco died and Damon was adopted by the Montclaires, Richard still wasn't allowed to contact him.

It was truly a horrible thing he'd been through even if he didn't remember some of it because he'd been so young at the time.

Dawn felt that those moments—the ones where he opened up and freely talked about his life, both present and past—were some of the most important ones in their friendship because she knew it was very unlikely they'd happen again.

Now, she dropped her head back onto the edge of the bench behind them and listened to the jingle of the tags on Nora's collar. "Don't you think it's interesting how both your adoptive fathers and your biological father are all in politics?"

"Yeah, I have thought about it. It is weird."

"And you're *sure* you don't want to follow their career choice?"

"Hell no."

Dawn giggled.

"Absolutely not. The only way I'd end up in politics by any means is if I was somehow forced into it. I don't see why people willingly go into politics. It's a minefield."

"I don't know." She lifted up her head, only to see Damon's gaze focused on Spot as he trotted happily along the perimeter of the fence at the dog park. "I think you'd make a great leader. Not, like, of a whole country though. Plus, no offense, I don't think you'd get that many votes, you know, to be president."

He chuckled at her. It wasn't often he laughed, but she could usually say something to at least get him to crack out his crooked smile.

"But, like, I could see you in a mayoral role."

The smile disappeared. "I don't ever want to be like him."

Dawn mashed her lips together in a straight line and nodded. "Understandable." She then reached into her brown leather bag—*I really need a new one; this thing is about to fall apart*—and dug around for a minute before finding what she was looking for.

She presented him with a Snickers, which he promptly took from her.

They watched the dogs run around and play together, as the sun set behind some trees off in the distance.

He silently pulled a pepperoni stick out of his pocket and took an aggressive bite out of it.

I hope he's feeling all right to drive back.

"What are you thinking?" It was Damon who broke the silence. Which was out of character for him.

"Are you feeling all right?"

"Just a little light-headed."

"I can tell …"

"What's your real question, Dawn," he pressed her.

Maybe I can ask him …

"Just remember, you don't have to—"

"I don't have to answer anything I don't want to. I know; I know. What is your question?"

She was always nervous to ask him anything because she knew that there were times when he took her up on the whole *not answering* deal. But she also knew that there were times when he answered her when it wasn't necessarily something she wanted to hear.

She plucked at a coil of hair on the top of her head before clasping her hands together and facing him. "Why are you in the program?"

His dark eyebrows knit together as he turned to look at her. "The master's program? Because that's part of—"

"No, no, no." She knew he hated to be interrupted, but she'd worked up the nerve to ask him, and it seemed to just be rolling out of her. "Why are you in the scholarship program?"

"Oh." He turned back to watch the dogs. "I honestly try not to think about that unless we're doing it."

Spot was trying to wrestle a toy out of Nora's mouth, but she was refusing to let go.

"I actually met Dwayne Kronos a few years ago. Before I met you."

"You did?" Dawn tried to make her voice seem casual so that he didn't get freaked out and stop talking. It took a big effort on her part to make sure he didn't know that *she* was the one freaking out on the inside, thinking back to what Hanna June and Amber had shared about their past experiences with the man prior to beginning the program.

"Yeah. I ... I did something stupid. Something I shouldn't have done. And I was going to get in a lot of trouble for it. But Kronos ... well, he was just ... there. And he helped me out but said that I would need to do something for him, no questions asked."

"Huh ... seems sketchy. You went for that?"

"I had to, Dawn. Didn't have much of a choice. He was already in the middle of cleaning up ... the mess when he told me that he'd reach back out to me and tell me what he needed from me."

"So, you ... you had a deal with him?"

"Yeah."

I feel like that's something I shouldn't share with HJ and Amber even though they said they wanted to know if I ever found out. I mean, he didn't actually say not to tell anyone, but that's kind of a given with him. And it's not like I can ask him if it's okay that I tell people that. Especially them. I really don't think he wants anyone on the show to know that he owed Dwayne Kronos a favor.

But something nagged at the back of her mind. "And you said he was just … *there?*"

Damon's dark eyes turned to face her now. "Yeah. He just showed up."

"That's really weird."

"It is, yeah. But … my life would've been so different if he hadn't shown up. I would not be sitting here right now talking to you—I can promise you that."

There was a sinister undertone in the words he was saying, and Dawn had to swallow over the lump forming in her throat.

"So, yeah, it's bizarre that he just showed up right when I needed help the most. And, yes, I was initially horrified that someone had been following me … but he just jumped right in and … fixed it."

"And you've never talked with him about it?"

"God, no."

Another moment of silence passed before Dawn turned to look at him. "How was your trip home?"

He rolled his eyes. "Pointless."

"Did your parents let up at all?"

"Nope. Still have to get married before I have access to any of the money."

She pushed some curls out of her eyes. "I'm sorry. That sucks. You shouldn't be forced to get married."

"Could be worse," he sighed as he leaned back against the bench. "Could be like that messed up thing Zach and Hanna June have going on."

She had to agree; it was a very complicated situation the two of them had been forced into and especially at such a young age. "I guess so."

"What makes it worse is that I am not marriage material. Imagine me being a husband, having a wedding and a wife and all that."

Damon had never talked about any of this with her before. As far as she knew, he never planned on getting married. She'd only known him for a year, but in that time, he never even dated anyone. He had once mentioned a girlfriend he had back in high school, but no other female had ever been brought up.

She honestly didn't know what to say to him, and that seemed to be okay because he didn't seem like he wanted to talk much more about it.

She decided to change the subject. "Can I ask you another question?"

"Yes, Dawn. You shouldn't be afraid to talk to me."

"I'm not afraid! I just don't want to push you too far," she explained to him. She felt like she constantly teetered on this tightwire, not wanting to be the cause of him going over the edge. She'd never seen that side of him, but she knew it was there. Witnessing it was definitely not on her bucket list.

"Go ahead and ask."

"You're not planning on staying in this program-slash-show thing any longer than you have to, right?"

"Right."

"Okay, good."

"Why?"

He shrugged. "Just don't want to be the only one leaving."

"And that's a for-sure thing you've decided on?"

"As soon as I can, I'm out of here."

"Even if you don't have a job lined up?"

"I'll always have a job lined up. I just don't know if that's what I want to do."

Dawn plucked at another tight coil. She still couldn't tell if he remembered telling her what he had the year prior, up on the rooftop.

She shifted on the bench. "Well, I think you should do whatever makes you happy."

He reached into the outside pocket of the bag that sat at his feet. He dug around for just a moment, and then produced a tiny chocolate bar. He offered the Snickers to her in his large open palm.

"This makes me happy."

Chapter 20

Labor Day meant that there were no classes on that Monday, which in turn meant that Zach, HJ, Kai, Amber, Damon, and Dawn were called to the third floor of the Student Center once again.

This meeting wasn't meant for interview purposes though. Instead, they'd been invited to watch the commercial and trailers for the show—which Zach and HJ had all but memorized by this point, having obsessively watched them on their own—and the director's cut of the first episode.

Kronos made a little speech right before, saying how he didn't particularly care that this was his directorial debut. What mattered the most to him was that he had been fortunate enough to have gotten to know all of them over the last three weeks and that the seven of them were working together to make something "incredible and life-changing." Then, he asked them to hold all their questions and comments until the end and stepped aside, and the pilot episode began.

It started off with an annoyingly catchy pop song, featuring candid footage of each of them in classes and walking around on campus, with their names splayed across the bottom of the screen. After the theme song, their introduction clips were featured, having been somewhat edited down. Their names faded in, displayed in their school colors—olive green and gold, which unfortunately just translated to green and yellow.

More clips were shown—Kai punching Zach, Damon and Dawn consuming too much coffee, Amber giving an apartment tour of all her plants.

Then, there were tidbits shown of Zach, HJ, and Dawn, giving their opinions of the other members. Dawn's views were valid, and she said them in such a way that the others honestly weren't upset by it. What *did* anger them was how judgmental and bitchy both of the freshmen were. Both Damon and Kai tried to walk out but were stopped. Whether they were bodyguards or just production assistants, they weren't sure, but the two half-brothers reluctantly took their seats after their exit route was blocked off. Amber, on the other hand, was holding in tears.

The scene cut to the girl's interview while Zach offered HJ his hand to hold. She toyed with the ends of her hair with her free hand and refused to make eye contact with anyone.

The reels from their spaghetti dinner were shown, and then the credits started rolling. Names flashed by on half of the black screen while the other half showed them sharing their favorite colors.

The lights came back up, and Dwayne Kronos stepped back to the front of the room. The six of them angrily blinked their eyes as the rapid change of light set in, and he clapped his hands together loudly.

"So, what do we think?"

"Cut the 'emo crap'? Are you fucking kidding me, Pruitt?" Damon was out of his chair again and had a finger pointed in HJ's direction. "Come talk to me when you see both your parents get gunned down in front of you at five years old, you bitch."

Damon had six inches on his youngest half-sibling, but that didn't stop Zach from getting up and defending his girlfriend. "Don't call my girlfriend a bitch," he ordered as he pushed his chest up against Damon's.

"Oh, don't even get me started on you, Alexander. Newport was right to knock you off your chair."

"Will you two please sit down?" Kronos stepped in and was trying to separate them, not that either of them had touched the other one.

Amber turned to HJ at the same moment. "Do you really think that about me?" Her voice didn't sound angry, like Damon's or Zach's. It just sounded hurt.

Hanna June didn't speak for a minute, but right before she did, she tucked her hair behind her ears and lifted her head so she was face-to-face with Amber. "I think you're doin' things that aren't your job. And I think you started it to be helpful, but now, it's expected of you, and *that* isn't fair."

Amber's voice rose, and her neck turned a slight shade of red. "I volunteered to do all that!"

"That's literally what I just said. Did you even listen to me?"

"Do *not* talk to me like a child." Amber's tone morphed, and her eyes turned cold.

Kai spoke up rather loudly and clearly annoyed from his tone. "Does everyone think I'm either hopelessly in love with Amber or high all the time?"

"Yes." Zach turned away from his argument with Damon.

"Yeah," HJ said at the same time.

"That's what it seems like," Damon agreed.

Dawn raised her hands slightly. "I said nothing about weed. But, yes, I think it's obvious to everyone that you feel something toward her."

His blue eyes moved around the room, holding everyone's gaze for just a second.

Well, everyone except Amber.

He looked like he was about to make a run for it the next chance he got, so Kronos gave Damon and Zach both a shove away from one another. "Everyone, just take a seat. Spread out if you need to be away from the others, but just sit down!"

Damon, apparently wired with a need to rebel, stood in the corner by the doors with his arms crossed. HJ rolled her chair over next to her counterpart. Kai slunk back down in his usual spot. Amber backed up to the far edge of the table. And Dawn stayed where she'd been the whole time.

"Well, most of you might not be happy with the finished product, but I need to inform you of something—audiences are."

"The show doesn't air until this Thursday night." Amber's voice was sharp when she spoke from the back of the room.

"Correct, Miss Hargrove. However, we've shown it to several test audiences in LA over the last two days. They love it."

Kai's head jolted toward the man in charge. "Wait, people have already seen this?" His blue eyes were wide with alarm.

"Well, the trailers and commercials have been out for a week and a half. Anybody can see those. But this version of the first episode, yes, we've had eight test audiences watch it."

"Jesus Christ."

HJ's blonde head whipped around to face him. "Do *not* say the Lord's name in vain."

"Do *not* tell me what I can and can't say," he dished back to her.

"Do *not* start this again!" Kronos took over the conversation. "Guys, come on!"

Rhianne took a step forward, lowering her clipboard. "Guys, just FYI, you're all free to leave after this. Honestly, we should've been done by now, but since you all want to verbally attack each other, we're running a little behind schedule." She tapped on the face of her watch.

HJ looked at her feet, and Amber fiddled with the ends of one of the six tiny braids in her hair. Damon seemed unfazed.

"We need more," was all Kronos said after Rhianne took a step back behind him.

HJ lifted her head to look at him with heavy uncertainty. "More what?"

"We need more of your personal lives."

"No." Damon didn't move as he said the word, and while everyone definitely heard him, Kronos ignored him.

"Our test audiences were extremely interested in your lives, in your stories. All of the feedback was that they liked learning about you all and watching you go about your day and your lives as students, but they had already gotten hooked on the things you were all going through."

Amber swiveled her chair back and forth, and you could see her mulling over what Kronos had said. Nobody else moved though, so he kept going with his spiel, trying to convince them.

"I hate to bring it up, but the whole thing between Mr. Newport and Miss Hargrove was a huge talking point. Same thing with Mr. Alexander and Miss Pruitt's setup. It's caused a major discussion on social media. Do none of you go on Twitter?"

Amber and Damon simply shook their heads. Dawn shared that she didn't have that particular app while Kai informed them that he hadn't been on his Twitter account in over a year.

Zach and HJ told the group that they were both very active on all their social media accounts—big surprise—and that people were talking about the show constantly.

"Guess I didn't pay much attention to the stuff with Kai and Amber 'cause, ya know … it wasn't about me," HJ sheepishly admitted.

Kai choked out a short laugh. "Wow."

"I'm bein' honest!"

"Look," Kronos interjected before it escalated again. "It's not a secret that several of you do not want to be in this program. But for better or worse, this is the situation. I suggest you make the most out of it while you can."

Another silence passed around the room before Zach spoke up again. "What do you mean, more of our personal lives, Kronos?"

"Think about the *Kardashians*, *The Bachelor* and *The Bachelorette*, *Jersey Shore*, or any reality TV show. We see the inner workings of their entire lives—that's what makes it entertaining; that's why people *watch*. We want to see the not-so-studious side of your college lives."

"I guess that makes sense." HJ was nodding as she spoke.

"Yeah," Zach joined in. "The show probably won't be very exciting if we're just answering generated questions all the time."

"Can I be honest with you all?" Kronos leaned on the chair. "If we get enough viewers, we get renewed for another season. That second season would bring you not only another free semester here, but also a salary."

Zach and HJ both sat up a little straighter at hearing that, and Amber leaned on the edge of the table, all ears. Even Damon, who had shoved himself in the corner behind the man, tilted his head just slightly at Kronos's words.

"I think you should all go out together. Go downtown and don't be afraid to … ya know, act like typical college kids in front of the camera."

Zach cleared his throat. "HJ and I are going out Thursday night. We were gonna have dinner together as a kind of, like, celebratory first-episode thing. We were thinking of going to one of the clubs on Fifth afterward, if anyone wants to meet us there?"

Kronos interjected, almost defensively. "We didn't want to do a viewing party or anything because we know you all do have classes and social lives, and scheduling interviews is hard enough for

Rhianne. But I think you should definitely all go out and celebrate together. Excellent idea, Mr. Alexander."

"You call it Fifth Street?" Kai questioned him. He hadn't listened to anything Kronos had just said.

Zach's tone came out so sassy. "Yes, Kai, I do call it that because that's the name of the street."

"It's called Court Street when you're downtown," he argued back.

"It has two names," Dawn interjected. She literally exuded peace.

They both shut their mouths and dropped the pointless debate.

"*Anyway,* that's our plan. You guys down?"

Damon rolled his eyes. There were seven years in between him and his blond half-brother, and there was an obvious language barrier to serve as a constant reminder. "No."

Dawn glared at him from her spot at the long conference table. "*Yes,* we will be there."

Amber stopped biting her nails to answer. "I guess I can show up for a little bit. But I can't stay too late. I have an eight a.m. tomorrow."

"Yeah, I'll be there too," Kai responded, his stare focused on the center of the table.

Kronos too loudly clapped his hands together again. "Okay, that's great. I personally won't be there; I have some business to take care of this weekend. However, we'll have two cameras on-site, and I'm going to send a new young man in to sort of play my role as interviewer. I figured you all could use a break from seeing my face. I also have no desire to step into downtown Olympia on a Thursday night!" He laughed, Zach and HJ semi-joining in. "I hope you all feel free to record or post anything you want on your personal social media accounts; I know people are going to want to be celebrating with you! I'll have the editing team put all your handles at the end of the episode! This is going to be great!"

Aside from his stars, no one else really seemed that enthusiastic.

Damon was out the door in a nanosecond—if you'd blinked, you might've missed him.

Kai heaved himself out of his chair, stopping to tell Kronos, "This was fun," before he walked out.

Amber picked up her oversize bag from the floor, mumbled, "I should probably go too," and was the third one to leave.

Dawn thanked Kronos for his time and again for the opportunity.

Zach and Hanna June stayed right where they were. She turned to look at him as soon as Dawn was out of earshot.

"We're going to be on TV!" she squealed, and he matched her excitement.

Chapter 21

SOLO INTERVIEW WITH AMBER.

Kronos: How are you doing today, Miss Hargrove?

Amber: [*slightly pouting*] My Geology lab tonight got canceled, and I really like that class …

Kronos: You're going home to visit your family this weekend?

Amber: [*lets out a big sigh*] No. My dad has some work thing he's going to Omaha for, and Fleur is going to be staying at my Meemaw's in Savannah.

Kronos: But you go home most weekends?

Amber: Yeah.

Kronos: Why though? Most college kids prefer to stay on campus. You know, go out with their friends and party and then sleep in the next morning.

Amber: [*shrugs*] Every once in a while, I do that. But I'm needed back home more.

Kronos: Your dad can't take care of things around the house?

Amber: [*looks down, swallows*] Not really. He's still upset about losing my mom. Some basic daily functions are sometimes too much for him.

Kronos: So, you're a daughter, but you also play the mother and caretaker roles? While being a student? Isn't that a lot?

Amber: [*shrugs again*] Sometimes, yeah. I really don't think about it much anymore. I've been doing it for so long.

Amber: Honestly, I like doing it, even when it gets stressful. It's one of those things that I feel like I'm just good at. [*facial expression quickly changes to slight panic*] Not that I want to think that! You know, that I'm thriving in a role my mom had before … before we lost her.

Kronos: How long ago was that?

Amber: Six years ago.

Kronos: How old were you?

Amber: I was thirteen. Fleur was eight.

Kronos: Would you mind sharing what happened? You don't have to.

Amber: [*pauses, contemplates*] We only moved to Charleston because my mom wanted to. That was her dream—to live in one of those colorful houses across from the water that everyone took pictures of. So, we left Nebraska when I was ten, and a year later, we adopted Fleur.

Amber: Well, we both initially went to school across the bridge, but Fleur got bullied there a lot, so Mom and Dad decided to enroll her in this private school just a few blocks from where we live. That morning, she had a meeting with CPS, just like a check-in type of thing. After the meeting, my mom took her to breakfast and then walked her to school. On her walk back to the house, this Cadillac drove up on the sidewalk and just … ran her down. Crashed into the front of a stationery shop. She—[*chokes up but quickly straightens*] She rolled up over the hood and landed on the concrete behind the car and was just … gone. [*one tear rolls down cheek, doesn't break eye contact with the camera*]

Kronos: That's horrible, Amber. I'm so sorry.

Amber: Yeah. [*sniffles*]

Kronos: Okay, let's lighten the mood. What do you do to relax?

Amber: [*looks alarmed, sits up straighter*] I just, you know … I paint. Take care of my plants. Boring stuff.

Kronos: You occasionally go out with the rest of the cast, right?

Amber: [*pauses*] Yeah.

Kronos: Are you planning on going out with them Thursday night?

Amber: [*clears throat, tries to seem put together but makeup is running, so it's not really working*] Yeah, I think so. I think it'll be nice to hang out and get to know each other better, you know, without all the dialogue prompts and questions from you—no offense!

Kronos: Nope, none taken. I know it's a strange situation, and I think tonight will be really great for the six of you. And hopefully, we'll get some great footage of you all actually acting like college kids—you know, targeting that audience we want.

Amber: [*nodding slowly, lost in thought, then looks up, slightly skeptical*] Kronos, can I ask you a question?

Kronos: [*slightly uncomfortable but tries to hide it*] That's usually my job! [*chuckles*] But, sure, I suppose so.

Amber: Why did you pick us?

Kronos: [*leans back in chair, folds hands in lap. Amber can't see that he's starting to sweat.*] What do you mean?

Amber: Well, you said that you handpicked us all during the application process, so, like, why? What made you pick us over other applicants?

Kronos: [*pauses*] Well, [*clears throat*] there honestly wasn't a whole lot of applicants. And you six … you all just gave me that feeling that you were going to do great things.

Amber: [*squints eyes at him, definitely trying to figure out what he means by that*] Huh …

Kronos: The idea is that this show will get a little bit bigger, and ideally, we can add a few more members, and this group, all of you together … you'll go down in history. I don't want this show to be easily forgotten, and if things go the way it looks like they will—the way I've planned for them to go—then you will all be unforgettable.

Amber: Wait, you want the show to get *bigger*?

Kronos: I do, Miss Hargrove. I know we've only released the pilot episode, but you are already huge. The whole country is talking about you and your costars. Are you really not aware of the fanfare you've caused?

Amber: [*quietly*] I don't have social media.

Kronos: You don't keep up to date with news? Even in pop culture?

Amber: [*shakes head, eyes are still huge, looks very unsettled*]

Kronos: [*pulls out phone, types, taps, and scrolls for a few seconds, then turns it to Amber*] Remember those numbers I shared with you, Miss Pruitt, and Miss Sutherland during our group interview session?

Amber: [*nods*]

Kronos: They've doubled; some have nearly tripled. We're anticipating over a million viewers for Thursday night's episode.

Amber: One—one million people?

Kronos: That's the hope. You guys have been trending on Twitter since Monday.

Amber: Oh God.

Kronos: We're going to be setting up a Snapchat account for you all to do those take over things from and to post behind the scenes on too.

Amber: [*inaudible noise*]

Kronos: You six are going to take over the world.

Amber: [*weak smile, then eyes dart back to the floor, hold stomach, rips off mic, and runs out*]

Chapter 22

INDIVIDUAL INTERVIEWS PIECED TOGETHER.

Interviewer: Be honest—why did you come out tonight?

Zach: Just wanted to go out with my girl, have a good time … [*eyes a group of girls as they walk in*]

Interviewer: So … if you want to go out with your girl, why did you just linger way too long on the four who just walked past?

Zach: Hey, man, shut the hell up! [*clearly offended*]

Interviewer: I said, be honest!

Zach: [*lets out a deep sigh*] Okay, look, being in a relationship is like being in a museum—you can look, but you can't touch. [*starts to walk away, but leans into interviewer, mostly off camera*] Unless you're really, really careful about it. [*slips interviewer a hundred-dollar bill, whispers*] Edit this out.

HJ: I love comin' out with Zach. We get dressed up, I get to show him off, he gets to show me off. This might sound silly, but I love knowing that every girl is seeing how good he looks, but I'm the only one who gets to have him.

Interviewer: Is that right?

HJ: Oh, yeah. Everyone always looks at us 'cause, I mean, look at us. [*shows lock screen on phone*] We look fucking amazing together— oh my gosh, I'm so sorry! I didn't mean to curse. Can you edit that out?

Interviewer: It's gonna cost you.

HJ: [*lets out an annoyed scoff as she scrambles in her purse before handing interviewer a twenty-dollar bill*] That's what I get for pre-gaming with Captain Morgan and SunnyD.

Kai: I'm only here because Amber is here.

Interviewer: You wanna get with Amber?

Kai: I've been trying for, like, two years. We went on one date, and I thought it was great, but I guess not 'cause she won't go out with me again.

Interviewer: Have you tried just talking to her? Seeing where her head is at and what she wants? There could be something else entirely that has nothing to do with you that's preventing her from opening herself up to you.

Kai: [*pauses*] No ... I haven't tried that. That's a good idea though. I'm gonna try that. Hey, thanks, man. You know what? [*hands interviewer a twenty-dollar bill*] Consider it a tip.

Damon: Dawn dragged me out.

Dawn: I honestly want to get to know these people more. They're considered my coworkers, but I'd like to get to know them outside of the office, if you know what I mean.

Damon: [*loudly from the doorway*] Everyone knows what you mean.

Dawn: Damon, get out of my interview! Can you just edit him out?

Interviewer: It's gonna cost you.

Damon: [*stepping forward and shoving a fifty-dollar bill into interviewer's hand, then grabbing Dawn's elbow and going inside*]

Amber: I allow myself to live the so-called "fun" college life for a few hours once a week. All the rest of the time is spent focusing on school or my family. So, this is my allotted fun time slot.

Interviewer: Yeah, you seem like you're having the time of your life.

Amber: [*biting nail, staring at sidewalk*] I really don't want to go inside.

Interviewer: What just happened inside?

Zach: I was defending my girl—that's what fucking happened.

Amber: [*looks physically upset*] Someone spilled their drink on me …

Dawn: Zach punched a guy because his hand happened to brush Hanna June's butt. But it was an accident. I saw the whole thing.

Kai: Zach clocked some dude for feelin' up HJ. He went flying into the bar, knocked, like, three people down. Someone's drink went all over Amber. [*pauses*] I actually feel really bad about that. I hope she's okay.

Damon: [*seems pissed off*] I don't know, and I really don't care. I do not want to be here.

HJ: This skeezy frat guy comes up and grabs my ass, and before I can even do anything, my wonderful boyfriend reaches over and sets him straight. Serves the creep right. Zach really is the perfect boyfriend. I'm so grateful for him. [*pauses*] I never said thank you. [*looks back inside*] Where did he go?

Interviewer: Kai, how you feelin'?

Kai: I feel fucking great.

Interviewer: Well, that's a nice change 'cause, ya know, you're usually pretty down.

Kai: Yeah, well, I'm fucking drunk. So, that's good.

Interviewer: Why is it good?

Kai: 'Cause exactly what you just fucking said, man. I'm always fucking depressed and shit. But now I'm not, 'cause I'm getting fucking wasted!

Interviewer: Why are you always depressed?

Kai: 'Cause I just … like, you know, fucking love.

Interviewer: Love?

Kai: Yeah. [*pauses*] I fucking love her. And she won't let me. So, I gotta keep fucking these sluts that don't measure up to her, and I swear to God, man, I feel so much fucking worse afterward.

Interviewer: Who do you love that doesn't love you back?

Kai: [*looks directly into camera*] Amber Hargrove.

Interviewer: Oh … wait. I thought you just wanted to hook up with her. Have, um … why won't she let you love her back?

Kai: [*exasperated sigh, throws his arms side to side like a child*] Says she's got too much going on. And I know that. I fucking know that. She's got this really complicated family setup, and she feels responsible for doing everything because she's just such a good person, and I just want to be there for her, and she won't let me.

Zach: [*comes outside*] Dude, where you been?

Kai: [*walking toward the camera, looking directly into it and ignoring Zach*] I fucking love her. And I just want her to love me back. [*tears up*]

Zach: [*to interviewer*] Shit, what the fuck did you do?

Interviewer: I'm doing my fucking job.

Kai: [*uncontrollable crying and incoherent blubbering*]

Zach: What the fuck?! Dude, you're supposed to be a fun drunk! There're four girls inside who have asked me for your number, man.

Kai: [*shakes head, still crying*] I don't care.

Zach: Well, you need to care. Actually, what you need is to get laid. Come on. You got four options. Maybe you can even get them all at the same time. That's pretty—[*glances at camera*] I've heard it's pretty great.

Kai: [*slumps against wall and slides down, lying on sidewalk*] I LOVE YOU, AMBER!!!

Zach: [*to interviewer*] I hope you're happy.

Interviewer: I'm fucking ecstatic. This is great TV.

Chapter 23

HANNA JUNE

AT ONE THIRTY IN THE MORNING, there was still a line outside of the club as HJ and Zach finally left.

Damon and Dawn had been the first to leave, right after the interviews about the whole butt-touching incident. Amber was twenty minutes behind them, and Zach had dumped Kai into an Uber within a half hour of his on-camera meltdown.

As they walked up the hill toward campus and Greek Row, they could hear the music fading behind them as they left the party scene.

There was something so peaceful about this part of the night that HJ looked forward to every weekend when they went out. The overstimulation of everything behind them, the quiet and the darkness ahead of them, her state of drunkenness, where everything was just really *good*. Every Saturday night, without fail, as they exited the club, Zach would extend his elbow, all chivalrous-like, and they'd walk that way, all the way back to whoever's place they had decided to stay at that night.

"Did you have fun tonight?" he asked her as the crosswalk lights told them it was safe to walk.

A smile spread across her face as she nodded. "I did. It was a little different with the cameras on us and the interviews in between … but I liked it."

"Yeah, me too."

Then, they were quiet as they slowly crossed over onto campus territory. There was a massive stone wall that read *Olympia College*, and every time she passed it, Hanna June imagined her and Zach taking their graduation pictures there someday.

"Are your feet hurting?"

She shook her head.

"Are you sure? Because I can carry you, if they're hurting."

Hanna June smiled at him and reassured him that she felt fine. She loved when he fell into the boyfriend role.

Which made it hurt even more when he didn't. And although she knew he had probably disappeared into the skeezy bathroom at High Life with some slutty freshman, she chose not to go down that road and changed the subject.

"How are Keanu and Skye?" She loved his little siblings' names; they were just so interesting.

The age difference between him and the younger two had always been kind of weird for Zach, but HJ loved the idea. His parents had had him and raised him and then added two more when he was older. They had a role model, and his parents had a babysitter. When they had still been in high school, Zach would take them to T-ball practice or dance recitals, and HJ had loved being a part of it. Watching him fall into the father-figure role was such a turn-on for her.

"They're fine. Key wants a dirt bike for his birthday."

"I'm sure your parents love that idea." She laughed.

He smiled back at her. "I told them if they don't get it for him, I will."

"Of course you did."

"You're coming to his birthday party when we're home for break, right?" The look in his eyes resembled worry, like he wasn't sure if she would actually show up. Even though she'd been at the hospital when he was born and not missed a birthday since.

"You know I wouldn't miss it."

His blond head bobbed as he nodded, and soon they were in front of Ash Residence Hall.

Such an ugly name. Who decided to name the dorms after trees?

He tugged on her arm, gently pulling her away from the main entrance to the building. "Come on."

"Why can't we stay at my place?"

" 'Cause you know your roommate is either gonna be awake and wanna stay up and talk or she's going to be *busy* with that English TA," he explained to her as he pulled her into his arms and cupped her face in one hand. She could feel the small calluses brush against her cheek.

"Probably the second one."

"Mmhmm, which means that I can't be busy with you. I, on the other hand, have only seen my roommate three times since we moved in," he reminded her as one of his hands slid around to palm her butt cheek.

A smile spread like a wildfire across her face. "Well, why didn't you just say so? But on one condition," she counterargued.

"Anything for you, Miss Pruitt."

"My feet are actually hurting now, so you're going to have to carry me."

Her sentence wasn't finished before he scooped her up bridal-style and was moving his legs as fast as he could down the sidewalk to his residence hall, and Hanna June didn't stop laughing the whole way, not even noticing the camera crew catching the moment.

Chapter 24

INDIVIDUAL INTERVIEW WITH DAMON.

Interviewer: Since the last episode was such a hit, Kronos asked me to conduct some one-on-one interviews … specifically yours.

Damon: Lucky me.

Interviewer: So, now, tell me, you've been on TV before?

Damon: Yes.

Interviewer: What were you on TV for?

Damon: [*sighs, looks at watch*] It was one of those talk shows run by a washed-up actress who had nothing better to do. They were doing a segment on the most eligible bachelors from the country's wealthiest families or something stupid and marketable like that.

Interviewer: So, was the spotlight on you or your family?

Damon: Both.

Interviewer: How old were you when you were on the show?

Damon: I don't know. Twenty?

Interviewer: Huh, I didn't know twenty was an acceptable age to be considered a bachelor. Seems a little young.

Damon: Yeah, well, that's Pau—that's my mom.

Interviewer: What do you mean by that?

Damon: She's always orchestrating things to draw attention to her family.

Interviewer: Well, your father is in politics, right?

Damon: Yeah.

Interviewer: Seems like she might've been doing those things in an effort to keep him in office.

Damon: Probably.

Interviewer: And your mother organized her own version of *The Bachelor* for you a few years after that, right?

Damon: Yes.

Interviewer: And that attempt was also unsuccessful?

Damon: [*crosses legs, looks at watch again*] Yes.

Interviewer: Now, a minute ago, you started to say her name. Do you normally call your parents by their first names?

Damon: Yeah.

Interviewer: You were adopted, right?

Damon: Yeah.

Interviewer: Is that why?

Damon: Probably. My real mother and father are dead. It seems disrespectful to pass the title along to someone else.

Interviewer: That makes sense … but isn't your biological father still alive?

Damon: [*long stare*] That man is not a father. To any of the children he's played a part in actually making, but me especially. He's nothing more than a sperm donor.

Interviewer: I feel like one of your costars would disagree with you.

Damon: Maybe, but that's because he doesn't know any better. I've had three father figures in my life. I know what a real dad is like. He doesn't because he has nothing to compare it to.

Interviewer: [*nodding*] That makes a lot of sense. So, how did the segment go? Find any possible contenders to be the future Mrs. Montclaire?

Damon: Fuck no.

Interviewer: [*laughs*] What makes you say that?

Damon: It went exactly how my ... how Paulina wanted it to go. My father's numbers did go up in the polls that election. She got invites to a dozen more fundraisers and galas in the following few months. And, yeah, girls started throwing themselves at me.

Interviewer: And you didn't like that?

Damon: No.

Interviewer: You didn't like girls throwing themselves at you?

Damon: That's correct.

Interviewer: [*looks unsure of himself, leans forward, and quietly whispers*] Are you, like ... you know?

Damon: [*completely unfazed by the question*] No, but you know, if I was, thanks for asking me during a TV interview.

Interviewer: Uh ...

Damon: I'm just not one of those guys. I have better things to do than just getting laid all the time.

Interviewer: And you weren't considering even one of them?

Damon: Not one.

Interviewer: Why not? What was it about them that turned you off?

Damon: Everything. Let's move on. [*clearly getting annoyed*]

Interviewer: Now, your adoptive mother seems exceedingly intent on making your romantic relationship happen now, rather than later. Why do you think that is?

Damon: I have no idea. You can ask her. I'm sure she'd be more than willing to set up an interview.

Interviewer: [*smirks*] We can change the subject. Tell me, why did you come *here*? You left one of the most esteemed universities in the country … to come to this rinky-dink little town—nowhere near your family, I might add—for your master's degree and your PhD. Why?

Damon: Guess I just didn't want to be in New Haven anymore.

Interviewer: Have you applied to any other PhD programs?

Damon: That's really not anyone's business.

Interviewer: Okay, okay. Heard. Can I ask one more question? It's not on the cards or anything, just something I've been wondering …

Damon: Sure.

Interviewer: Why are you doing this? Like you've made it obvious that you don't like sharing personal information, you don't like having the cameras on you, and you hate being the center of attention. So why did you agree to it all?

Damon: [*prolonged silence before he gets up, takes off mic, and leaves*]

Chapter 25

DAWN

DAWN SAT AT AMBER'S KITCHEN table across from her. Amber had made a pot of coffee for them, and it tasted better than any brew she'd ever had.

"I spend more than fifty dollars a week on coffee, and this is the best cup I've ever had!" She laughed at her friend across the table. Well, she wasn't quite sure if friend was the right word, but she couldn't think of a better one to use.

"Well, thank you," Amber proudly smiled, her rust-colored hair swaying as she shook her head giddily.

Dawn had gotten the feeling that she didn't really have many friends. When she had approached her with the idea of a coffee date—just the two of them, no cameras—Amber had been hesitant at first but ultimately accepted the invitation.

Honestly, Dawn just felt like she needed someone to talk to. If the rumors were true, she had a complicated home life and too much on her plate. Not that Dawn listened to rumors. She much preferred to go right to the source and figure out the truth instead of poisoning her mind and the minds of others with, *Well, I heard this,* and, *I bet it's like this,* and, *What if …*

"How are your parents handling the whole you-being-on-TV thing? Sorry, I didn't mean for that to sound like an after-school special!" Amber laughed.

"No, no, it's okay! Honestly, they've been really supportive. My dad pretends to be paparazzi sometimes, like when I'm brushing my teeth," she let her in on.

"Oh my gosh, that's hilarious!"

"What about yours?"

Amber tapped her fingertips on the ceramic edge of her mug and stared into her coffee. "I haven't really talked to them about it."

Dawn was confused. "What? You talk to your family all the time."

"I stay away from the show though. Like … I don't know. I just feel weird, having it be a topic of conversation. Like, it's fine right now, between me and you because we're both doing it. But, like, my dad still gets super depressed sometimes, and Fleur is so impressionable. I don't want her to think this is normal. She's already obsessed with the whole idea of it."

Dawn smiled at her. She really liked talking to Amber. She liked talking to HJ, too, but she had more in common with Amber, and she wasn't as judgmental and harsh as HJ could be. "I think if you explained it to her that way—that this isn't reality—instead of purposely not making it a talking point, then she might be more understanding."

Amber scrunched her eyebrows together, seemingly lost in thought. She nodded, holding her gaze on the wooden table in between them.

She kept going. She loved giving advice—maybe it was because she felt like she was actually helping people; maybe it was because she was just good at it. "And as for your dad, he's probably going to have those really sad moments for the rest of his life, and unfortunately, *that's normal.* But your job is to be there for him, to support him in the bad moments and to celebrate the good ones with him."

The redhead smiled sadly at her. "Thanks, Dawn."

They both quietly took tiny sips of their drinks, and then Dawn pushed a handful of coils out of her face. "So, I have to admit something."

"What's that?" Amber asked as she sipped from her mug. It looked hand-painted, and Dawn saw when she picked it up that it was signed, but she couldn't read it upside down.

"Out of us girls, you're the one I would rather talk to …"

Amber leaned back, laughing. "The only other one is HJ!"

Dawn laughed with her. "I know! It's not that I dislike her; it's just that you're so much calmer than her. You know, you don't crave the spotlight, drama doesn't follow you … it's just much more enjoyable, spending time with you."

"Well, thank you again. I feel the same way about you—but don't tell anyone I said that!"

"No, no, of course not!"

They both sipped their drinks before Amber changed the topic. "So, what's the deal with you and Damon? I know you tell everyone you're just friends, but is it really something else …"

Dawn stared back at the redhead across from her.

"Sorry, I didn't mean to pry! You don't have to tell me." The words flew out of her mouth, and she looked sheepishly down at her hands in her lap. Her cheeks turned a slight shade of pink, though Dawn didn't know why *she* felt embarrassed. She wasn't the one who had just gotten asked if she was secretly hooking up with her best friend.

She should've seen it coming though. Kronos had asked them in an interview, and people had been asking the both of them for years. It was only a matter of time before one of her other costars asked. She had just assumed it would be Zach or HJ.

"It's okay. We get asked that a lot." She tried to keep a calm demeanor for Amber's sake. She never liked seeing other people feel embarrassed or ashamed. "We've been friends for almost six years, but we've never been anything more than that."

"Never? Not even like, you know, a drunken accident?"

Dawn laughed. She was the oldest out of the six, but she'd never had a sip of alcohol. "Not even a drunken accident."

Amber seemed disappointed in her response. "But … he's so … and you're so …" She shook her head. "Never mind."

"Don't ever shy away from sharing your feelings about a situation. Tell me what you're thinking," Dawn encouraged.

Amber stared at her for a moment, almost like she was trying to decide if she'd end up twiddling her thumbs after she voiced her opinion again.

"I just think you guys would kind of balance each other out. He's so dark and broody and kind of … scary? And you're just so kind and warm and inviting."

Dawn repeated her words over in her head at least six times. She liked her description, and she felt like Damon wouldn't be able to argue if he were here.

She must've been quiet for too long because Amber spoke again. "Are you seriously telling me you're not and never have been attracted to him?"

Dawn laughed again. She really liked laughing. She didn't laugh much with Damon, but she'd laughed now five times in the last half hour. Amber's filter seemed to have a mind of its own, but for the most part, she really liked her.

She leaned in closer to the table, feeling like she was sharing secrets with her friends at the lunch table in elementary school again. "Wanna know something?" She didn't know why she lowered her voice—they were the only two here.

Amber nodded excitedly.

"I did have a crush on him when we first met. For almost a year."

Amber's green eyes were massive. And then a wide smile splayed across her face. Dawn tried not to focus on how perfectly her teeth were all aligned. It reminded her of her brace-face era.

No, thank you.

"And what? It just faded away?"

Actually, I found out that he had committed murder in the past and was planning to do it at least one more time, and that was kind of a deal-breaker for me.

"Yeah," she said instead as she sat back against her chair, the fun, gossipy moment over. "Sometimes, you learn more about a person, and the way you see them just changes."

Amber was still staring at her, as if she knew Dawn wasn't telling her the whole truth, but she didn't ask any other questions. Instead, Dawn turned the tables on her.

"What about you?"

"What, do I have a crush on Damon?"

Dawn laughed. Again. *Six.* "No, like, what's going on with you and Kai?"

Embarrassed Amber was back. Not looking at her hands in her lap though, but frozen, facing Dawn. She didn't even blink for almost a minute. "You don't have to tell me if you don't want to. I was just curious."

She could visibly see Amber swallow. "No, it's just …" The sigh that she let out as she unfroze and dropped her elbows to the table and her head into her hands felt *heavy*. Dawn could see that her shoulders were tense, and she gripped the roots of her hair.

"I don't know."

Somehow, she sensed that Amber wanted to say more but just needed a minute. Dawn waited patiently.

Her parents had always told her she was the most patient person in the whole world, and that was something Dawn remembered being so proud of as a little girl; she did all she could to practice patience every day, so she could remain the most patient person in the world, especially as she got older.

"Your generation grew up when technology became as big as it is now, and it just keeps growing. And some of that is good; it makes things a lot easier for a lot of people. But it's also doing the human race a disservice—having the world available to us in just a few taps of our fingers is teaching us to become more and more impatient. We simply cannot wait for things anymore, and when that happens, we lose the appreciation we once had for things that we had to wait for. We are losing our patience. But not you, Dawn Avery. You're the most patient person in the whole world, and I hope you never lose it." It was one of those core memories that Dawn had imprinted right at the front of her mind.

"We went out once. We kissed once. And, like, I wanted to do it again. And again and *again*, but I can't."

Dawn already knew the next thing she was going to say. It was a vague response she always gave, but one that she seemed to have a valid reason for giving. "Because of your family?"

Amber nodded again, keeping her head in her hands.

She let a silent moment pass between them before voicing what she wanted to say next. "Can I ask you some questions? You obviously don't have to answer anything you don't want to; I completely understand privacy."

Her head nodded, so Dawn continued, "You know he … has feelings for you, right?"

"I think everyone in the world knows. I can't believe he did that."

Dawn shrugged even though Amber wasn't looking at her. "They say drunk words speak sober thoughts."

The only response to come from her was an upset groan.

"Did you have a good time with him when you two went out?"

"Yeah." Her voice was weak, like she didn't want to admit it.

"And when you guys kissed, did you like it?"

She looked up now, and Dawn immediately picked up on the sadness in her eyes. She stared at her for another minute before finally answering the question. "I *loved* it." Then, she dropped her head back down again.

"So, would you want to go out with him again?"

"I would love to, but I can't because of my—"

"Family. Yeah."

More silence hung heavy in the air, but Dawn refused to fill that space. She had asked Amber a lot of questions. Questions that she had the feeling Amber hadn't been asked before. Or maybe she had, but Dawn didn't think Amber had ever fully admitted the truth, even to herself.

When Amber finally picked up her head and took another sip from her hand-painted mug, Dawn lowered her voice and offered her last tidbit of advice.

"I think your family will understand if you feel the need to take some time to explore a relationship. I think that's only fair. And as far as Kai goes, I think it says a lot about him that he knows about your home life and all that, but still wants to be with you. So, I think he might be worth another shot. Especially considering he yelled to anyone who would listen that he loves you and didn't ask Kronos or Rhianne or anyone to take it out of the episode."

"He was drunk, Dawn. He probably didn't know what he was saying."

"I think he knew exactly what he was saying. And I think you know that too."

Chapter 26

PARTNER INTERVIEW WITH ZACH AND HANNA JUNE.

Interviewer: So, you guys are quite the *it* couple.

Zach: Sorry, where's Kronos?

Interviewer: Oh, uh—

Zach: Like, no offense. I just kinda thought you interviewing us was, like, a onetime thing because he wasn't available. Actually, I think it was really just because the old man didn't wanna go downtown. Which, I get, ya know … [*fake laughs*] But, so, like, is this a permanent thing, you doing this?

Interviewer: No, no. Kronos just isn't always around. He arranged his schedule so that he could be the interview conductor for the first few weeks, so it wasn't such a huge transition for you guys. But he *is* the head of a television network and can't always be here, you know, in bumfuck, North Carolina—

HJ: South Car'lina.

Interviewer: Yeah, whatever. So, when he's not here, it's going to be me doing it, and then the backup for me is Rhianne. That cool?

Zach: Uh, yeah. Yeah, sure.

Interviewer: Great. So, is it okay if we get back to the topic of you two?

HJ: Absolutely.

Interviewer: So, lots of viewers will frequently go to social media to say things like, *I want a love like Zach and HJ*, or *Waiting for my Zach*. There're even shirts that say things like that. What do you guys think about that?

HJ: [*visibly excited*] I've seen that! It's so sweet!

Zach: Yeah, it is. But just, like, keep in mind that, you know, we're not perfect. We've had our struggles.

Interviewer: Oh yeah? What kind of struggles?

Zach: [*laughs*] Like, all of middle school. You know, hormones.

HJ: [*swats Zach's arm playfully*] Stop it.

Zach: Well, it's true!

Interviewer: What do you mean by that?

HJ: [*looks slightly alarmed, puts a gentle hand on Zach's forearm*] Oh, no. I don't think that's really appropriate to be sharin' on TV. [*looks at him with a distressed look on her face*]

Interviewer: [*leans forward, as if he's trying to level with them*] Look, guys, you're the hottest thing right now. Not just the hottest show out there or even the hottest cast, but you two are it. Everyone is talking about you; they want to know as much as they can. And when fans get that inside line to your lives, it makes this personal connection with them, which will keep bringing them back. You get what I'm saying?

Zach: [*vigorously nodding, sitting back to his regular position*] Yep, sure do.

HJ: [*still uncertain but trying to follow her boyfriend's lead*] I guess so.

Zach: [*turns to face her, throws an arm around her shoulders, and pulls her in for a forehead kiss*] C'mon. It'll be great. Promise.

HJ: [*relaxing slightly*] Okay.

Interviewer: God, editing is gonna hate this. Okay, so, Zach, can you elaborate on that please?

Zach: So, try going through puberty, which is hard enough, but then you're being told that you're, like, supposed to be with this girl for the rest of your life. Like princes and stuff in the olden days— what was that called? Like, when you're born and your marriage is, like, already set up for you?

HJ: Betrothed.

Zach: Yeah, that's what we are. We're betrothed.

Interviewer: But why do you consider that a struggle?

Zach: 'Cause, like, you know, it's awkward. Like … [*pauses*] Okay, I'm introduced to this girl when we're, like, four, right? Five, whatever. And whatever, she's my friend. When you're a kid, you don't think about relationships and sex and stuff, right? But then, as you get older … you do. And these people—my parents and everyone—are telling me that she's *my person*. She's the person I'm gonna have my first kiss with. We're gonna lose our virginities to each other. We're gonna say *I do* someday, we're gonna have a house and kids and shit, and, like … look, I'm saying that I love this girl right here next to me, [*gestures to HJ*] but it's super weird when adults set it all up for you and when everyone knows about it.

Interviewer: Huh …

Zach: Like, think about it. Think about all six of us. I couldn't tell you who any of them—Grain Brain, Damon, any of them—had sex with for the very first time. *If* they've even had sex. But everyone knows that about me. Everyone knows that about HJ.

Interviewer: Right, right. And you don't resent your parents for not even giving you the option to, like, find your own person and all that?

Zach: Nah.

HJ: Oh good Lord, no! Can you imagine all that anxiety and wondering if you made the right choice and all that?

Interviewer: [*eyes darting back and forth between them*] I see …

HJ: Yes, it's definitely strange. But all in all, I think it's only made us stronger as a couple. We've had these … scenarios that most people don't end up in, and we've found a way to get through it together.

Interviewer: I think that's a beautiful way to look at it. What is the most difficult thing you've had to overcome as a couple? The worst thing you've gone through together?

HJ: [*nervously looks at Zach*]

Zach: [*shakes head*] We've never had to deal with anything *that* bad.

Interviewer: Hanna June, is that true?

HJ: [*slowly nods*] Yes, it's true.

Interviewer: Hanna June, I hate to tell you this, but you're not a very good liar.

HJ: [*bites lip, looks back to Zach, then back to camera*] I'm really sorry, but I think some things are just meant to stay between the people who actually went through it.

Interviewer: [*nods slowly*] I understand.

HJ: [*tears well up in her eyes, bites lip nervously, breaks down crying*]

Zach: [*reaches over to hold her*] Shut off the cameras. [*pauses*] I said, SHUT THEM OFF!

Chapter 27

AMBER

JUST UNDER AN HOUR AND A HALF was all it took for her to get home. *Thank God.*

The Olympians had been out for two weeks now, and she hadn't been home since. The first weekend was because they weren't there—her dad had shipped Fleur off to Savannah while he flew to Nebraska for work. And this past weekend, Amber had felt so sick that she didn't think she could make the drive.

But in all honesty, it was probably just nerves. She was so worried about what her dad and sister would think after seeing her on a reality TV show, that the anxiety got to her. She had spent most of the weekend sitting in her apartment, high as a kite, and accidentally double-ordering Cookie Dude deliveries.

But Fleur was ecstatic about her big sister being on TV, wanting nothing more than to gossip about *everything* that had happened in the first two episodes.

And as for her dad, he had simply told her that he was proud of her. Then, he'd changed the subject and asked if she needed money for anything, practically boasting that he'd paid the electric *and* water bills this month, "so you don't have to!"

She barely pulled all four tires into their driveway and past the throng of tourists taking pictures of the Rainbow Row houses when the fifteen-year-old ran outside. She was barefoot, and it looked like her hair hadn't been brushed in a few days.

"Ahhhhh! It's Amber Hargrove from *The Olympians!*" she screamed as she bounded toward Amber.

Onlookers passed questioning looks at each other but turned their cameras to take pictures of the two girls anyway. Just because they didn't know who they were now didn't mean the pictures might not be worth something someday.

"Fleur, stop! Don't yell that out," Amber pleaded with her.

"Oh, come on. I'm just having fun!" She threw her untamed mane of hair over one of her shoulders.

"Yeah, but you're attracting attention," Amber pointed out as she hurried inside, towing Fleur along with her.

"Amber, you're on a TV show. Attracting attention is something that just happens to you now. Get used to it."

She hated when Fleur was right. She was the older sister; she was supposed to be the smarter one between the two of them.

They ran up the stairway inside the house, their feet pounding on the old wooden steps into the kitchen.

She heard him before she saw him. "There she is! My superstar!" Her dad came around the corner from the dining room, his arms outstretched. He pulled her in for a hug, the proximity making Amber's nose immediately wrinkle up at the horribly strong smell of scotch.

Shaun pulled her back and poked at her stomach. "Have you been eating?"

"Yes, Daddy, I have. I promise."

He definitely *looked* happy despite his odor. His face was significantly rounder, and his belt seemed to be working hard to hold his belly in.

He's eating at least. He's drinking, too, but that's another discussion.

"How are you feelin', baby girl?" Her father had placed himself at the head of the small kitchen table while Fleur and Amber slid down the bench.

"I'm good. How are you guys?"

Her quick assessment of Fleur told her that she definitely wasn't eating as much as her dad was. Her shirt was extremely baggy on her, but the vertebrae going down her spine weren't as clearly visible as she was afraid they'd be.

I wish I could take online classes.

"Okay, seriously, we do *not* want to talk about us. You're on TV! What's it like?" Fleur was practically vibrating with excitement. "Is everyone really nice? Or are they super stuck-up? Because some of them—I won't mention names—seem like they would be *really* snobby …"

Amber was all in favor of letting Fleur babble until she passed out from lack of oxygen, but her dad leaned forward, looking like he might want to add something halfway intelligent to the conversation.

"The only thing I need to know is, do you like it?"

"Like what?"

"The program. Or the show or whatever."

Amber preferred to think of it as the program because she did not want to be on a TV show at all. Ever. For any reason.

"Yeah, I guess the program is fine." She shrugged as she pushed herself up from her seat and went to the cabinet to take out three glasses.

"Now," her dad continued, "when does the whole financial aspect of it kick in?"

He lasted longer than I thought.

Amber had been prepared for that to be the first question he asked his daughter, always worried about money. Which was ironic because he was the reason they'd lost so much of it. He was the sole purpose of her being in the program.

"Rhianne said that it was all taken care of already," she reassured him as she filled their glasses with sweet tea.

Her father crossed his arms and leaned back in his seat. "Who's Rhianne?"

"She's the production manager, and I guess she handles the financial side of the program too. I don't know. I think she's kind of in charge of most things."

"Then, what does Dwayne Kronos do?"

"He's in charge of the whole program. And the show. And us and Rhianne and everyone else we work with."

"He's the creator of the show," Fleur explained, using more hand gestures than anyone else in the room. It wasn't very often, but sometimes, you could easily tell she hadn't been born into the Hargrove family.

"Hmph, seems to me like he just likes making you kids answer mind-numbing questions while you could be getting an education."

Amber finished squeezing fresh lemons into their tea and passed them around. She assumed the little one had cut them up, as her dad only entered the kitchen to get a beer or heat up frozen chicken wings.

"Oh, no, I never miss class. Rhianne makes the interview schedules around our classes."

"So, she's a secretary?" Her dad was still hung up on her role.

"You know what, Daddy? I don't know her exact job title, but I will ask her when I see her Monday morning at ten, okay?"

He looked like he was about to say something when his phone rang. He yanked it out of his pocket, turning it inside out, a harsh frown immediately shadowing over his face as he stared at the screen. "I gotta take this," he grumbled as he got up and pulled himself around the corner by the old post, trying to get out of earshot.

As soon as he was gone, Fleur turned her entire tiny body to face Amber. "So, is he really in love with you?"

Oh, God.

"What?"

Fleur rolled her eyes. "Kai. Is he really in love with you? Because *wow.* Imagine your babies."

"Fleur Juliet! Don't say things like that!"

She scoffed at Amber. "Why not? It's true."

"Fleur!" She was so embarrassed; she could feel her pale skin turning red, creeping up her neck. Her mind was drawing the biggest blank as she tried to think of something else to say.

"Okay, no, seriously, picture it: your freckles, his eyes, and the skin tone they would have—*oh my God.* They would be born with modeling contracts." Fleur stretched her arms out to reach Amber, making the whole thing more dramatic.

"Fleur, stop."

"So, do you love him back?"

"No!" Bright red—she could feel it. Her face had to be the same color as her hair, if not a darker, more tomato-like color.

Fleur's mouth twisted up into a smile. "Why are you getting so defensive, Am?" She didn't give her a second to answer. Not that Amber would have been able to since her brain was still short-circuiting. "I'll tell you why. I think you *do* like him!"

"I do not!"

Amber, you have got to do better than that. She might only be fifteen, but she knows when you're lying.

"Have you guys kissed?"

She knows when you're lying. You can't lie.

But ... you can't tell her the truth either ...

Say something.

Anything.

LITERALLY ANYTHING, AMBER.

"Holy crap, have you guys had sex?"

If her head could have exploded, it would have.

"Fleur!"

"It's okay. You don't have to tell me." Fleur deflated as she slunk back against her spot on the bench. "But just know that until you deny it, I'm going to think that you did ... and if you *do* deny it, I probably won't believe you. There's too much evidence."

Amber tripped over her words. "I—I'm sorry, there's what?"

Fleur got up from the table. "Evidence," she repeated herself. "There're several fan theories about you guys and how you've been hiding your relationship ever since filming started. Maybe even before that."

"What?!"

Fleur sat back down and popped a red bendy straw into her drink. "Mmhmm. See, I know they're all lies because my big sister would have told me if anything was going on, *right?*"

Amber threw a sideways glance her way. "Of course," she replied, which made Fleur smile proudly and sit up a little straighter.

Her dad came back around the corner, wearing a forced grin. "Sorry, work."

Fleur propped up on her knees, took a long sip of her tea, then announced, "I have to go to the bathroom," and promptly left the room.

As soon as *she* was gone, Amber turned to her dad, serious mode switched on. "What's going on?"

"What are you talking about? There's nothing going on," Shaun answered her, beads of sweat dripping down the side of his neck.

"Daddy, don't lie to me."

Her father flipped up the collar of his shirt, dabbed at the moisture, and answered her, refusing to make eye contact, "I just have a lot of things going on. The company is expanding *again*, which is great, but it means I'm gone more, and that means—"

She cut him off, already knowing where he was leading, "Dad, you cannot leave Fleur alone for that long. A few hours is one thing, but a few days is another. She's only fifteen."

"But she's very responsible for fifteen!" This grown man, her legal guardian, was actually arguing back with her.

"Don't tell me that. Tell a judge—after they've looked at your record. I'm sure they'd have no problem deeming you an unfit parent."

"What do you want me to do, Amber? You're not here to watch her, and her staying with Meemaw for a weekend isn't the same as sending her to live there! The woman is starting to lose it anyway. I'm running a company around the country at the same time, so if you have any parenting tips, I'd be open to hearing them."

She had about a million things to offer him, but he would just argue back. He was getting upset and defensive and flustered, and it would only go downhill. She had to leave tomorrow afternoon, and she knew that there were times where he didn't resurface for days. Amber couldn't allow that to happen.

She reached forward and held his clammy hands in hers. "I'm going to think of something that will make this whole situation easier on all of us, Daddy, I promise. I'll come up with something."

He nodded, and they sat together quietly for a minute.

Hours later, Amber made them all dinner. The three of them sat around the dining room table, which Amber could tell hadn't been used as frequently since she lived two hours away for most of the week. They laughed together, and none of them brought up the show the rest of the night. Afterward, they all went for a walk down King Street, stopping to get gelato on the way.

This is how it should be all the time.

Sunday morning, Amber woke up to Fleur in her room. She was kneeling on the floor, just staring at the plants on her windowsill.

She rubbed her eyes and groggily asked the little one, "Can I help you?"

"What are the chances of me being on the show too?"

Amber sat straight up. *Shit. Head rush.* "What?"

"I mean, not yet, obviously. But in three years, if I wanted to go to Olympia, too, then do you thi—"

"No, Fleur. Absolutely not." Amber wasn't a fan of interrupting anyone, especially her family. But there was no way she would ever let Fleur be in the same situation as her.

Although she'd never mentioned it, both she and her dad knew that Fleur would most likely want to go to college. He had replenished some of Fleur's college fund, and Amber stashed whatever she made from selling weed to anyone who'd buy it. That was the whole reason for her selling—being a technical drug dealer was definitely not something she wanted, but she didn't see any other options.

Yes, when Kronos had first pitched the idea to Shaun, he'd immediately gone along with it. The papers and everything were signed for Amber, but nothing was ever done for Fleur because she was in elementary school at the time and it just didn't make sense. As time went on and they got older, Amber had talked with her dad, and they decided that unless it was necessary, Fleur wouldn't have to be in the program. They were both saving money to be able to afford for her to go wherever she wanted without some crazy scholarship scheme. Amber had also done the math though, and by the time she was supposed to start her undergrad, Amber would've been working for almost three years, and based on the salary her dad had quoted her a few months ago, she'd have more than enough to cover her little sister's education.

None of this had ever been brought to Fleur's attention, and Amber didn't think there was any reason to ever tell her.

But now, she *wanted* to be in it?

Absolutely not. She wouldn't allow her little sister to be in the public eye any more than she already had been.

She got up out of her bed, put her glasses on to turn her distorted figure clearer, and walked over to her. She sat on the floor, and they stared at the mums blooming in the hanging basket outside her window.

"Fleur, I don't ever want you to be in this situation. I know you think it looks like fun, and maybe there's some kind of fun moments, but it honestly just makes everything more stressful. You'll be able to go to whichever school you want for college even if it's all the way across the country! Anywhere you want!"

"See," she started slowly, "I've actually been looking into Olympia, and I'd think I really like it. They have the major I want, and I know because it's the same one as you." She smiled as she bumped shoulders with Amber. Amber didn't smile back. "It's a small school, which is good because I don't think I'd want to go anywhere too big—even C of C is too many kids for me. It's less than two hours away. Plus, I love that campus."

Amber paused before she answered, "I guess if you really like it …"

"And by that time, you'll have been on the show for a few years, and I bet Kronos would love to have two sisters on the show!"

Amber knew she wasn't going to let up—Fleur was persistent, if nothing else.

"I'll talk to him."

Chapter 28

HANNA JUNE

"WE NEED TO HAVE A PARTY."

Zach finally looked up from his phone. "What?"

"You heard me. We need to have a party."

He blinked. "What do you mean, we?"

Hanna June walked around the edge of his bed and hopped up next to him. "The six of us."

His nose wrinkled up, and she immediately knew he would need some convincing. Good thing she had rehearsed her argument on her short walk over to his dorm.

"Okay, listen. The more viewers *The Olympians* gets, the more money we can possibly get, right?"

"Go on," he urged, though he still seemed skeptical.

"So, how do we get more viewers? We make a scene. Think about it. Think about all the pointless and trashy TV we watch. How do they keep getting renewed? How do they have so much buzz? *They make a scene.* What better way to make a scene than to have a party, no cameras? We are in full control of what we post on social media. Obviously, it isn't enough to fill in all the blanks. We're not making a full episode or anything. Just some blurry pictures and thirty-second-long videos of drunken chaos. Enough to get a stupid article by *The Daily Mail*, a few thousand more followers on Instagram for us, and more viewers for the show."

End debate. Argue with that, Zachary.

She could see him mulling it over and waited patiently for his rebuttal.

A few seconds later, it came. And it was something HJ hadn't prepared for. "How are you going to convince Damon to come?"

Shit.

She hadn't thought of that. How *was* she going to get the King of Darkness and Death and Complicated Backstories to a party?

"I haven't thought of that … but I'm sure Dawn will have no problem helping me come up with something. I doubt she'll want to show up without him anyway."

Zach nodded slowly and went back to thinking. "You're talking, like … a *party*, party, right? Not like the lame-ass spaghetti thing we did a few weeks ago, right?"

"I mean, a *party*, party," she reassured him.

He turned to look at her for a moment and then pulled her in for a kiss. "You're so fucking smart. That's a great idea."

She couldn't help the smile that spread like a wildfire across her face. "Thank you." She leaned in to kiss him back, and seconds later, she was on her back, and his tongue was inside her mouth. She reached down and ran her hand over his zipper, and he groaned into her mouth.

"*Fuck.* Let me get a condom." He rolled off her and propped himself up on his knees to lean over and reach into the drawer on his nightstand.

HJ turned her head to watch him and noticed something.

A hickey.

One that she hadn't put there.

She knew for an absolute fact that she had *not* put that there.

He crawled back, straddling her, condom in between his fingers.

"Where did you get that?"

"What?" He didn't look at her as he tried to rip it open.

"The hickey on your neck."

That got his attention. The little unopened square literally slipped out from his hand and landed on her stomach. Neither of them moved.

"You put it there."

"No, I didn't."

"Yes, you did. When we fucked last night."

"*No, I didn't.* You bent me over your dresser when you fucked me last night. My mouth never once touched your neck."

He stared at her in disbelief. "It came from you, baby. Where else would I have gotten it from?" He still hadn't bothered to pick up the condom off of her, and it only made her angrier.

"I don't know, Zachary. That's why I'm asking you because I know for a fact that I did not put it there."

He sighed. She hated it when he fucking sighed. Like she was such an inconvenience to him. He slumped over onto his side next to her and finally removed the condom and dropped it behind his back.

"Baby, sometimes, when, you know, things are heating up between us, you get kind of lost in the moment, and I don't think you always remember things the right way. It's not your fault. Like, I don't want you to feel bad. I think everyone gets that way. Our brains kinda turn to mush when we have sex."

She stared back at him. She knew she hadn't put it there because she remembered everything they did. She just didn't think *he* did.

"Zachary, I didn't put it there. Trust me, I'd know if I did."

It happened. His switch flipped inside. He leaned forward toward her, and his eyes lit up. She could see his jaw tense up, and she almost felt herself cower. "What are you suggesting, Hanna June? Are you saying I cheated on you? Is that what you're saying? 'Cause that's what it fucking sounds like."

Retreat. Retreat.

"No, no, of course not. I just don't remember putting that there, like, at all. But … you know, if you say it was me who put it there … then it was me."

The fire dwindled in his eyes after a minute, and his shoulders relaxed. His breathing returned to normal, and he leaned back. "Okay."

Her big eyes stayed glued to him though, watching for any signs. There was usually a sign.

He stretched an arm behind his head and let out another sigh. Another fucking sigh. "I hate when you ask me that. You know that. You know I love you. Like, more than anything. And when you suggest that I've been with someone else …" He turned to look over at her, and there it was.

An intense look of hurt and betrayal in his eyes. His bright blue eyes looked like he was going to drown, and HJ immediately felt horrible. Like she had failed him. Like he had promised to love her and be there for her even though it hadn't been his own voice he was going to see it all the way through to the best of his ability and how DARE she question his fidelity when she was probably the one who had put it there in the first place and she just didn't remember because she'd been so focused on the show and how to be the star and, honestly, she had kind of been neglecting her relationship and that was probably the reason she was questioning it in the first place because she felt guilty for not spending time in her own relationship and she was finally getting to spend time with just him after class and having cameras follow them around and she'd had to go and ruin it.

"I'm sorry," she mumbled, though something in the back of her mind nagged her, telling her that she shouldn't be apologizing.

He rolled over closer to her and sighed *again*. "I'm sorry too. I didn't mean to jump down your throat and get mean a minute ago. I shouldn't have done that. I just hate when you ask me that."

I hate when you give me a reason to ask that.

Instead, she only nodded and said, "Yeah, I know."

"I just really missed you. I feel like we have less alone time with the show now. I was looking forward to … ya know." A tiny smile spread across his face, and she felt like she was in seventh grade again.

It had been the first day of starting at a new school, where she only knew Zach and Zach knew everyone. She was late getting into class because her mom had to fill out some last-minute paperwork with an updated physical exam, and the secretary offered to walk her upstairs to her new room once it was completed. The bell had already rung, and the hallways were empty. She felt tiny as she approached the door, knowing that she was about to have one of those awkward *new student's first day of school* moments, where she stood in front of the room and got introduced to the entire class by a teacher who really didn't know anything about her.

The classroom door opened, and the secretary passed her name along to Mr. Sanders and told everyone that she'd just transferred here from North Carolina. Hanna June stood at the front of the room, frizz around her head, pimples on her face, and braces on her teeth. She could feel the heat start to settle in her cheeks as her new classmates judged her and made mental assumptions about her. And then she was saved.

All of her embarrassment and nervousness faded quickly as Zach yelled out from the center of the room, "That's my girlfriend!"

She had already known she liked him and that a long-term relationship was inevitable between them, but that was the moment when she had fallen in love with him. His crooked smile, his eyes that were too bright to look at sometimes, his ability to control a room without even trying—but mostly the way he claimed her. He announced to anyone who would listen that she was *his*. And that was how to everyone had seen her from that moment on.

She couldn't help but smile back at him. "I was looking forward to that too."

He reached behind his back and pulled the little metallic package back between them. "So, should I open this?"

She nodded, and a few chaotic seconds later, their clothes were off, and it was on. He was back on top of her, instructing her to, "Brace yourself."

She closed her eyes as he began, but the second his head dropped against her shoulder, they snapped back open.

The hickey was directly next to her mouth, and it was accompanied by a scent.

HJ strictly wore Chanel No. 5. She didn't even have a backup perfume.

And the smell coming off of his collarbone was fruity, combined with the stench of stale cigarettes.

But she didn't say anything. She just stared at the ceiling and waited for it to be over.

Chapter 29

SOLO INTERVIEW WITH KAI.

Kronos: Kai Newport, you are my final solo interview.

Kai: Is that a good thing?

Kronos: Well, personally, I always prefer to go last—that way, you can see your competition.

Kai: Hmm.

Kronos: Mr. Newport?

Kai: Hmm?

Kronos: Are you high?

Kai: [*prolonged silence*]

Kai:

Kai:

Kai: What?

Kronos: Okay. [*turns over shoulder and gives cameraman a hand signal*] You never went to traditional school before college, did you?

Kai: Nope. Homeschooled.

Kronos: And you didn't have an actual house?

Kai: House*boat*.

Kronos: That must've been fun.

Kai: Went swimming whenever I wanted. And fishing.

Kronos: Just you and your mom?

Kai: Most of the time. Uncle Kris comes and goes.

Kronos: Now, there was something that seemed to upset you after you watched the first episode—that your costars seemed to think of you only as a stoner who's hopelessly in love with Miss Hargrove. Would you like to address those opinions?

Kai: Oh God, [*rubs his face*] I guess. Uhh, first of all, I'm not a stoner. Yeah, I smoke once in a while, but I don't *need* it.

Kronos: You seem to be high during most interviews.

Kai: I hate doing these, Kronos—you know that.

Kronos: [*nods*] I do. Now, what about the part involving Miss Hargrove?

Kai: [*stares into the camera, then rolls head dramatically back to Kronos*] We went out once last year, kissed once at the end of the night. Nothing has happened since then, and I really don't think it's ever going to.

Kronos: Do you want it to?

Kai: That doesn't matter.

Kronos: Sure it does.

Kai: Kronos, why am I answering these questions? Everyone—the whole fucking world—saw me. I don't want to rehash this shit again. It's never gonna happen. Every time I think it's going somewhere, it doesn't. I'm proven wrong time and time again.

Kronos: Would you like to change the subject?

Kai: Yes, please.

Kronos: In the introduction segments you all filmed, you shared that you were studying marine biology, but that you might fail out. Why get a degree in something so challenging?

Kai: It was the only thing I was halfway interested in.

Kronos: And you haven't considered switching majors?

Kai: No point in it now. I'm so far along; it wouldn't make sense to.

Kronos: You're a junior; you still have time.

Kai: I took summer classes online last year and the one before, so I'm actually a semester ahead. My mom didn't want me taking a ton of classes, so I got a bunch out of the way while I could.

Kronos: Oh, so you'll be graduating early?

Kai: Well, *now*, I'm planning on taking the minimum number of hours. I'm sort of in this program that's taking over my life.

Kronos: [*smirks*] Well, that was a very smart plan—to get most of the work out of the way early while you were able to.

Kai: My mom's a smart woman.

Kronos: You don't speak to your father?

Kai: No.

Kronos: Have you ever met him?

Kai: Nope. I only know what he looks like because he's been on TV a few times.

Kronos: Mmhmm, he spoke *about* you on TV, didn't he?

Kai: [*raises hand*] I'm the bastard son.

Kronos: [*nodding*] Have you ever spoken to Mr. Alexander about this?

Kai: Uh, yeah, shortly after our … altercation.

Kronos: What about Mr. Montclaire?

Kai: No.

Kronos: Why not?

Kai: I doubt he's up for talking about any of this.

Kronos: I think you might be right about that.

Kai: It's like the three of us are on a spectrum.

Kronos: [*skeptically*] What do you mean?

Kai: Like, Zach is totally open, and Damon is completely closed off. And I'm kinda right in the middle.

Kronos: That makes sense. I can see that.

Kai: And, like, the girls are the same way, but not with openness.

Kronos: Then, with what?

Kai: With empathy. HJ can be pretty judgy, Dawn is totally accepting of everyone, and Amber is right in the middle.

Kronos: Just like you.

Kai: Yeah.

Kronos:

Kai:

Kronos:

Kai:

Kronos:

Kai: I like her.

Kronos: [*pretends to be shocked*] No!

Kai: But it'll never happen.

Kronos: You don't know that.

Kai: [*long pause*] Can we be done with this?

Kronos: [*takes a deep breath and nods*] Sure, Mr. Newport. Sure.

Chapter 30

ZACH

GOD, I HOPE THEY DON'T BUG OUR PHONES.

Honestly, he was grateful they hadn't come up with the idea to put cameras in places they met often, like Amber's apartment, although he did feel like it was just a matter of time before they did.

They'd only met there a few times, but it worked pretty well as a meeting place away from the cameras. He and HJ were in dorms since all the freshmen and sophomores were required to live on campus, which was stupid. Dawn lived with her parents, and there was no way Damon would ever invite anyone over. She was really the only other option, but she seemed to be on board with it. She'd texted Zach back right away when he asked her if they could have a party at her place.

Coordinating was going to be a bitch though because not everyone had each other's numbers, and for some fucking reason, Kai didn't want to text Amber.

"I don't want her to think I'm needy …"

Like, dude, grow a pair.

Guess I'm gonna have to do it, he thought as he pulled up a new text and began to add everyone's numbers.

Thank God everyone has an iPhone.

Zach: okay we need a group chat

Amber: oh thank god

Amber: I've been wanting to start one, but I didn't want to step on your toes Zach

Zach: why would that be stepping on my toes?

Amber: Because you're kind of like the leader. I didn't want you to feel like I was taking away from something that I felt was your place to do.

Zach: am you can start a group chat if you want idc

Damon: Quick question: how do you leave a group chat?

Zach: you dont

Damon: Never mind. I'll figure it out.

Kai: Hi

Dawn: Who's number is that?

Kai: It's Kai

Dawn: Hi, Kai! I'm so glad you started this, Zach. I've been wanting to get everyone's phone numbers, but I feel like there're always cameras around

Zach: which is kinda why I made this

Zach: HJ had the idea for us to have a party

Zach: but not like last time, like a real party

Zach: no offense grain brain but it was kinda lame

Zach: meatballs were rlly fucking good tho, def the best i've ever had

Amber: It was my mom's recipe.

Zach: so amber said we can do it at her place, this thurs nite, maybe get there around like 9?

Dawn: Sounds like fun! We will be there

Damon: What do you mean by "we"?

Dawn: Don't ask me questions you already know the answers to.

Kai: sounds good- can I bring weed?

Zach: yes

Kai: Amber, is that okay?

Amber: Is what okay?

Damon: Fine, I'll go. But I'm going to hate every second of it.

Kai: Is it okay that we smoke weed in your apartment?

Kai: Sorry, I should've asked first

Amber: It's fine, but yeah, you're good.

Kai: Okay, cool

Kai: Thanks

Dawn: Damon, you're going to enjoy yourself. And Amber, thank you for having us over.

HJ: omg what is happening??

HJ: I just got out of my geology lab and my phone is blowing up

HJ: going through messages now

Zach: baby you know all this, you don't need to read it

Damon: Why can't she read it, Alexander?

Zach: just don't want her to waste her time

Zach: since she IS my gf i know her pretty well, so i know that she's got a psych paper due tomorrow that she's got to work on

Zach: she doesn't like to write papers in order, she goes backwards. so i know she hasn't done her intro and she hasn't even started a bibliography

Zach: i also know that she's got a volleyball game she has to go to tonight with her sisters, so she's not gonna have as much time to work on it as she should

Zach: im trying to look out for her by telling her she doesnt have to waste her time reading all this shit

Damon: Wow.

Zach: don't be a fucking asshole man

HJ: You said that my mom's meatballs were the best you've ever had!!!

Damon: Looks like you're the asshole now.

Zach: i told you not to read it babe

Zach: stfu d

Kai: Wow can't wait for Thursday

Zach's phone was ringing in his hand. He slid the bar to open it, answering the call before it was even up to his ear. "Hey, baby."

"Hi. So, I completely forgot about the bibliography until I saw you say that."

"Good thing I said it then."

"Mmhmm. Listen, can you email me that link we used in high school? It's the one where, like, we just input the information and it auto-generates the bib for us?"

"Why would I have that?"

"I bookmarked it on your laptop—you don't remember?"

The only bookmarks I know are ones I can't tell you about …

"Yeah, I'll look for it. Hang on," was what he told her instead as he logged in to the slim laptop on his desk.

As he typed away, she started talking.

Again.

"Do you really think hers are better?"

What? "What?"

I have a lot of porn sites bookmarked. Shit.

"Her meatballs."

Oh my God.

"No, baby, of course not. She's just, you know, she's so quiet and stuff sometimes. I felt like I had to give her some sort of compliment."

"Oh, yeah, okay. That was a really nice compliment," she forced out through gritted teeth. He could tell she was chewing on her fingernails.

"Get them out of your mouth."

Where the hell is it?

"How do you know that?"

"Six years, HJ. We've been together six years. And I've known you for, like, thirteen. I can tell pretty easily when you're biting your nails after that long."

Literally the last one.

"Well, I'm glad you know me so well. Kinda makes me love you even more." He could tell she was doing that flirty little smile of hers as she talked—the one where she kind of leans her shoulders side to side as she tilts her head.

"I just found that link for you."

"Just email it to me, baby."

"Your school email? What is it again?"

He knew their email addresses were the initials of their first and middle names, followed by their last name. There was a number added at the end if there was already an active student email with the exact same initials.

The problem was that June wasn't HJ's middle name. In fact, he'd forgotten her middle name years ago. He couldn't exactly tell her that though. He was supposed to be the poster child for the perfect boyfriend, so indicating in any way that he'd forgotten the middle name of his future wife—and someone he'd known since before either of them could even ride a bike—wasn't something he could ever admit to. He'd hoped their former principal would announce it at their high school graduation, but she'd chosen to only go by Hanna June Pruitt.

HJ hated her middle name—Zach had learned that really early on in their relationship. There was absolutely nothing in her room or even in her parents' house with all four of her legal names on it.

But he figured it would be on their marriage certificate though, so he really just had to wait a few more years to find out what it actually was. But for now, an initial would do.

"You know my name, Zachary," she teased him.

I actually don't though.

"Just spell it out for me. There's a guy in my writing class who had his last name spelled wrong on his school email."

"Wait, are you serious?"

No.

"Yeah, the admissions office fucked up, and apparently, they can't change it now because it's linked to his account. It's this whole IT mess. He doesn't know if they're gonna get it fixed or what."

"Oh my gosh, that's awful. What a headache." She sounded genuinely upset for his fictional classmate.

"Yeah. Guess the girl who assigned it to him was dyslexic or something."

"Zachary, you stop it. You don't know that."

Can't even take a joke.

"I was joking, baby." He softened his voice.

"Hmm," she hummed into the receiver, clearly annoyed. "Well, it wasn't very nice."

His autopilot switched on; he knew when to spit out the two meaningless words. "I'm sorry."

"Can you send me the email, please? I need to get this done." Her tone said that she was done with the conversation and with talking to him.

Whatever.

"Baby, I need you to tell me your email address, remember?" He used an even softer voice, trying to get her to feel calmer.

She took in a deep breath, and then static filled the phone as she blew it out. "You know my first three initials—H-J-M—and then my last name, Pruitt."

M.

He had to stall her while he made a note of her middle initial in her phone contact.

"Spell it out for me, just to double-check."

"H-J-M P-R-U-I-T-T."

"No numbers at the end?" He mentally referred to this as his therapist voice, when he had to talk gently to her.

Sometimes, she just coiled up like a fucking rattlesnake within seconds, and it did nothing but piss him off. But he knew she'd end up calming down and apologizing. And there was usually sex involved, so he was okay with it.

"And you're sure they spelled your last name correctly?"

"Yes, baby." She spoke slowly. "I'm sure."

"Okay. You know I don't want what happened to Alex to happen to you too, especially if you don't even realize it."

Wow, guess he has a name now.

"I know, baby. Thank you. I'm sorry. I guess I'm just stressed."

There it is.

"I know. It's okay. We have a lot going on."

"Yeah, we do."

"I sent it to you."

"It just came through. Thank you, baby." She almost sounded sad now. "Maybe I can come over later?"

Two for two.

"I think you definitely should do that."

"Okay, good." He imagined her sitting up straighter, that big smile plastering across her cute little face.

"Oh, would you go to the volleyball game with me tomorrow night?"

Tall girls in short shorts, jumping up and down? Abso-fucking-lutely.

"Yeah, I think I can. What time is it?"

"Uh, it starts at seven, but we were gonna pregame at the house first. I know Bree and Hadley are bringing their boyfriends too."

Shit. What's-her-name is coming over at six thirty ...

"Baby, I'm so sorry, but I actually told Alex I'd do this peer editing assignment with him around that time, and that's kinda the only night he can do it. I can probably be at the game around seven, but I might not make it to the pregame."

"Oh, okay."

You couldn't actually hear a smile fading, but Zach easily picked up on it.

"I'll come over as soon as we're done, I promise. It shouldn't take me that long. I'll make it work."

"Okay. Thank you, baby."

"Of course."

"I love you."

"I love you too, HJ."

Chapter 31

DAMON

THE ONLY PERSON ON THE entire campus who'd ever been inside Damon's apartment was Dawn, and he could count on one hand how many times she'd visited.

Checking his Rolex, he saw he had exactly four minutes until her last class was finished, and then she was planning to drive over to his place right after. Having timed it before, he knew she could make it to his apartment from the Grad Studies building, to the parking lot across the street, and to his apartment in eleven minutes—as long as you didn't get stuck at the light at the Arlington Boulevard and Carolina Avenue intersection. That would add on another three minutes.

The campus layout didn't make any sense to Damon. There was an entire building for graduate students, yet not all of their classes were in that building.

What annoyed him was when he ran into underclassmen on his way to and from class. Especially when Zach was with his frat brothers, and for whatever reason, he decided to acknowledge him.

Like today.

"Hey, man. What's up?" He'd said it so casually too, like they hung out outside of their mandatory meeting times.

And of course, everyone else had turned to look at him, to see who the golden boy was talking to.

He hated it.

Damon had done such a good job of building up his walls and his "scary" demeanor, so people purposely wouldn't interact with him. If he didn't have to be on the show, he never would've even considered participating in something that forced him to be so social with other people.

Zach and HJ want to be in the spotlight, and that's fine. Let them. But don't drag me into it, he thought as his long legs carried him down through the filthy stairwell back to his car.

He had managed to cram twenty-five balloons into the back of his Lincoln for the occasion. He grabbed the last handful of them, balanced the box of cupcakes he'd picked up at a bakery downtown, locked his doors twice, and bounded back upstairs.

He dragged the handful of brightly colored balloons into his otherwise dark living area, feeling bad for Dawn. She deserved better—so much better. He knew none of the others remembered it was her birthday, and even though she was going to be having a big party at her parents' house this weekend with her family—that both of her parents and Dawn herself had invited him to-he still felt like she needed to celebrate at school, with her friends.

Even if these "friends" were all too wrapped up in their own things to even know that it was her twenty-fifth birthday.

Zach was a selfish prick, so it made sense that he probably didn't know any of their birthdays. Honestly, it wouldn't surprise Damon if Zach didn't know his own girlfriend's birthday.

He's a complete piece of shit. But he's his father's son, so that makes sense. Certain people shouldn't be allowed to breed, I swear to God.

Now, Hanna June he could understand. It was probably really hard to just make it through day to day, doing basic things for yourself, knowing that the so-called love of your life was out there, screwing whatever he could find, and you couldn't even leave him.

How could her parents do that to her? He pulled out his phone and made a note to research the legality of arranged marriages for children.

Then, there were Kai and Amber. First of all, out of his two biological yet estranged brothers, Damon liked Kai the best, but, *wow,* did he have a lot going on.

He didn't look anything like either Zach or himself. He had dark skin, like his mother, but he had those bright blue eyes that Zach had also gotten from their father, Richard. Damon had heard Hanna June talk about how nice Zach's eyes were, but they looked significantly better on the middle brother than they did on him. He was also taller than Zach, and you could look at his arms and tell that working on boats his whole life had done nothing but good things for him. Kai was a catch—there was no doubt about it.

There were girls who were all but throwing themselves at him, and, as he'd willingly offered to share after he had five beers in him when they went downtown together—before his public display of emotion—he'd entertain them for a little while, but nothing made him forget about her.

"Dude, I think about her *during* it," he had confessed to Damon, who definitely did not want to be hearing about Kai's sex life.

As far as Amber went, Damon couldn't seem to figure out what her deal was. Kai had filled him in on *everything* that had happened between the two of them since they'd met, and he struggled to draw a conclusion. She seemed interested sometimes when they texted, but then a while later, she'd be closed off and constantly using the "family" excuse that they were all too used to hearing.

But he saw the way they stood too close to each other and how they looked at one another when they talked to each other. They both seemed genuinely happy—and that was painfully obvious because any other time Damon had seen either of them, they were both very clearly *not* happy.

Yes, the situation had become more of an annoyance than anything, but Damon did feel bad for both of them. Kai knew exactly what he wanted while Amber couldn't seem to make up her mind.

It's like she's afraid to do something for herself that might make her happy.

His phone buzzed.

Paulina: Tell Dawnie we are sending her happy birthday wishes from NYC!

He was glad she wasn't actually in front of him, so she wouldn't have to see him roll his eyes. He hated when they called her Dawnie even though she seemed to love it.

After carefully unboxing the cupcakes, he stuck a candle in one. He wasn't particularly a fan of sweets, but he had to admit that the buttercream frosting looked really delicious.

Six minutes left.

He pushed his way through the floating latex mass taking up too much space for his comfort and began to separate them and spread them out when the door opened.

He wasn't a jumpy person—he couldn't be, as he'd been taught at a young age—but he was very type A. Dawn hadn't been expected until a certain time, but what made his anxiety really climb for just a second was that he hadn't been ready for her.

"Umm …"

"Surprise."

"Damon, what did you do?" Dawn let out a short laugh as she began to examine the scene in front of her.

"I know you're having a party this weekend, but it's your actual birthday, and you need to celebrate. So, I tried to give you what I'm now seeing is the world's lamest surprise party ever."

Dawn dropped her bags onto one of the chairs at the island and walked over to him. "Do not say that. This is amazing. You did all this for me, all by yourself. I'm gonna go out on a limb and say you've never thrown anyone a birthday party before."

A sarcastic snort came out. Damon and parties didn't really mix, no matter how Paulina might try to change him.

"This is so sweet, and I really was surprised." She laughed and went in for a hug. "Thank you."

Damon wasn't a hugger—that much was clear as day to anyone. But for his only real friend, on her birthday, he made an exception and hugged her back.

"I got cupcakes."

"You did? Thank goodness. I've been craving sweets all day." She clapped her hands together excitedly and walked over to where he'd arranged them on a plate. "Oh, wow, these look so good." Her eyes widened as he pulled out a lighter, and the tiny flame on the single candle grew.

She glanced up at him, waiting.

"I will not be singing to you."

A stifled laugh made it past her lips as she explained, "You hugged me, so I figured you were in a giving mood."

"Ah, no, see, that's where my favors stop. My deepest apologies."

Dawn rolled her brown eyes, thought of a wish, and then blew out her candle. Her next movements were almost animalistic as she tore off the paper wrapper around the cake portion and began to lick off the frosting.

"Why on earth do you eat cupcakes like a four-year-old?" His voice came out judgmental as hell, and Paulina just might've given him a whack upside the head if she had heard him.

He felt bad when he heard his own tone of voice, not wanting to offend her, but her loud laugh drowned out his own thoughts.

She threw her head back, and her shoulders shook with her. "What did you just say?"

"It's true. You do," he defended himself.

"Well, how do you eat them?"

Quietly demonstrating, he pulled the bottom part off with a slight twist. Then, he turned it over and placed it on top of the frosting, creating a cupcake sandwich.

"Of course you have some thought-out method."

He just shrugged his shoulders and took another bite out of the frosting segment. He'd never had buttercream that tasted like this. It was so ... *good.*

Seeing how Dawn was almost done devouring hers and was already reaching for another one, he assumed she was thinking the same thing.

They ate like they were starving, shoving the dessert into their mouths.

Damon had just finished his second one when he broke the silence. "So, what did you wish for?"

"I can't tell you that."

"Oh, please." Damon shook his head at her, pushing himself up from the barstool and walking over to where he'd slid her present behind the end of the couch. As he held it out and approached her with it, her eyes nearly doubled in size.

"Damon James Montclaire, you did *not* get me a present!" She was squealing and clapping again, and as much as those things annoyed the absolute crap out of him, he didn't say anything about it.

"I honestly didn't do anything, except pay for someone else to make it," he explained, although she didn't seem to be listening as she tore off the wrapping job he'd put together better than he'd expected to.

Her dark eyebrows pulled toward each other as she slid it out and stared at the immense detail in front of her. She ran her fingers down the edge of the frame. Her mouth opened a little. He held his eyes on her, trying to figure out just what she was thinking … but failed.

And what made it worse was that she *wasn't talking.*

No words. Nothing was coming out.

She hates it.

This was such a stupid idea.

Good job, Damon. Get some artsy high school kid to make a map of her college campus for the past six years. Good fucking job. She's got the damn place memorized—why the hell did I think a map was a great idea?

This is why everyone gets Amazon gift cards.

She sniffled.

Then, she did it again.

Then, a tear fell out of one of her eyes and landed on the edge of the frame.

"Oh shoot," she forced out, wiping it away with her cardigan sleeve.

"Don't worry about it. I can get you something else."

"You absolutely cannot." She picked up her head and looked at him. "I love it."

It was his turn to be surprised. "What?"

"I said, I love it."

The look he gave her was so skeptical; he could see his eyebrows in the top of his peripheral vision as they knit together in confusion. "You do?"

"I really, really do," she assured him as she gave him her smile—the one that was calming just to look at. It wasn't huge, nor did it take up her face, but it wasn't tiny and forced. Instead, it was sincere and real.

"Even the style of it?"

"Are you kidding? Especially the style! It reminds me of that Historical Architectural Styles class I took last semester!"

"Good. That's what I was hoping for." He finally sat down.

Damon also wasn't much of a gift giver, if you couldn't tell. He hadn't realized how nervous he'd been to see her reaction.

Dawn began to study the entirety of the map. "Oh my gosh, you included Ground Floor! By the way, Amber makes better coffee than them. I don't know how, but she just does."

"Good to know." *I'm never going to use that information, but she's in too much of a good mood for me to ruin it.*

"Washboards is on here! We haven't been there since before finals last year. Maybe we should take them," she suggested, practically bouncing on the heels of her feet.

"Take who?" he asked, although he already knew her answer and didn't want to hear it.

"The Olympian kids."

When it was just the two of them, that was their nickname for the youngest four. They'd agreed not to say it in front of any of them though. Amber and Kai might be offended because they were older than the other two; both of them would be turning twenty-one before the school year was done. And Zach and HJ both seemed to run hot, and there didn't really seem to be a good reason to piss them off.

Again, Damon didn't want to ruin her day, but he knew that if he went along with the suggestion of going out with them again, she would hold him to it. They were already all getting together at Amber's place tomorrow night, and Damon had been dreading it since Zach had started that stupid group text. The first time they'd all been forced to go downtown together had been enough. He had had no desire to go clubbing with some underclassmen and a camera crew. And although, this time, it would be limited to just the six of them and their social media accounts, he still did not want to have any part of it.

He'd even told Kronos how he felt to see if there was any way he could get out of it. But of course, Kronos only reminded him that he had agreed to this, that it was in a binding contract. That he could leave in two years, but until then, he had to be an active scholarship participant. He'd closed the conversation by reminding Damon about his slipup a few years ago and how if Kronos hadn't been in the right place at the right time, Damon would be in a prison cell right now.

"I'm afraid you don't have a choice, Mr. Montclaire. I suggest you enjoy it while you can. Remember, everything can go away in a split second."

Using Spot as an excuse hadn't worked either because Kronos had just scheduled a dog sitter for him.

"Dawn, I want to spend as limited time with them as possible."

"Don't worry; I don't think they're too fond of you either." She tossed him a smile and went back to scanning her fantasy-style campus map. "Your apartment isn't on here."

"It's so far from campus. I would've had to get a bigger map. And at that point, it would've been one of the whole city," he offered.

"So, that's what I can expect for my next birthday then?" She smiled at him again.

He rolled his eyes at her, and the faintest trace of a smile crawled across his mouth. "Oh yeah, I'll make sure that high school kid who made this gets right on that."

"You know I'm kidding. It's perfect. I love it so much. I really, really do. Thank you," she told him as she came in for a second embrace.

Hugs were funny because they said things without actually saying anything.

For instance, when Damon hugged her, he was saying, *I got you this because it's the place where our story started, our friendship.*

And when Dawn hugged him back, what she was telling him was, *I know.*

Chapter 32

THE FOLLOWING TRANSCRIPTS TOOK PLACE *on the night of the party at Amber's apartment. Some recordings made it to social media. Others did not and possibly never would.*

Kai: I'm the interviewer tonight.

HJ: What? No, I wanna do it!

Amber: I kinda want to do it too. It looks like fun.

Kai: You can interview me first, Amber. If you want.

HJ: I want to do it!

Dawn: All of you do it! Post on your own accounts, from your own phones. We should each do it.

Damon: Hard pass.

Dawn: Not you, child of darkness. I meant the rest of us who enjoy interacting with other people.

Zach: That's actually a good idea, Dawn.

Dawn: Thank you.

Zach: [*walking behind the counter*] So, who wants what? We have rum, vodka, lots of Jose …

Amber: I probably shouldn't drink tonight …

Zach: No, you're drinking. You're getting drunk tonight. We all are. Classes are canceled tomorrow for the game, and I happen to know your car's in the shop, so you won't be going home this weekend. You have no excuse, Hargrove.

Amber: How did you know that?

Zach: I know a guy who works at Campus Auto Care. He texted me when he saw your name in the system and asked if we were on the show together.

Amber: That seems like some sort of violation …

Zach: I repeat my question: who wants what? I'm opening the tequila first.

Kai: [*raises hand*]

Dawn: [*to Damon*] Do you want anything?

Damon: No.

Zach: Bro, you should drink something. I feel like you're the kind drunk who eats ice cream out of the carton, sitting on the floor while revealing your deepest, darkest secrets.

Damon: I'm not your bro.

Zach: [*puts hands up defensively*] Whatever, man. I was just suggesting you lighten up a little.

Damon: I don't need your suggestions.

Zach: No, what I think you *need* is pussy.

HJ: OKAY! Zach, I'll take a vodka soda.

Zach: That's my girl. Let's get you plastered tonight.

Kai: I brought weed … if anyone wants.

Amber: Yes!

Everyone else turns to look at her, surprised.

Amber: What? It's a party, right? And I never get to … you know, get messed up. And like Zach so kindly pointed out, I get to let loose tonight. So, pass the weed, Kai.

Kai: You want a joint? I have three rolled already. I also brought my bowl.

Amber: Umm …

HJ: Have you ever been high, Amber?

Amber: [*pauses*] No.

Kai: Okay, come sit with me. I'll go over the basics with you.

They retreat awkwardly to Amber's living room area.

HJ: [*to Zach*] Can I get high?

Zach: Fuck yes! God, you remember when we both got high as shit a few weeks ago and ate a whole box of cereal and fucked for, like, three hours?

HJ: [*grimaces*] I couldn't walk the next day.

Zach: Fuck yeah, you couldn't. Go get blazed, baby girl.

HJ: [*joins Kai and Amber on the couch*]

Zach: What are you drinking, Dawn?

Dawn: Oh, I actually don't drink. But thank you for the offer.

Zach: What do you mean, you don't drink? You're, like, twenty-six.

Dawn: I actually just turned twenty-five.

Zach: When?

Damon: [*interrupts*] Yesterday.

Zach: Oh … well, happy late birthday. Sorry we, uh, didn't do anything. I'm sure HJ would've planned something if we knew.

Damon: You did know. It was on the stupid cheat sheets Kronos passed out at the second meeting, and it was written across the screen when we did our initial introductions in the first episode. But you were all too wrapped up in your own shit to even notice.

Zach: Okay, don't act like you know everyone's birthdays, Montclaire.

Damon: You're the youngest, born August 6, 1996. Hanna June is only slightly older than you, born two months and five days before you, on June 1. Next comes Kai on March 11 and then Amber on April 27, both in '94. Dawn and I were both born five years before them, and it shows. Me on December 22 and her on September 18, making her the oldest out of all of us.

Zach: [*pauses*] Big fucking whoop, you read the cheat sheet.

Damon: [*walks over to the bar, staring at Zach*]

Zach: [*tentatively moves aside*]

Damon: [*pours himself a drink, then silently retreats to the balcony*]

Dawn: Don't mind him. He's just protective.

Zach: [*sighs*] He's *that* protective, and you've seriously never tapped that?

Dawn: [*confused*] I don't think a girl can technically tap that.

Zach: Whatever. You know what I mean.

Dawn: I do, and, no, I have not.

Zach: Dawn … can I ask you a question?

Dawn: Sure.

Zach: Are you a virgin?

Dawn: [*smiles softly*] I am.

Zach: Why?

Dawn: [*looks amused*] What do you mean, why?

Zach: Like, why are you still a virgin? You could've gotten laid by now.

Dawn: [*laughs*] I just don't want to have sex yet. Not everyone wants the same things, you know.

Zach: I think you'd change your mind if you actually did it.

Dawn: [*shrugs*] I'll do it when I'm ready. Or I won't, and I'll never know what I'm missing.

Zach: Hmm.

Dawn: I'm gonna go watch Amber get high for the first time. I feel like it'll be interesting. [*leaves*]

Amber was high, sitting on the couch by herself, when Zach came over to join her, sitting on the arm of the couch.

Amber: This was a great fucking idea.

Zach: How you feelin', Hargrove?

Amber: I feel so good, Alexander.

Zach: [*eyes Amber*]

Amber: Don't look at me like that.

Zach: Like what?

Amber: [*dramatically rolls eyes*] Don't act fucking stupid. You know *exactly* what you're doing, and the only reason you keep doing it is because you keep getting away with it.

Zach: I don't know what you're talking about, Amber.

Amber: [*scoffs*] God, I'm so lucky I'm not Hanna June. Which is so sad because I used to *want* to be her.

Zach: Why?

Amber: 'Cause she's fucking perfect. Look at her. Wait, why am I telling you that? You know what she looks like. Better than any of the rest of us. She looks like a model. She has a perfect life. Perfect family, perfect you, perfect *arranged marriage* …

Zach: [*smirks*] Yeah, I guess you're right.

Amber: [*pauses*] And then I realized it was all a lie.

Zach: [*pauses*] What are you talking about?

Amber: It's all a fucking ruse. And it's all for you. And you don't give a shit.

Amber: She never talks about her family. Ever. She only talks about you. Because she's desperately trying to communicate to you and to anyone who will listen how much she fucking loves you. And you continuously cheat on her. Like, all the fucking time. And she knows it. Everybody knows it. And she can't do anything about it.

Zach: [*pauses*] That doesn't mean her whole life is a lie.

Amber: She colors her hair because you told her back in high school that you liked her better as a blonde. She fucking starves herself sometimes because she's trying so hard to stay skinny for you, so you will maybe find her attractive enough that you stop picking other girls over her. You told her when you two first met that your favorite fucking colors were gold and blue, and ever since then, she's tried to wear those colors more than any others even though, apparently, gold doesn't go with her fucking skin tone and her favorite color is pastel pink—but I'd put money down that you didn't even know that. That you didn't know *any* of that. Because you don't fucking care.

Zach: [*long pause*] You say *fuck* a lot when you're high.

Amber: [*stares in disbelief*] That's what you took away from everything I just said? [*scoffs and walks away*]

Hanna June was drunk. She was sitting around the table with Dawn and Damon.

HJ: Dawn. Damon. You guys are so lucky.

Dawn: [*amused*] What do you mean?

HJ: You're about to fucking graduate! That's… tha's so great for you guys.

Dawn: You'll graduate in three years.

Damon: Maybe.

HJ: But, like, I mean, like, that you are, you know, you're gonna start your lives. You're grown-ups. Like, you're gonna have like, actual, like, bills and a 'partment that's not on campus, and you're gonna have a job and a 401(k).

Dawn: Actually, we're both staying here for another few years.

HJ: [*wrinkles nose, disgusted*] Oh my God, why?

Dawn: [*chuckles*] We're both still waiting to hear about our doctorate programs. But even if I don't get accepted, I've got my tutoring job here, and that pays me well.

HJ: [*turns to Damon, trying to impersonate Kronos*] What about you, Mr. Montclaire?

Damon: I'm not done with school yet.

HJ: [*shakes head drunkenly*] You're about to have your master's degree. Do you really need a PhD?

Damon: Yes.

HJ: [*pauses*] So … you'll be Dr. Damon?

Dawn: [*holds in laughter*]

Damon: I won't be a doctor.

HJ: Yes, you will. That'll be your title.

Damon: I won't be a doctor.

HJ: [*taunting him*] You'll have a PhD, so you'll be a doctor. Don't argue with me! I might be drunk, but I'm right!

Dawn: You're both right. He'll have his doctorate, but he won't technically be a doctor, which is why he feels the need to clarify that he won't be a doctor and doesn't really want to be called one.

HJ: But … like, you did all that fucking work … I'd wanna be called a doctor.

Dawn: [*mumbles as she sits back in her chair*] Yeah, me too.

Damon: [*sips drink*]

HJ: Are you drunk yet, Doctor?

Damon: [*annoyed*] Not yet.

HJ: Well then, catch up! I'm the drunkest out of everybody!

Damon: There's only six of us.

Dawn: [*looks around*] Do you think there will ever be any more of us?

HJ: [*nods vigorously while drinking, sloshing and spilling all over the table but somehow not on herself*] Oh yeah. Soon.

Damon: [*looks questioningly at Dawn*] You say that like you're sure about it.

HJ: I am. [*tries to catch the straw from her drink in her mouth, misses*]

Dawn: You're sure there's going to be more of us?

HJ: Yep.

Damon: [*long pause, then turns to Dawn*] She doesn't stop talking for twenty-five minutes about how she ranks the Kardashians, but now, she can't divulge information that *she* offered up.

Dawn: Shh. [*to HJ*] HJ, how do you know that?

HJ: [*still trying to get the straw in her mouth*] Zach told me.

Dawn: How does he know?

HJ: Kronos told him.

Damon: [*brow furrows in confusion*] Why would Kronos have told him information like that and not shared with the rest of us?

HJ: [*shrugs bigger than a sober person would and takes a sip of her drink after successfully getting that damn straw in her mouth*] I don't know. He tells him a lot of stuff.

Dawn: [*pauses*] He wouldn't have told him that when the cameras were rolling, so when would he have shared that?

HJ: Probably on Tuesdays.

Damon and Dawn both stare at her, waiting.

HJ: [*violently slurring her words*] They have lunch together every Tuesday.

Damon: What?

HJ: [*big shrug again*] I don't know. That's what he told me.

Damon: How long have they been doing that?

HJ: Since the week before we started.

Dawn's eyes get huge, and Damon grips the edge of his chair.

Dawn: And Zach just told you this?

HJ: Oh no, you see, he was, [*jokingly clears her throat*] ahem, not sober. I don't know if he even remembers telling me.

Damon: Christ.

HJ: [*obnoxious gasp*] Don't you say the Lord's name in vain!

Damon: [*completely ignores her*] You're sure that they've been meeting every Tuesday and talking about things that don't get discussed with the rest of us?

HJ: [*nods, then pauses*] Unless he made it all up and he's been lying to me about where he's been for a few hours every Tuesday for the past month and a half.

HJ: Which wouldn't surprise me.

Hanna June pulls her knees up to her chest, stares at the table in front of her, and chugs the rest of her drink. Dawn and Damon watch in silence.

Dawn: [*sitting down next to Kai, who has been sitting by himself since he gave Amber a crash course in Cannabis 101*] You're pretty quiet.

Kai: [*nods*]

Dawn: Any particular reason for that?

Kai: Kronos said I talk more when I'm high. Which is true. And the last time I was drunk, I professed my love for Amber. And it was on TV.

Kai: And now, I'm high *and* drunk. And she's right there, and she's so pretty, and she smells so good, and she's smoking my weed, so I figured it was best if I kept my distance.

Dawn: [*nods slowly*] Can't argue with that logic.

Amber: [*runs over to them*] We're gonna watch Twilight with the sound off and make up our own words! I call Alice! [*jumps up excitedly with her hands flying and accidentally hits the chain on her ceiling fan*] Oh shit. [*runs back to living room*]

Kai: [*keeps his eyes on her as she leaves for a moment, then turns to Dawn*] Do you know that I didn't agree to be in the program until I found out she was in it?

Dawn: Really?

Kai: Yeah. Kronos told me, like, about you and Damon. Said you two were the first ones and he had two incoming freshmen he was waiting on paperwork from, and then he said the last person was someone I knew, and he told me it was her.

Dawn: You like her.

Kai: [*gives her a sad smile*] The whole country knows I … like her.

Dawn: I've been wondering why you didn't ask Rhianne to have them edit it out.

Kai: [*shrugs, leans head back*] I did actually. But they showed me the footage of it, and … I don't know. [*sighs*] I feel like so much of the shit that actually ends up on the show just seems so fake and forced. We're literally sitting in front of a fucking backdrop and being asked questions on cue cards, you know?

Dawn: Yeah, I know exactly what you mean.

Kai: Yeah, so, like, I told her I wanted them to get rid of it, and she had me actually watch the footage first. And it just … I don't know. It seemed like one of the first real moments on the show so far. At least for me. So, when Rhianne asked if I was sure I wanted to get rid of it, I said I didn't know, and then Kr—[*cuts off sentence, stares at Dawn with huge eyes*]

Dawn: What?

Kai: Nothing.

Dawn: Kai, you can talk to me. If you don't want to, I understand that. But just know that if you decide to tell me something, anything, I won't share it unless you ask me to.

Kai: [*stares at her, contemplating*] He offered me money.

Dawn: Kronos did?

Kai: Yeah. Just like a onetime thing. But my mom needed it 'cause something on the boat broke again, so she couldn't send me money for groceries, so, like, I kinda needed it too. So, I took it.

Dawn: [*nods slowly*] I understand. It makes complete sense.

Kai: [*nods*] Thanks.

Dawn: And I agree with you.

Kai: What?

Dawn: I agree with you. That moment is probably the first authentic thing they've ever filmed of us. I'm glad you decided to keep it. Even if it took a little bribing.

Kai: Thanks.

HJ: [*walks out to the balcony to find only Damon*] I deserve an Oscar for my performance as Bella. I really do. I totally brought that bitch to life.

Damon: [*glances over his shoulder at her but turns back away*]

HJ: [*slowly approaches him*] You okay?

Damon: Fine.

HJ: [*nods, looking at the ground but then back up at him*] 'Cause you don't seem like you're fine.

Damon: Hanna June, why are you out here?

HJ: I'm checking on you! You're normally very antisocial and broody, but it's magnified by, like, a million tonight, so I'm just checking on you.

Damon: [*lets out an annoyed sigh*] Are you still drunk?

HJ: Not as much as I was before *Twilight*.

Damon: [*turns to face her, clearly still annoyed*] Do you remember what you told me and Dawn?

HJ: [*looks off into the distance, purses lips*] When?

Damon: Two hours ago.

HJ: No.

Damon: [*single nod*] Okay. [*turns away from her*]

HJ: No, tell me! What did I say?

Damon: Never mind, Hanna June.

HJ: [*whines*] Tell me!

Damon: Oh my God, stop.

HJ: [*still whining*] Only if you tell me!

Damon: [*annoyed sigh*] Fine, okay. You told us that Kronos meets with Zach every Tuesday. That they talk about things, things he hasn't bothered to tell the rest of us and likely never will. And that just ... really, really bothers me.

HJ: Oh yeah. That definitely happens.

Damon: You're one hundred percent positive? There's not even the slightest chance that you're wrong?

HJ: [*pauses*] Well ... there's *always* a chance ...

Damon: Tell me exactly what you know about these meetings.

HJ: [*glances at the door inside over his shoulder, hears someone*] Bev's, two o'clock tomorrow.

Damon: What?

Zach: [*comes outside*] Hey, what's going on?

HJ: I was just checking on Damon.

Zach: He looks like he's fine. Especially considering how extremely close he's standing to my girlfriend ... [*cocks his head at Damon*]

Damon: We were just talking.

Zach: Mmhmm. Do me a favor. Don't get that close to her again.

Damon: Oh, 'cause you weren't that close to another girl less than twenty-four hours ago? Maybe even twelve—does that sound right?

HJ: [*drops her head, takes a step back*]

Zach: Man, shut the fuck up.

Damon: Am I wrong?

Zach: I said, shut the fuck up!

Damon: [*gets right up close to him, towering over him*] Don't worry; *I* wouldn't do that. She's not really my type. But you should really treat your girlfriend the way she should be treated.

Zach: [*sneers up at him*] Get away from me.

Damon: Gladly. [*walks back inside*]

Amber: [*drops onto couch, slurring her words*] This … this was so mush fun, yous guys.

HJ: Yeah, I think we're gonna head back 'cause it's almost two … [*glaring at her phone screen*] I think. Reading is hard.

Zach: Thank you for having us, Amber. You were a wonderful host.

Amber: Hostess with the mostest, bitches!

HJ: [*laughs*] Amber, you should go to sleep.

Amber: I will, I will, I pinkie promise! Now, go, go, go, go, go. Text me when you get back!

HJ: Okay, okay, I will!

Zach: [*raises an eyebrow at HJ*] Well, maybe not. 'Cause … ya know, we might be busy.

HJ: [*playfully hits him on the arm*] Zachary!

They laugh as they walk out the door.

Kai: I should probably head back too.

Amber: No. No, *you* should stay.

Kai: [*sharply turns his head to look back at her*] What?

Amber: I said, you should stay. [*reaches out to grab his arm even though he's too far away*]

Kai: [*nervously looks down at her extended arm*] I don't think that's a good idea.

Amber: Why not?

Kai: You're slurring your words. It looks like you can't even hold yourself up right now.

Amber: Tha's 'cause I can't.

Kai: I think if you were sober, you'd be telling me to go home.

Amber: Not true.

Kai: No?

Amber: Nope.

Kai: [*pauses, speaks quietly*] Then, why do you, like, reject me?

Amber: [*dramatic sigh*] It's just easier that way.

Kai: What do you mean?

Amber: [*blankly stares at him, then slowly blinks and mumbles*] I'm so tired.

Kai: You should go to sleep.

Amber: You can't leave.

Kai: [*pauses to look at her*] I'll stay if you really want me to stay.

Amber: I do.

Kai: Who am I?

Amber: What?

Kai: What's my name? Who am I? I need to make sure you're at least aware enough to know who you're asking to stay in your apartment while you're shit-faced drunk and high off your ass for the first time.

Amber: [*snorts*] You think I'm high for the first time? That's *high-larious.*

Kai: [*pauses again*] What?

Amber: I've been smoking weed since, like, my sophomore year of high school.

Kai: [*dumbfounded*] Seriously?

Amber: I'm not, like, a stoner, [*facial expression pretending she's high*] but, yeah, I knew what I was doing.

Kai: So … so why did you ask me to teach you and stuff?

Amber: I can't have everyone know that I do it! They have this, like, image of me, and I don't wanna ruin it. I don't want Fleur to find out.

Amber: [*yawns*] Plus, I kinda wanted you to just, like, be close to me.

Kai: [*long pause*] Who am I?

Amber: [*sighs, closes eyes*] Your name is Kai Beckham Newport. Your mother is a lovely woman named Leticia, and you share a dad with Damon and Zach, you being in the middle out of the three of you. You grew up on a houseboat, sailing around the Outer Banks of North Carolina, and you were homeschooled most of your life. You live off campus in your uncle's old RV, which is, like, the coolest thing ever, and you kissed me after the Theta Chi party about a year ago, and I really want you to do it again. [*rolls her head in his direction, opens eyes, and stares right at him*] I know who you are, and I want you to stay.

Kai: [*gulps, nods*] Where am I sleeping?

Amber: You can sleep out here on the couch, if you want, but I'd like it better if you slept with me.

Kai: Okay.

Amber: [*locks the front door, starts down the hallway with Kai in tow, turns around quickly, and points a finger in his face*] I mean, literally *sleep* with me. Like, nothing … else.

Kai: [*nods*] I'm okay with that.

Amber: [*stares at him for a few seconds before turning around and walking back into her bedroom*]

Chapter 33

DAMON

DAMON TURNED THE CORNER ON Carolina Avenue and headed toward the downtown area of Olympia. His apartment wasn't anywhere near campus, as he didn't want to be near all the chaotic undergrads. He lived out in between the sad excuse for the Medical District and the few businesses that didn't revolve around the campus.

He pulled into the visitors lot near Bev's Taproom, already dreading this meeting. He didn't know why he was even wasting his time—he knew she wasn't going to show up. She'd given him extremely vague instructions while she was drunk and stoned out of her mind, and there was no way she remembered doing it.

He just knew he was going to walk into the place, have everyone look at him—because, apparently, that was what people did even though he always hated it—and she wouldn't be there. He'd then be left with two options: one, awkwardly sit down by himself, or two, turn and leave.

But as he approached the entryway on the corner of Carolina Avenue and Sullivan Street, he saw a figure that resembled her. Her short frame, blonde hair pulled into a ponytail on the top of her head, manicured fingers tapping away at her phone while her other hand held a cigarette.

Damon had always been stealthy, which he found odd because he was so tall. It would've been nice to use that skill on siblings during games of hide-and-seek or manhunt, but he was destined to be an only child, and his parents' staff never wanted to play with him when he was growing up. The skill had gone unused for years until Ernesto showed him how to use it *properly*.

She didn't hear him walk up behind her.

"I didn't peg you for the smoking type."

Hanna June turned around fast and nearly dropped her phone. "Jesus, you scared me."

"Did you just say the *Lord's name* in vain?"

She glared at him. "I'm not perfect"—she gestured to the cigarette in her hand—"as you just found out. And I'd appreciate it if you didn't tell anyone. *Anyone*."

"Secret's safe with me."

She took another drag, then tossed it onto the sidewalk and put it out underneath her Jack Roger. "Let's go. I'm starving."

Damon followed her inside, assuming she must already be tightly wound. She never pronounced the *G* on the end of words.

Inside, it was fairly empty. They sat across from each other in a small booth at the back of the restaurant, behind the bar. Damon made sure he could see the door from his position.

A too-skinny server came by to hand them grimy, plastic-covered menus and to take their drink orders—sweet tea for her, water for him.

"They have really good buffalo fries here," HJ informed him, crumpling up the wrapper from her straw and poking it into her tea.

"I'm not here to eat, Hanna June," he explained as his eyes panned back and forth between her and the menu she had pushed toward him.

She peered at him from over the top of her trifold, her dark eyebrows rising up on her head. "Okay. But I am."

The waitress came back, jotted down her order, and left, taking the menus with her. Damon cleared his throat and watched Hanna June as she picked up her phone and checked something, quickly placing it back on the table, facedown.

"They meet at one every Tuesday for lunch at Philomena's, off one of those streets behind campus. I can't think of which one off the top of my head right now."

"It's on the corner of 3rd and Center Street."

Damon had been there once but hadn't dared to step inside. In Dawn's attempt to make him more social, she had taken him to something called Mug Night last year. After taking in the scene of half-dressed girls and skeezy guys in boat shoes from the parking lot, he promptly turned around and headed back toward campus. There had never been anything that he'd *not* wanted to participate in so much.

"I have no idea what they talk about, if it's the same thing or always different, or if it's related to the program or the show, or what. But … I know there're some files."

Damon's interest was piqued. He leaned in slightly, getting hit with wafts of vanilla rolling off of her. It baffled him that Zach cheated on her repeatedly—she was attractive, she was good to him, and she really loved him. Which made the whole thing even sadder.

What the hell is wrong with him?

"What kind of files?"

"So, there's a locked computer file because, ya know, we don't live in the Stone Age. But there's also, like, actual paper, envelope files. One for each of us with just, like, basic info, I'm assuming. But"—she leaned forward and lowered her voice—"there're also files for people who aren't in the program. Some for kids who don't even go to school here, like high school students."

"Do you have their names?"

"No. That's as much as I know." She looked disappointed in herself.

"What's in the computer file?"

"I'm assuming it's more of the same stuff, maybe just more in depth?"

Damon leaned back against the cracking fake leather cushion, shaking his head. "No, that doesn't make any sense." He rubbed his jawline, pushing his stubble in the opposite direction. *I need to shave.* "Why would they need files on us?" He didn't mean to say it out loud.

But he was glad he had.

"Apparently, Parthenon has been watching us for years—like, this has been a plan for a while now. Zach said Amber has the biggest file out of all of us."

"Amber?"

Hanna June sipped at her tea. "Yeah, she's technically been in the program since she was in middle school."

Wait, what?

"Middle school?"

"Yeah. But Zach said he saw his file and it's huge too. So is yours."

What the fuck?

Kronos already knows more about me than even Dawn. What the hell is in those files?

"You said that he might not remember telling you this."

Hanna June's cheeks turned bright pink as she leaned back against the booth. She cleared her throat and took a sip of her drink, avoiding eye contact with Damon.

"He, umm, he wasn't exactly … sober when he told me."

"Yeah, you said that last night. He was drunk?" Damon didn't see the big deal. Sure, he was technically related to him, but he'd really only just met him a month or so ago, and he'd already seen him drunk multiple times.

"He was … well, *we* were very high."

He nodded slowly.

HJ's massive brown eyes met Damon's black ones. "Do you remember last night when he mentioned how we had gotten stoned a few weeks ago?"

It was a memory Damon had tried to put out of his head. "I forgot it until just now."

"Yeah"—she made eye contact with the edge of the table again—"that was that time. That was his … second, maybe third, meeting with Kronos. He came back with this, like, crazy amount of information, but Kronos had told him he couldn't tell anyone, and Zach was, like, literally buzzing with energy and said he had to calm down. One of the guys in his dorm had given him some weed, so me and him got high, and he told me all that."

It was coming together now. It wasn't necessarily a picture Damon wanted to see the finished product of, but nevertheless, it was all making sense to him.

"I guess I asked too many questions because he stopped talking and just started making out with me, probably to distract me, and then we …" Her gaze volleyed in between his face and her fingers in her lap that she couldn't seem to stop moving. "Well, you know. Anyway, I didn't forget what he'd told me. But when he asked me the next day if I remembered anything from before we started smoking, I said no."

"You lied to him?" It came out as a tease, although he hadn't meant it that way. Zach would have something to say to him if he were here right now, no doubt about it.

She rolled her eyes. "He lies to me all the time."

"Then, why are you still with him?"

A long pause passed between them, neither of them breaking eye contact this time though.

"I love him too much to lose him."

"I guess," Damon started, knowing that it was a losing battle. She wasn't going to listen to what he had to say anyway. "But wouldn't you rather be with someone who is honest with you and doesn't … you know?"

The smile she offered him was so sad. "I don't really have a choice."

Another empty moment passed before she kept going. "Damon, have you ever been in love?"

He scoffed unintentionally. "No, I have not."

"Well then, you really don't have any right to tell me that I'm making a bad choice when you have no idea how you'd react if you were in my position. Love makes people do stupid things. You'll see one day."

Another scoff slipped from his lips, and he realized he really needed to stop doing that. Paulina would not approve—and honestly, neither would Lydia.

"Why are you laughing?"

"I just don't think that love is in the cards for me."

The face she made said that she might agree with him. "You never know. Don't write it off. It can be pretty great."

He held back an eye roll and changed the subject. "So, how are we getting these files?"

Hanna June's expression dropped. "I never said we were going to get them."

"That *is* the plan though, right?"

There was no way in hell he had been given this information—that there was a file on him, not far from where they sat, which dated back to his time before he had even been at college—and he'd *not* go confiscate it.

And it seemed like Hanna June was on the same page as him. A slow smile spread across her face as she leaned back in.

"Oh, that's absolutely the plan."

Chapter 34

AMBER

"Thank you, Heath!" She waved to the student mechanic who'd only charged her for the parts and not the labor he'd put in and turned her yellow VW bug onto the main road by the campus and headed for the highway.

It would be a short trip home, but it was better than nothing. Besides, if she didn't go home, no one would go grocery shopping or take the trash out or get the mail. The one thing Fleur was always good about was taking care of the plants. Amber's mom had died years ago, but Fleur had managed to keep all her massive gardens somehow thriving over the years.

Amber knew that the loss of her mom had hit everyone hard, but her dad had definitely taken the brunt of it. They'd been together since high school, and one day, she was just gone. Amber imagined that, six years later, she'd still be a wreck if she was in his shoes too.

I just wish he wouldn't disappear for days at a time and leave the fifteen-year-old home alone.

The idea of getting married appealed to her, but not as much as staying away from the possibility of having to balance her family and someone else … someone who could very well just end up hurting her.

Not that Kai would do that.

Wait. No.

Why am I thinking about him? It's not like I've thought about marrying him. We'd be really cute together though …

Fuck, wait. Why am I thinking about this?

They had made out all night. He never once tried anything more, just like she'd told him not to. He fell asleep, facing her, his hand outstretched so his fingertips were brushing hers. The morning had gone so well … until she checked her phone and saw a text from Fleur that had arrived just after they drifted off to sleep.

Fleur: so I don't wanna worry you but dad never came home last night

Fleur: everything's fine tho! Like I don't need you to come home or anything. I'm still eating and everything, just wanted to let you know

A little while later, Amber had left to pick up her car, which, thankfully, one of the student mechanics had finished working on last night, and Kai had walked back to his RV.

But now, she felt like she was buzzing. Maybe it was the lack of sleep; maybe it was because of the text she'd gotten early that morning from Fleur. But she knew that it was probably him.

A little while later, she watched as the surroundings blurring by her became more and more colorful and frequent. Although she much preferred to be in the Midwest, she finally felt like she was home as she crossed the border into Charleston County. She didn't even necessarily need to be in her driveway to get the feeling; it was just knowing that she was back in South Carolina Lowcountry.

After her mom had died, Amber had flawlessly stepped into her role. She took up the cooking, the cleaning, the gardening, all of it. No one had asked her to, not her dad or eight-year-old Fleur at the time. They both showed ways to say thank you to her, and it made her feel better that her work didn't go unnoticed. What had made it all easier was that Amber actually liked doing it. She'd rather live back at home and just be a homemaker full-time, but she also knew that wasn't rational.

Her father made enough money to support the lifestyle they had been living before Rose passed, but in the last three years, things had changed. After she had left for Olympia, Amber had assumed that the realization that she wouldn't be around to take care of things all the time had sunk in for him, and as a way to cope with the added stress and responsibility, he'd picked up on drinking and occasionally gambling. He still went to the country club for dinner on Mondays, and their boat was still docked at the marina—it was important to keep up appearances. He never participated in either of his newly established bad habits to such an extent where he might do something stupid and not be able to take it back. At least, not since his Vegas incident. But the fact that he still did it and she wasn't around to just keep an eye on him worried her.

She was always worried, which was why she had chosen to let loose last night—getting high alone in her apartment only worked so much. She had really thought that she'd checked all her boxes and was sure she could have the night off. But that changed after Fleur's texts came through early this morning.

She had wanted to go get breakfast at the bagel shop downtown with Kai this morning. She wanted to curl under her covers with him and go back to sleep. She had wanted to just sit with her plants today and eat some macadamia nut cookies.

But she had responsibilities to take care of, so everything else would have to wait.

She turned down a few side streets, and the small groups of tourists still wandering around at the end of September had disappeared completely. No one came down these roads—there were no impressive historic buildings or houses this way, no fancy restaurants or shopping areas. Just quiet, old, secluded houses with massive front doors and creaky floorboards.

But then she turned another corner and was down by The Battery, and it seemed as though she was brought back to civilization.

She drove past the first few houses, then pulled into the tiny drive with the mailbox at the end that had flowers and vines wrapping all around it. Fleur had done that when she was ten.

Amber immediately saw her father's Mercedes sideways in the driveway, parked a little too close to the back staircase that went up to the kitchen door. She pulled up next to him and got out.

She hadn't even touched the first step when she heard the yelling. It was a man's voice—his voice. There were some inaudible words being screamed and then the sound of breaking glass.

Amber took the steps two at a time, still able to hear the yelling.

"It's all your fucking fault! It's your fault she's gone!"

She swung the door open as soon as she could reach it with her long arms.

Her father had her stepsister pinned against the refrigerator and was holding her by her neck. Fleur's face was bright red, and her feet were off the ground. She was clawing at his hand wrapped around her neck.

"Dad, what the hell are you doing?!" Her voice came out high-pitched, and her words were rushed.

He dropped her before her sentence was finished. Fleur fell to the ground and immediately began coughing as Amber rushed to her side.

Her dad stumbled back against the counter, breathing heavily and refusing to make eye contact with Amber.

"Dad!"

The color from his face faded, and he raised a finger, pointing at Fleur. "It's her fault."

"What? What is?"

"It's her fault Rose is gone! She took her from me!" He took a step toward her, and Amber jumped to her feet and pushed him back.

"Dad, stop! It's not her fault! She didn't do anything wrong!" She looked at his face and waited for his own manic gaze to connect with hers. His eyes were bloodshot, and he smelled like a liquor cabinet.

He stared back at her for a moment until his face screwed up and tears welled up in his eyes. "She's gone, baby. She's gone." He started sobbing, and his shoulders dropped.

Fleur began to push herself off the floor at this moment, and apparently, the sadness in her dad's body hadn't completely taken over the anger he'd been feeling seconds ago because he lunged at her again and slapped her across the face, sending her sailing back into the fridge.

"It's your fucking fault she's gone!"

"Dad, what is wrong with you?!" She shoved him back with one hand, which ended up not being hard at all. She didn't want to hurt him though. She just needed to try and redirect his attention, in hopes that he would lose the violent streak running through him.

Instead, he reached for Fleur again, but this time, Amber anticipated his move. She held him back with all the upper body strength she could muster, wished she were the type of person who enjoyed working out, and held him back.

"My keys are on the counter behind you! Lock yourself in my car and don't open it until I come to get you!"

Fleur grabbed the keychain off the counter and dashed out the door in nanoseconds.

As soon as she was gone, her father stopped struggling against her. His breathing became heavy for a minute or two, and then he turned back into a blubbering mess.

"Okay, get up," Amber instructed as she tried to help him walk to the bathroom off the master suite.

He stumbled down the hallway and dropped into the tub, fully clothed in his business-casual ensemble he'd most likely worn to work the day before. Amber turned the nozzles to cold water and shut the door, leaving him alone.

She snatched a travel mug out of the cabinet, filled it with hot water from the Keurig, dropped in a tea bag, and raced down the steps. She scooted around to the driver's door, where Fleur was seated.

"Are you okay?" She opened the door, thrust the insulated mug into her tiny hands, and immediately began inspecting the fourteen-year-old's neck. Huge blue-and-purple welts were sprouting up, and Amber could see that she was still shaking.

"I'm fine," she breathed but didn't look her in the eye as she reluctantly took the drink being offered to her.

"Fleur, what happened?" Amber was gripping the doorframe, her knuckles turning white.

"I don't know. I got home from school yesterday ... and he wasn't here, which is normal. A little while later, he ran in—literally *ran*—while I was doing my homework. He went into their room, but I don't know what he was doing."

"You didn't hear anything?"

"Just some, like, shuffling around. A few bangs against the wall, like maybe he was looking for something. He was only in there for two or three minutes. And then he left."

"And then …"

"And then, today, he got home, like … ten minutes before you came here. I think he fell, coming up the stairs, 'cause it made a loud noise, and that was what made me get up and see what it was. He slammed the door open—I'm pretty sure there's a hole in the wall—and started yelling about Ro—about Mom. Then, he started screaming at me, saying it was my fault. He broke all of those vases in the living room and punched the mirror in the hallway by your room. Next thing I knew, he picked me up by my neck, and I couldn't breathe. I couldn't really see, like everything started to kinda go black … and then you got here."

Amber glanced over Fleur's body, checking for any more bruises or signs of distress. She seemed to be calming down … but now what? Was she really supposed to send her back inside, and the three of them would pretend to be one happy family? What about tomorrow night, when Amber went back to school? What was she supposed to do then?

"Okay," she breathed, trying to buy herself a minute. "Just … just stay here. I'll be back in a few minutes. Lock the doors again."

She shut the door and went back up the wooden staircase after hearing the car doors lock. She traveled through the house quietly until she found her father, still fully clothed and lying on the floor of the walk-in shower. The water was streaming out of the showerhead, the steam hanging in a heavy cloud over him, as he stared off into the abyss. The alcohol stench was still extremely potent.

Amber went into full guardian mode, her hands on her hips as she stood in front of the condensation-covered mirror. "Fleur gave me her version of events. What's yours, Daddy?"

"I gambled away Fleur's college fund."

There had been no pause before his response. He had known what Amber had come in to ask him, and apparently, he wasn't even going to try to deny what he had done.

Amber shut the water off. "Please tell me that's a lie."

"Amber," he groaned. "I'm telling you what happened. Why would I lie about it?"

"I don't know! Maybe some sick joke?"

He shook his head slightly as he lay on his side, the water dripping off his chinos and seersucker. "It wasn't all of it. Just a few thousand."

"Oh! Just a few thousand! Daddy, what the hell? You gambled away money that wasn't yours? Again?!"

Amber was trying really hard to be mad, but it wasn't easy. She was more worried than anything. She'd seen her dad depressed plenty of times—the better part of the last six years. He had gone through some extremely low lows, but he'd never done anything like this. He'd never been violent.

"You slapped her. And you choked her. You could have *killed* her!"

"I know," he whimpered as his face screwed up again. "I know. I'm sorry." His words came out as breaths in between sobs. It was awful to see him like this. He would have killed Fleur if Amber hadn't gotten there when she did, and it looked like the severity of his actions were finally catching up with him.

"Is she okay?"

"She says she's fine, but I doubt that's the truth. You left huge bruises all over her neck. She can't go to school like that. She can't go anywhere."

"I know," he wailed.

How is this the situation I'm in? He was fine yesterday when I called him, so what the hell happened in the last twenty-four hours?

"I think," Amber began, "that I should take her. For a few days."

Her dad was nodding, making the tears roll faster down his cheeks.

"Her bruises need to heal, and honestly, I don't think she's too keen on the idea of being left here alone with you. I know I don't like it."

"Okay." His hand shot out and grabbed the tips of Amber's fingers, pulling her back to him. "I didn't mean it. What I said. And I didn't mean to hurt her. I didn't mean it." The tears welled up in his eyes, and he only had to blink once for them to fall out onto his pudgy cheeks and roll down his face.

"Just … get up off the floor. Drink some decaf and maybe sleep the rest of it off."

"Okay."

"I'll bring her back on Thursday."

"Okay."

With that, Amber exited the bathroom and made a beeline for Fleur's room. She grabbed the first bag she could find and started tossing clothes in. After she felt like she had enough clothes for a few days, she picked up Fleur's backpack, shut the door, and went back out to her car. Neither of them said a word as Fleur got out of the driver's seat and went around to the other side of the car. Amber started her bug and backed out of their bumpy cobblestone driveway.

As she pulled back onto I-26, heading in the opposite direction she'd come from just a half an hour earlier, Fleur turned to her. "Can you tell me what's going on?"

Amber took a breath. "You're not going to school for a few days, probably the rest of the week. We'll see if you can do your work online. You're going to just hang out at my apartment with me, aside from when I'm in class or …"

"Or doing something for *The Olympians*?" Fleur finished for her.

"Yeah." Amber didn't like the idea of her being around with the cameras and Kronos and the other five. The thought of it made her cringe and want to hide her sister away from everyone and everything.

Fleur had been her responsibility from the moment she was adopted. For the first two years, it was her duty to be the best big sister ever. She'd always wanted to be one, and at eleven years old, her wish had finally come true. But after her mom passed, she had to suddenly be a parent too—helping Fleur with her homework, packing her lunch, washing her clothes, and giving her "the talk" a few years later. That was hands down the most awkward, having to inform her of things that were going to happen to her body and how to prepare for them—although some of those things hadn't even happened for Amber at that point.

It had been difficult, but ultimately, she felt as though she had found the perfect balance between being her friend, her sister, and her mom, and that was something she was very proud of.

Fleur timidly asked if she could play her music, and for the rest of the drive, Amber just tried to focus on figuring out the next best step for her family and how to erase from her mind the image of the man who had given her life trying to take that same thing away from her little sister.

Chapter 35

KAI

CLOUD FUCKING NINE.

That was where Kai was. In fact, that was where he'd been for the past twenty-four hours, and he didn't care if he never came back to earth.

Thank God he had stayed because he really was going to leave, pull a good-guy card and not stay the night, even though Amber was very far from sober.

They went into her room and sat cross-legged on her bed, facing each other, talking about *everything*.

Amber told him how she felt like her dad and sister were maybe finally both in a good place and how things seemed to be working out in that department. She was listing off the fan theories Fleur was following on Twitter when Amber suddenly broke off her sentence and looked at him.

"Are you hungry?"

He laughed at her abruptness but went along with it. Instead of touching any of the food the six of them had picked at in the earlier hours, she threw some dinosaur chicken nuggets into the oven, mixed up a "special sauce"—he didn't ask her what it was because she seemed to love the idea of it being a secret, and he loved the look on her face too much when she told him it was confidential—and placed an order for Cookie Dude.

The two of them ate and talked for hours and smoked a few more joints. But as the clock got closer to four in the morning, she got closer to him. But he knew better.

Until he didn't.

She leaned forward, making Kai completely freeze. Her eyes darted in between his lips and his eyes, holding eye contact.

"I need you to kiss me."

Kai *almost* asked her to repeat herself, but he knew what he'd heard her say, and he also knew that there was a chance she would take it back.

So, he did it.

And oh.

My.

God.

It was perfect.

So much better than the last time they'd kissed.

She was warm and soft, and one of her arms slid up his chest while the other one went around the back of his neck and pulled him in closer.

This was it. This was what he'd been waiting for so long for.

They made out for what felt like hours, not doing anything past that. Kai had waited a year to kiss her again, and he'd gladly wait longer than that to take the next step if it meant he got to have her.

He wasn't sure how long their tongues painted each other's, but at some point, they both passed out.

Kai woke up because Amber had rolled into him, causing him to lock up again, not sure of what to do. Her arms slid around him, and she nuzzled her face into his chest and let out this peaceful little sigh.

Without consciously thinking about it, he slid his arms around her, too, and rested his chin on top of her head.

He was about to drift back off into sleep when he heard her mumble, "Hi," against his pec.

He gave her a gentle squeeze and repeated her greeting back to him, and they lay together like that for a while-until she reached onto her nightstand and retrieved her phone from its charging position.

Kai didn't stretch over for his yet—he wasn't ready to rejoin reality.

She only scrolled through her notifications for what seemed like nanoseconds before she bolted upright and announced that she had to go.

She's got family stuff going on. At least you got a whole night. The best night you could've asked for.

Kai didn't want to push her by asking too many questions—things had finally turned around for him, and he was determined to make sure there were no setbacks.

She simply said, "A family thing came up," and she had to go home pretty much right away.

They both dressed quickly, and she threw some things in a backpack as she called Campus Auto Care to find out if her car was ready. They were about to walk out the door together when she threw in that she really enjoyed him spending the night and that if she didn't absolutely *have* to leave right away, they'd be going to get breakfast right now.

Well, almost lunch at that hour, but still.

Yes, their time together had been cut drastically short that morning, but Kai was over the moon with what he had gotten.

Guess my drunken profession of love for her didn't totally push her away.

Unless she hasn't watched it.

She probably hasn't. She doesn't seem like she watches reality TV. And I feel like she'd get uncomfortable, watching herself . . .

Kai knew what he'd done downtown that night was not exactly smart even though everyone was praising him for it.

See, this is why I prefer to just get high. Alcohol just makes me stupid. And fat. And Amber probably won't like me if I'm fat.

Wait, but . . . smoking gives me the munchies . . . shit.

I need a blunt.

Wait, shit.

Episode five would air later this week, and in their Sunday meeting with Kronos—which Amber had been excused from for a family emergency—he'd shared that Kai was already voted Most Relatable Cast Member.

Everything was becoming more and more real, and he didn't know how to feel about it. Some parts of it were really cool, like when girls asked him to take pictures with them or sign their chests—those were the best. Obviously.

But then there were lots of times where it was kind of just *a lot.* Everyone in his classes seemed to be obsessed with him—whether they were whispering to him, trying to sneak a picture, or just plain staring.

And what was worse was that he *had* to pass Organic Chem 2, Ecology, *and* Modern Genetics this semester; otherwise, it would completely mess up his last three semesters, and he'd probably have to enroll in summer classes again. The last thing he wanted was to have to stay here for an extra three months when he could be home with his mama.

But, *God*, everyone was making it so difficult.

Zach and HJ had both been talking about getting bodyguards for when they traveled across campus while Damon was already transitioning his classes to be online.

And even though Kronos had personally thanked him for making the show's first episode such a "kick out of the park" and for becoming an internet meme, none of it made him feel any better.

What would make him feel better was if he was back home, on the water.

People used to ask him a lot, "Doesn't that bother you? Not having a stable home? Not even knowing where you're drifting to sometimes?"

"Why would that bother me?" was always his answer. That was the exciting part. Sometimes, you'd end up in a place you'd already visited, and you'd get to go back and stop by a spot you'd had a good time at during your last visit. But there were also plenty of times neither his mom or him recognized the dock in the distance, and they'd take a chance and anchor there. They usually found some great reason to want to come back.

Kai had also found out during his first week of his freshman year at OC that he couldn't sleep soundly through the whole night unless he was rocked to sleep by the waves.

That's it. Amber and the water. That's all I want.

And to have Mom close by.

Just not actually there.

'Cause, ya know ... privacy.

She had called him a week or two ago, absolutely ecstatic that there'd been a huge deposit in her account. She had called the bank to try and find out where it had come from, but all they would tell her was that it was an anonymous donor paying her the money she was owed and that there'd be four more installments over the next few months.

"You know, baby, I think it was your daddy—horrible thing that he is. Because I don't know anyone else who has that much money *and* would want to remain anonymous! You and I and everyone else know that man likes to flaunt his money, and if he was donating to some library or hospital or, hell, even that school of yours—and now, his *other* sons'—he'd want that to be public news! But since it's to me, it needs to be all secretive." She was completely right though.

Not that he told her that.

"You're probably right, Mama. I'm just glad you finally got it."

"Me too, baby. Now, I can get you some of those Christmas presents from when you were little that I couldn't afford back then," she joked with him.

This woman was always able to put a smile on, and that was something Kai was proud of her for doing … but also really jealous of.

Why do I feel like I'm drowning for days at a time?

Nothing that bad has happened to me.

I shouldn't feel like this—she should. She's been through so much.

Not that I want her to feel like this. I don't want anyone to feel like this.

Shit, I'm not allowed to be so depressed. I'm on TV, for Chrissake. I'm gonna have no student loans. I have girls fighting over me on social media and shit.

So, why do I feel like this? What's wrong with me?

It was Uncle Kris who brought it up. "Do you like it?"

"Like what?" Kai asked him after his mom handed her phone over to her brother to talk to him.

"The show. College. All of it."

"Oh, yeah. Yeah, it's great." That was his usual answer, and it just slipped out of his mouth without much thought to it.

"Kai …"

"Yeah?"

"What's wrong?"

Kai's face screwed up. Not that it mattered since Kris couldn't see him. "What do you mean?"

His uncle's voice stayed calm and smooth as he explained through the receiver, "Something isn't right. So, what's wrong?"

"Nothing!"

"*Kai Beckham.*"

"Kris, there's nothing wrong!"

"I don't believe you, kid."

They went back and forth for another minute before Kai broke. He should've hung up the phone. He *knew* he should have. Instead, he exploded.

"Everything's wrong! I hate this school, I hate this city, I hate this stupid show that's made me look fucking stupid in front of the *whole* world! I hate my classes! I hate it all!"

There was a long silence on the other end while his breathing slowly regulated, and then his uncle said, "Do you want to come home?"

Of course I do.

"No, it's fine. I'll be fine. Look, I'm just tired. I'm—I'm sorry for yelling. I'm sorry. I think I just need to get some rest."

The embarrassment and regret immediately set in as his uncle let him go, after reminding him that fall break was coming up and he'd get to come home for a few days.

He paced the length of his tiny RV. He contemplated rolling a joint, and then realized that it didn't matter. Even if it worked for a little while, it would wear off eventually, and he'd end up feeling like shit again.

And *that* thought didn't make him feel any better, as true as it was.

So, Kai did something he hadn't done in a very long time.

He cried.

And he cried. And then he cried some more.

When he finally couldn't see his hands in front of him and his body felt like it was going to collapse, he dropped onto his bed, curled up in a ball, and that was the first night in his two years at Olympia College that he slept through the night.

Until he had spent the night with Amber.

So, maybe, just maybe, things were finally falling into place.

Chapter 36

HANNA JUNE WAS ON THE phone with Dawn, walking across campus with Damon. The conversation was on speakerphone.

Dawn: Are you guys almost there yet?

HJ: Almost. We would already be if Damon would walk a little faster! Come on. Your legs are as long as my entire body! How am I in front of you?

Damon: [*heard in the background*] Unlike you, I haven't had three cups of coffee in the last hour.

HJ: Ugh, just come on! Are Kai and Amber with you, Dawn?

Dawn: Kai is.

Kai: Hi.

HJ: Hi, Kai.

Dawn: Amber isn't here though.

HJ: Oh, have you finally heard from her? She's been MIA since the party …

Dawn: Yeah, she texted me a little while ago and said that she wasn't going to be able to make it. I hope she's okay.

HJ: Huh, that's weird. She seemed real eager to come when we talked about it on Thursday night.

Kai: Yeah, she told me she was coming on Friday morning.

HJ: You talked to her on Friday? *Morning?*

Kai: Yeah, just for a little.

HJ: Like … did you text her? Or did you talk in person?

A long pause passes between the group as Kai realizes what HJ is insinuating. HJ and Damon reach the office they're looking for.

Damon: We're here. [*ends the phone call on HJ's phone*]

HJ: Hey!

Damon: What? [*kneels down and pulls out lock-picking tools and begins on opening the door*]

HJ: I was in the middle of a conversation.

Damon: No, you weren't.

HJ: [*scoffs*] Excuse me?

Damon: You weren't having a conversation. You were trying to extract personal information from someone you barely know, just because you're nosy and you want something to gossip about.

HJ: [*highly offended and also upset that she got called out*] I'm not nosy! I was just tryin' to find out if Kai and Amber hooked up or not! I want to know what's goin' on with my *coworkers*, so I can anticipate any drama. Why are you actin' like you're not interested too?

Damon: It's not my business, and it isn't yours either. Now, if you'd please let me get back to work so we can get inside before someone comes down the hall, I'd appreciate it.

HJ: [*rolls her eyes and waits*]

Seconds later, the door glides open.

Damon: Go. Get inside.

HJ: [*slips into the room and flicks the lights on, groans*]

Damon: What? [*enters room behind her and relocks the door from the inside*]

HJ: Just a whole lot of file cabinets …

Damon: Then, we'd better get to work. You're sure this stuff on us isn't on his computer?

HJ: [*shakes her head*] Zach said they started the files so long ago and they've gotten so big that they just haven't transferred everything over.

Damon: That just doesn't make sense to me. Everything is online now. It would be easier for him if all the information was virtual, so what's the purpose of keeping tangible documents? And why have one file on the computer, but not the rest of them?

HJ: [*shrugs*] I don't know. Let's just get lookin'. I'll start on this set over here, and you start on that side.

Damon: [*nods, begins working*] Just take pictures of everything you find with any of our names, or the program, or—

HJ: I know; I know. We already went over it. I know what to do. [*slides a drawer open, starts singing the Mission: Impossible theme song*]

Damon: [*jerks his head up and stares at her*]

HJ: Oh, come on! I'm trying to make it fun!

Damon: Don't.

HJ: [*shakes her head, rolls her eyes, and silently gets to work*]

Roughly forty minutes later, they hear footsteps and keys jingling outside.

Damon: Hide. [*ducks into a tiny coat closet and shuts the door*]

HJ: [*looks around for a space to hide in, begins to panic, dives under the desk, and curls up into a ball, knowing that she will be found*]

A janitor comes in, empties the trash, walks right in front of Hanna June, but does not acknowledge her. Leaves seconds later. Damon slowly opens the door about thirty seconds after the janitor shut the door behind him and relocked it.

Damon: Hanna June?

HJ: I'm here. [*uncurls from under the desk*]

Damon: He didn't see you?

HJ: [*shakes head*]

Damon: How is that possible?

HJ: I don't know. He was right in front of me. I swear he looked right at me. Maybe he was blind?

Damon: Maybe.

HJ: We should probably get back to work. We don't have much time, and we've still got four full file cabinets to go.

Damon: [*nods, gets back to work*]

Five minutes later, Hanna June's phone rings.

HJ: Dawn?

Dawn: They're leaving now. You've got about ten minutes.

HJ: Copy. [*hangs up*] Less than ten. They just left.

Damon: Okay. Honestly, we should just pack up and get out. We can come back and go through the rest next week.

HJ: That's a good idea. I really don't want to have to explain to Kronos what we're doin' here.

They pack up the files they went through, put things back where they were, and leave in time. They leave down the back stairwell.

HJ: Oh shit.

Damon: [*sighs*] What now?

HJ: We were supposed to meet at Amber's to go over everythin'. But I guess we can't do that now … eh, I'll just call her and see if she's up for it. She usually likes playin' hostess anyway. [*calls Amber*]

Amber: [*on speakerphone*] Hello?

HJ: Am? Quick question.

Amber: Okay …

HJ: So, we all planned to reconvene at your place and go over everythin'. Is that still the plan or no since, you know, you're not here?

Amber: Oh … umm …

HJ: It's fine if you say no. We just need to know if we need to come up with another meeting place.

Amber: No, no! It's fine! Just, umm … how long until you get here?

HJ: Well, me and Damon are right around the corner. We left the Admin building a few minutes ago. We're about to pass the Rec Center. [*to Damon*] Will you *please* keep up with me?

Amber: Okay, yeah, um, that's fine. Just, uh, text me when you get here.

HJ: 'Kay. [*hangs up*] She seemed weird.

Damon. Stress.

HJ: Yeah. Wonder what about.

Damon: Probably her family. Isn't that what it always is for her?

HJ: Yeah. [*eyes him skeptically*]

Damon: What?

HJ: Nothin'. I just … just didn't know you actually listened to us.

Damon: [*annoyed*] Don't tell Paulina you thought that. She'll think those etiquette classes didn't pay off and I'm not receptive to others.

HJ: You took etiquette classes?

Damon: Yeah.

HJ: Hmm.

Damon: What?

HJ: [*shrugs*] Just weird to hear things about you, I guess. You're so closed off.

Damon: I just don't like people knowing my business.

HJ: [*nods slowly*] I guess that's fair. [*lost in thought for a moment*] Oh shoot, I never told Dawn we're still going to Amber's.

Damon: I texted Kai.

HJ: Oh … I didn't know you had any of our numbers.

Damon: Thanks to your boyfriend and his stupid group text idea, I have all your numbers. I just choose not to use them as frequently as the rest of you.

HJ: Does that … never mind.

Damon: No, ask your question.

HJ: [*pauses*] You might not like it.

Damon: I've done a lot of things I don't particularly like. Answering a question from you isn't going to kill me.

HJ: Um … does your lack of participation have anything to do with your, um, half-brothers?

Damon: [*stops at the bottom of the stairs to Amber's apartment building and stares at Hanna June*] Probably.

HJ: Probably?

Damon: I've honestly tried not to think about it.

HJ: Yeah. That's probably, like, really awkward.

Damon: [*zones out for a second*] Let's go. [*starts up the stairs*]

She follows him up the stairs, and she texts Amber that they're there. A minute later, the door swings open.

Amber: [*somewhat frantic*] Hi.

HJ: [*excited*] Hi! Guess what we found.

Amber: [*trying to match her excitement but still very cautious*] What?

Damon: Nothing.

Amber: [*confused*] What?

HJ: [*rolls eyes*] He's lying. [*pushes past Amber to walk inside*]

Amber: [*slightly perturbed at HJ once again inviting herself into her house*] Oh, you're … okay. Come on in, Damon.

Damon: Thanks. [*walks inside*]

Chapter 37

DAMON

AMBER'S APARTMENT WAS TOO HOMEY. It didn't make sense to Damon. Why spend the time and the money on a temporary establishment?

She had clearly put a lot of effort into making her apartment look a certain way, and even if she stayed there until she graduated, she only had another two years left. And Amber was never here anyway, so why did it matter so much?

Her space was a dizzying yet comforting combination of every possible color. There were flowerpots everywhere that had clearly been hand-painted. Throw pillows and blankets with earthy color schemes and geometric patterns on them. Mirrors with designs on them that made the fixtures take up way more space than necessary. Curtains that were too long and gathered on the floor in shades of dark green, mustard yellow, and rusty terra-cotta.

Hanna June sat down at the table, and Damon followed. The furniture piece was clearly pre-loved with its warped wood and nicks in the surface. Paulina would have flipped a lid if he had accidentally left a ring from a drink on the table, much less made a clearly visible indent in the surface of it.

"So," Hanna June started as Amber shakily passed out water among the three of them, "Dawn and Kai should be here any minute, but we found a lot of stuff with our names on it."

"Really?" Amber sank down into a chair on Damon's right. She nervously glanced down the hallway, then redirected her attention to HJ.

"Yeah, nothing super old though, like you were thinking."

"How far back does the stuff you found go?"

"Less than a year."

"Hmm." Amber chewed on her bottom lip. "I don't know. I know this has been going on for a while. I have this feeling that Kronos … picked us. You guys didn't have to write an essay or anything to get accepted into the program, right?"

Damon spoke up. "No."

"I didn't have to do anything aside from fill out most of the same information I'd put on my application. Name, date of birth, home address, intended major, stuff like that."

Amber was nodding. "Me too. Even though I was already technically in it."

There was a brief knock at the door, but before Amber could get up to open it, it swung open.

Kai waltzed in, explaining to Dawn, "You can just go right in."

"I don't think that's very polite, Kai. You should always wait for the homeowner to invite you in," Dawn said, trying to convince him.

"Amber doesn't own this place. She rents it." He turned to look at the redhead, who was uncomfortably watching the conversation unfold in her kitchen. "Hey, Am."

She made a sound. It was so low and so quiet that she must've assumed nobody could hear it, but Damon did. It was a sound of distress.

"Hey, Kai," she mumbled back.

He glided over and sat down next to her, and Dawn leaned against the counter.

"Oh my gosh, Dawn, come sit, please!" Amber jumped out of her seat and shuffled Dawn into it, all too willingly.

Hanna June must've picked up on the awkwardness of the whole situation because she clapped her hands together loudly. "Okay, let's just get down to it. We found a lot of stuff, and we need to all be on the same page, and my guess is that I've got about twenty minutes until Zach calls me and asks where I am, so I'm just gonna dive right in."

She opened the Photos app on her phone and propped it up so the other three could see. "This is the earliest one we found—well, Damon found this, not me. But it's from this time two years ago. This has everyone's name on it, except mine and Zach's. Probably because you guys were all students here last year, is my guess."

She explained another few pictures, but nothing was all that exciting—mainly student files from OC and the high school she and Zach had gone to back in DC. There was a newspaper clipping from when she had won Miss Maryland Teen, copies of all of their college acceptance letters, and an article the local newspaper had written about Dawn from when she graduated with her bachelor's degree.

Damon only half-listened to the conversations going on around him—the theories and questions. On Thursday night, when he'd found out that this was likely bigger than he'd guessed, he'd been mad. But when he'd found out that Zach was somehow in on it, he had been livid. He wanted to ... well, to be honest, he wanted to kill.

He wanted to have a direct target with valid reasoning behind the hit and take them out of the earth's orbit.

His vision started to close in, and he knew that if he didn't redirect himself, he might hurt someone or something.

He shoved his chair out from underneath his long legs and darted toward what he hoped was the bathroom. Slipping inside, he kept the light off as he locked the door, pinched his eyes shut, and leaned his frame against the door. His shoulders dropped, and he let out several ragged breaths, trying to regain a steady pace so he could rejoin everyone before they began to question where he'd gone and why he'd gotten up so abruptly.

"Umm ..."

He jumped.

He knew he shouldn't have, but after thinking that he'd been alone, combined with his growing murderous appetite, he jumped and spun around.

I recognize her.

In the middle of the empty bathtub sat a young girl, holding a plant. She was fully clothed in a white dress, and some of the dirt had spilled into her lap, but she didn't seem to care. Her dark green eyes were almost as big as Hanna June's, staring at him with unease.

The girl from the pictures in Amber's room.

"Sorry," he whispered to her, trying not to stare too intensely back at her. He couldn't be too loud and risk the others hearing him. "I didn't know anyone was in here."

"It's okay," she offered back in her own hushed tone, not looking away from him. "I'm not supposed to be in here anyway. Amber thinks I'm in her room. Still."

"How do you know Amber?" He tried playing dumb but hated the idea of lying to her, which was stupid because he didn't even know this girl. "And why would she think you're still in her room?"

"She's my stepsister."

Damon slowly nodded his head, affirming what he'd already guessed.

"And because she told me to stay in there while everyone was here."

A silence crept in between them, and Damon felt like she had more she wanted to say. "But ..."

She didn't miss a beat as she took his bait. "But I'm sick of being in her room. I'm sick of being in this apartment. I've been here since Saturday, and I haven't gone outside once. Hence ..." She held the long, potted plant up.

Damon struggled to hold in a smile. They had just met and only spoken a few sentences to each other, but he already knew he liked talking to her. He needed to keep going. "You like being outside?"

"I *love* being outside. It's warm most of the time, and you can feel the grass and smell the air and the flowers and breathe better." She paused, eyeing him up and down. A slow smile crept across her thin lips. "You look like you don't see much sun."

He couldn't help the smirk that drew up at her comment. "Yeah, I'm more of a homebody."

Holy shit, is she flirting with me? Nobody flirts with me. Well, I shut it down when they do, but ... I like this.

She nodded but didn't respond. Damon wanted to keep talking to her though, so before the silence went on for too long, he interjected, "I'm Damon."

"Fleur." She smiled back at him.

"Your name means flower."

"Yeah." She giggled. "I, uh, I usually get a *Harry Potter* reference when people hear my name. But you're right; it does mean flower."

"So, I guess it's fitting that you *love* being outside then."

Her smile hadn't gone away, Damon noticed, and it stretched further up into her cheeks.

His smirk was back, and he took a step forward and maneuvered around the small bathroom to lean against the sink. This angle had a much better view of her, of her eyes.

"Well, Fleur, may I ask why you're sitting, fully clothed, in an empty bathtub?"

"I, uhh … I was feeling very overwhelmed."

Her answer hit his gut when he remembered his reason for coming in here—the discussion and possible implications being tossed around, which had caused him to get so infuriated that he had to leave the room.

He took in a deep breath, and as he let it out, he replied, "Yeah, I get that. So, um, why, exactly, are you holding a plant?"

"Oh, umm, yeah, that's kind of a weird thing for other people, I guess. Amber does it too. Probably not in front of anyone though. Umm, this specific plant is as close to indestructible as a plant can get. And the last few days, I've been feeling kind of like I'm going to break, so I figured this was a good one to kind of latch on to."

Damon nodded, listening intently to every word she said. "I like it. I think I've seen a few similar to that one, but the one you're holding is the greenest one I've ever seen." He gestured to the greenery she was holding, meaning every word of what he was saying.

"Yeah, you've probably seen one before. It's a pretty common house plant."

"What's it called?"

"Well, its real name is golden pothos, but most people just refer to it as devil's ivy," she informed him, eyeing his stance curiously.

His gaze blinked down to meet hers, and for several long, silent seconds, neither of them moved.

She blinked twice and slowly pursed her lips before saying, "I can bring you one, you know."

Damon snapped out of his trance, rewinding the words she'd just said and playing them back. "Bring me what?"

"A plant. Not this one because, you know, Amber will notice if one of her forty-eight plants is gone. Trust me."

A story he definitely wanted her to tell him, but it didn't seem like she was offering it now.

"But I can bring you a different one. I think I know one that might work better for you ..." She trailed off, tilting her head to the side and staring at him some more.

Damon hated being looked at. He hated being the center of attention and knowing that all eyes were on him. But her ... he didn't really mind having her stare at him.

"Okay."

"Um ..." She shook her head and refocused her attention to his eyes instead of his mouth. "Do you have class tomorrow?"

"I'm done at ten."

She sat up a little straighter, slightly shaking the long ivy as she readjusted. "Okay, that's perfect! Amber leaves for class at nine forty-five and won't be back until, like, three—tomorrow is her long day. I'll tell her I need to go for a walk or else I'm going to really be diagnosed with cabin fever and start to lose my mind, so she'll give me her key, and then ..."

Damon was only half-listening to her words. This girl wanted to meet up with him.

This pretty girl.

Girl.

Girl.

He cleared his throat and adjusted his button-down. "I don't think that's a good idea."

Her face screwed up, and she looked like he'd just insulted her. "Why not?"

"It's just ... well, it's probably not a good idea for us to spend time together."

Her eyes darted around the darkened bathroom. "We're spending time together right now ..."

He waited a moment before he asked, contemplating if he really should. "Fleur ... how old are you?"

"I just turned sixteen a few days ago. How old are you?"

"I'm almost twenty-five."

"Okay, great." She shook her head at him and started to reach for her phone on the ledge of the bathtub, where it was sitting. "Now that we've established that, what's your number?"

"Fleur ..."

Her eyes narrowed slightly at him. "Damon, I'm bringing you a plant, not sucking your dick! Calm down!"

Fuck. I like her.

She was looking at him in disbelief, as if she was appalled that he'd even think such a thing. As if they had known each other so well that him suggesting that she'd do that was so out of character for him.

He wanted to laugh, which he rarely did, but instead, he put his hands up, as if to indicate that he was innocent. "Okay, okay. If you want to, you can bring me a plant tomorrow."

They exchanged numbers, and then Damon realized he'd been in the bathroom for the last ten minutes and informed her that he needed to go before they started asking questions. She told him she was going to stay in her little cove, gripping on to her ivy plant, but added in that she was glad he'd barged into the bathroom and that she felt slightly less overwhelmed than she had been feeling.

He didn't share that he was feeling calmer too.

He said good-bye, and as she responded, she turned her head up toward him from where she'd been looking down at her plant, and the hair covering the right side of her neck slipped away behind her shoulder.

Dark blue-and-purple bruises were all down the side of her neck and under her ear. A huge right hand, by the looks of the size of it.

The marks didn't have any makeup on them—there was no intention of trying to hide them. *Probably because she wasn't supposed to be seen by anyone.*

His gaze lingered too long on the spot though because Fleur quickly dropped one corner of the flowerpot into her lap and pulled her hair back forward, staring only at the leaves in front of her and the newly dumped pile of dirt in her lap.

Damon couldn't just walk away with her covered in soil. "Uh, do you want me to—"

"Just go."

His anger was back. His fury and his hatred for horrible people had returned, and he wanted to eliminate whatever sick son of a bitch had done this to her.

He didn't know a whole lot about her, but that didn't matter. *How fucking dare someone touch her like that.*

He ripped the door open and left, slamming it behind him. He didn't make eye contact with anyone as he tore back through Amber's kitchen and left. He was crossing Fifth Street before Greek Row began when he sent the text.

Damon: You got anything local for me?

A response came almost instantly. He must not be very busy. *Either that or he's so busy that he needs some help.*

Ernesto: You feel like driving to Florence?

Damon: Walking to my car now. Send me the info.

Chapter 38

By mid-October, The Olympians had gained international attention. Six episodes had aired by the time Olympia College began their fall break, and the six students returned home for a week.

When they returned to campus once classes resumed, they all had difficulty going anywhere on campus without being swarmed by other students. They were constantly asked for their pictures or autographs. Their followers on social media platforms had skyrocketed by the time midterms came around.

Damon managed to switch all of his classes to online instruction. Amber changed delivery methods for all her courses, except her labs, as well. Dawn and Kai tolerated the attention but didn't particularly like it and occasionally had to push their way out of crowds. Zach and Hanna June, however, loved being in the spotlight and posing with fans, and they both began traveling to their classes with bodyguards.

The students were given a two-week break from filming, so they could focus on their midterms.

The following transcript was from a closed meeting, and not recorded via camera; therefore, it did not appear in any episode.

Kronos: You all amaze me. No, you astound me.

Kai: [*whispers to Damon*] Is that a good thing?

Damon: [*rolls eyes, nods*]

Kronos: Three things I want to discuss with you all today. [*shows on his fingers*] Number one, our projections figured March 2015 would be when this show took off and viewers would really get hooked on the show.

Kronos: We are halfway through October, just six episodes in, and viewers cannot get enough. We've had to hire more people to edit the show, so it can hit the network as soon as possible. We've literally got people working twenty-four hours a day, piecing this thing together, because the country cannot seem to get enough of you.

Zach: I mean, that's good, right?

Kronos: It's fantastic! This sort of thing hasn't happened since *Jersey Shore!*

Zach and Hanna June pass a proud look back and forth to each other, Dawn has a soft smile, everyone else seems to be indifferent.

Amber: I don't get it.

Everyone turns to look at her.

Kronos: Miss Hargrove?

Amber: Like, we're not doing anything crazy or whatever. Yeah, sometimes, we get a little drunk, and Kai gets high, but aside from that … I just—I don't understand why people are obsessed with us. We're nothing special.

Kronos [*a kind of creepy smile spreads across his face*] Oh, but you are, Miss Hargrove.

Damon: She's right. It doesn't make any sense. There are dozens of other shows that are far more exciting than ours.

HJ: [*teasing him*] Aww, you called it ours!

Damon: [*glares at her*]

Dawn: [*nodding*] I'm with Amber and Damon actually.

Kronos: Kids, I have no idea why everyone has to watch you all every Thursday night—not a clue. But for whatever reason, they do. They have this compulsive need to see you all as you go about your college lives, but I'm not sitting here questioning why, and neither should you.

Kronos: Besides, if most of the country wasn't obsessed with the show, I wouldn't have number two on my list of good news for you all.

Damon: Oh, yippee.

Kronos: The network wants to officially reward you all with salaries.

Kai: Holy shit, really?

Kronos: Mr. Newport, you should know I never joke around when it comes to money. You're bringing the network more viewers and therefore more money, so they want to repay you properly for your hard work, beginning next semester once filming has resumed in January.

Kronos: Speaking of, you're the one to thank for the most played clips. Between you punching Mr. Alexander and drunkenly professing your love for Miss Hargrove, you're quite the internet sensation.

Kai: [*mumbles inaudibly and sinks back against his chair*]

Kronos: Everyone loves the little clips of you guys hanging out together outside of the show that you post on, what is it, Instagram? Keep doing that.

HJ: Easy.

Damon: I have a question.

Kronos: Yes, Mr. Montclaire?

Damon: Is it just going to stay the six of us? Or will you be adding more of us? Or possibly getting rid of any of us?

Kronos: [*chuckles*] No, no. Definitely not getting rid of you. You're all very much needed. But bringing in more of you is part of the plan. It's just a matter of … well, we need to make sure that we bring in the right people. We don't want to add anyone to the mix who doesn't necessarily belong with the rest of you.

Zach: [*nodding along with Kronos*]

HJ: [*eyes him questioningly*]

Kronos: Interviews resume on Monday. We've added in some viewer questions that were sent to us through Facebook, so it should make things a little more interesting!

Kronos: Now, on to number three. Miss Sutherland, would you care to share?

Dawn: [*big smile on her face, sits up a little straighter*] Damon and I have both been accepted to the PhD programs here!

HJ: That's amazing!

Amber: Congratulations, you guys!

Kai: You're gonna do more school?

Dawn: Thank you! Yes, Kai, we both want to further our education. Well, I need to. I think Damon just wants to though.

Kai: [*turns to Damon*] God, why?

Damon: [*shakes his head gently, doesn't make eye contact with anyone*]

Kronos: Isn't it great? Mr. Montclaire and Miss Sutherland will be sticking around for another two years!

Damon: [*glares at him*]

Chapter 39

ZACH

Zach: Where the hell are u guys??

Dawn: Still trying to drag Damon down College Rd…

Damon: I'm absolutely not going to this.

HJ: yes you are, child of darkness! This is your holiday!

Zach: dude you dont even have to dress up

HJ: but it would be so much more entertaining if you did…

Kai: wait we don't have to dress up?

Amber: I'll be there in five minutes!

Amber: I'm dressed up lol

Kai: Oh nvm

Loser.

"Zach, baby, can you hold my phone? I need to pee *again*, and I almost dropped it in last time." His girlfriend giggled as she caught her balance, using his arm as leverage. HJ handed her device over to him, grabbed two of her sorority sisters by the arms, and then left the room.

I would never give my phone to her.
But if I did, maybe she would be less paranoid …
But then she might go through it.
I could just wipe it before I gave it to her …

"Havin' a good time, Alexander?" Kyle Parkin gave him a slap on the back. He was the frat president and a linebacker for OC's very pathetic excuse of a football team.

He was in a suit and had stuffed the pockets with Monopoly money, announcing to everyone that he was dressed up as Jordan Belfort. He had stood on the back of a couch an hour earlier and drunkenly stated, "I'm the Wolf of fuckin' Wall Street!"

"Yeah, yeah. You?"

"Good. Yeah, listen, are these TV friends of yours comin'?"

"I just texted them. They should be here soon."

Kyle was nodding way too much, and his bloodshot eyes seemed to be vibrating inside his skull. "Cool, cool. 'Cause, ya know, I got a lot of people who are waiting to meet them. Well, you know, party with 'em."

"Oh, yeah, no, they'll be here any minute." Zach could hear his voice shaking. *They'd better show up.*

"'Kay, cool." He started walking away. "You come find me when they get here! I want a photo op with the Olympians!" He pointed a finger back at him, brought his beer to his mouth, and then was swallowed up by the crowd.

Zach was about to text Kai and tell him to hurry up when he felt a much lighter hand land on his shoulder and slide down to his elbow.

He turned to see … Sam. No, wait. Sarah. No, no, her name was definitely Sam … maybe.

"Hey, sailor." She walked around him and leaned against the island counter and held a drank wine cooler in her hand. "Nice robe."

"Hey." He mimicked her stance, while shifting himself so he could see when HJ came back. "I'm actually Hugh Hefner."

S stared back at him. "Who?"

"Hugh Hefner!"

But she still just shook her head, not knowing who he was talking about. The coins around her skirt made a jingling noise that made Zach want to grind his teeth.

Jesus Christ.

"The old guy who fucks the Playboy Bunnies?"

Her eyes widened with realization. "Oh! Yeah, I know him. So, where's your Playmate?"

Wow, she doesn't waste any time.

"She'll probably be back any second."

She nodded slowly, pursed her lips, and then made him an offer. "Well, if you can find some way to distract her, I'm going upstairs around eleven thirty, so ..."

Yes.

"I'll see what I can do. You know my costars are gonna be here soon, right?"

"Oh shit, really? That brother of yours is cute, by the way," she admitted as she adjusted the scarf on her head.

He snorted—mostly in disgust. "Which one?"

"Exactly."

There was a loud applause from the front of the house, and Zach assumed it was the other four. At least, he hoped it was.

He turned back to her, still unsure of what to call her. "So, what are you supposed to be?"

She finished downing her drink and smiled at him, pushing the empty cheer beer bottle to the middle of the countertop. "I'm a fortune teller," she said and shook her hips to make the coins shake again.

But Zach wasn't paying any attention to the sound this time. "Oh yeah?" He held out his palm. "What do you see in my future?"

S smiled, took his hand, and then jerked him closer.

As she leaned up and whispered in his ear, there was a small part of Zach's brain that was reminding him, *HJ is in the next room!*

The problem was that there was a much bigger and significantly louder part of his brain that was screaming at him *She's so hot, and she was so good last time!*

Her lips grazed the edge of his ear as she shared her prediction. "Me."

Then, she released him just as HJ was coming around the corner, heading straight in their direction. "I'll text you later."

"Hey," HJ announced herself. She pushed her body up against Zach's and intertwined their fingers somewhat aggressively.

"Oh my God! Now, I get it!" The girl with no definite name pointed at the two of them in their couple's costume. "You guys are so cute!"

"Oh, thanks!" Hanna June gushed at her.

"Oh, wait! Would it be totally uncool of me to ask for a picture with you guys? You know, like, the stars?" She let out a horribly fake giggle, but HJ went right along with it.

They both posed for a picture on her phone, and she thanked them. "I love you guys together, ugh!"

"Oh my God, thank you!"

Sam/Sarah left, and HJ changed her response as soon as she was out of earshot. "Slut."

Zach laughed at her and tucked a loose piece of her hair behind the headband of her bunny ears. "I love you," he reminded her.

"Mmm, I love you too, handsome man. Come on. We have photo ops waitin' for us!"

Zach tried to get Kai to stay in his Waldo costume, but he literally threw the shirt off the front porch after taking five tequila shots and drunk yelling back to him, "Amber cannot see me like this! Red is not my color!"

Amber had arrived just before Kai but didn't get a chance to see him in his full costume because HJ whisked her away so that the three girls could take pictures together. They also had a throng of people waiting to pose with them—girls with not enough clothes on, which Zach didn't mind, and guys with too much alcohol in their systems.

Which should've bothered him, but he was also one of those guys.

The six of them took a few pictures together, but Damon's photo limit was apparently two. As soon as he stepped away, Kai headed straight for the keg in the closet.

And now, not even an hour later, he was wasted on the front steps of the Zeta Upsilon Sigma house with no shirt on and sweat dripping down his back.

"I'm gonna leave you out here if you don't get your shit together," Zach told him, completely annoyed with his behavior.

What the hell is wrong with this guy?

"I'm good. I'm good. I just don't know what's fucking wrong with me." He rubbed at his face.

Zach shook his head at him as his phone vibrated in his robe pocket. Twice.

Unknown Number: about to go up

Unknown Number: see you there

Jesus, I need to not be here right now.

"The problem is that you need to get laid, man."

Kai didn't even look at him. "That's not it."

Wait. Uncrossing his arms, Zach pushed off the post on the porch and sauntered over to him, bending down to where he was seated on the front steps among empty aluminum cans. "Wait, is that it?"

Kai didn't move.

"Holy shit, that's it, isn't it? You fucked Hargrove?"

"No, I didn't—we didn't. Whatever."

The push on his shoulder he gave Kai was playful, and Zach immediately regretted it. Alcohol in their systems or not, they were not that friendly with each other yet. "Yeah, *sure*."

"Zach, I swear, we didn't have sex."

He stared back at him as their blue eyes met. If you looked closely, you could see that the shapes of their features were all the same—their faces, their eyes, even their noses. The thing was that hardly anyone ever picked up on it because, after seeing the startling symmetry in their eye colors, the main hang-up was their difference in skin tone.

Hanna June had actually been the one to point it out to Zach actually, after their first meeting. "You know, you guys are almost identical-looking, right?"

"What are you talking about? I look nothing like Damon." Which was true—neither of them did.

Honestly, Damon looked almost exactly like his birth mother, which was probably why their father had gotten away so easily with claiming that he wasn't his father. But if you really focused, you could see that he and Zach had the same facial features—the sharp chin and long, dark eyelashes. And that Kai and Damon had the same body structure—long arms and legs. Although Damon was by far the tallest out of them all, Kai was not far behind him.

"I meant, Kai! You guys are the exact same, if you really look at your faces," she'd explained to him. And she was right.

She usually was though.

Not that he'd ever admit it to her.

Even now, as she stepped outside. "Where the hell have you been, Zachary? I've been lookin' all over for you!"

Oh, this is perfect.

Zach turned to her and gave her a not-now face as he walked over to where she was standing. "Listen, babe, Kai is really upset. Like, he's not doing good."

"Oh." She peered at the very drunk, very sad Waldo on the tiny set of stairs. Her expression quickly changed from annoyed to concerned. "Is he gonna be okay?"

"Yeah, yeah. I think he just needs a good distraction. I'm, uh"—he leaned in closer to her—"I'm gonna take him upstairs …"

HJ's big eyes widened, and she nodded, silently letting him know that she understood what he was talking about. "Do you want me to come? You know, like, for moral support?"

"Nah, it's okay. You've got that photo shoot in the morning, and I don't want you to be … tempted. Plus, I think it'll be, like, a bonding moment for us, ya know?"

"That's so sweet of you, baby." She smiled proudly up at him. Pushing up on her toes, she gave him a kiss. He reached back and pulled at her bunny tail, making her squeal. "Zachary!"

He just smiled back at her. *Wow, I love her.* "I'll come find you in a little bit, okay?"

"Okay, baby." And then she chasséd back inside to the party.

Zach turned back to his excuse of a big brother, his robe completely askew. "Get up," he instructed him, dusting off the dirt from the velvet.

"Where are we going?" Kai put his hat with the stupid pom-pom back on and straightened his fake glasses on his face.

"Somewhere that'll make you feel better."

Minutes later, Zach had seated Kai in between two girls, who had less than the bare minimum of clothing on, with a blunt in his hand. He definitely didn't *look* sad anymore.

Kyle pulled Zach to the side. "Here, do this." It was a key bump. *Shit.*

Zach had done coke a few times, but never like this. Off of Jenna Collin's back at the after party for prom? Yes. But he couldn't turn this down. He plugged a nostril and threw it back.

Kyle gave him a few nonsensical words of praise, saying he was the most promising pledge they'd had in a long time.

Zach turned back to Kai. "You good?"

Kai just gave him a quick nod, then took the blunt back from one of the girls for his next hit.

That was his cue to leave.

Except that he got held up again in the hallway. Sam/Sarah was waiting in the next room for him … but Amber was slumped down at the end of the hall in almost the exact same position Kai had been in a little while ago.

"Amber?" He had to make sure she was okay. Knowing she was upset and leaving her alone would just be cruel.

Her head jolted up, revealing red eyes—not red from weed, but instead from crying.

"Oh my God, what's wrong?" He raced over to her, placing a hand on her knee and sitting beside her.

She immediately jerked away from him, pulling her skirt down. "Don't touch me." Her facial expression was wild with alarm and fear.

He scooted back a few inches and put his hands up defensively. "Okay, okay. Sorry. I was trying to help. Sorry for being worried about you."

"Ugh, no, it's not that." She sighed, dropping her head again. "Midterm grades just went up for my Historical Ag class—a class I have to pass to graduate—and I barely passed. *Barely.*"

Zach's face screwed up. "I thought you were, like, smart?"

Amber's eyes narrowed, and she looked like she might throttle him. "I am smart. But my intelligence level doesn't matter if I can't sleep and can't focus and just have lots of other stuff going on."

"You can't focus?" He leaned his head back against the edge of the windowsill. "I have something that might be able to help with that, you know."

"What's that?"

"Adderall."

Amber's thick eyebrows furrowed as her eyes grew in size. "How do you have Adderall?"

"Don't worry about it, Grain Brain. You want it or not?"

She shifted uncomfortably, her pirate costume not covering much of her long legs. "What's the catch?"

Well, if we weren't on a TV show together and you weren't becoming semi-friendly with my girlfriend and future wife …

"No catch. I won't even charge you." He flashed a smile at her.

She tilted her head to the side in annoyance. "I *can* pay you, you know."

"I know. We were at the same meeting the other day, remember?"

She rolled her eyes at him, but still didn't answer right away.

A few moments passed before he broke the silence between them. "Look, I have somewhere I need to be, somewhere I'm actually late to." He glanced at the door just a few feet away from them. "So, you need to tell me, like, now."

"I'll take them."

Zach stood up and offered her his hand. "Okay, come with me. Quickly."

They went around a corner into another bedroom. Zach slid the closet door open and rifled through some of the things on the floor until he found his backpack. He'd come right here after class to help set things up. After fishing around in the dark for a few seconds, he found the orange pill bottle, realizing that he probably should transfer them into something less obvious next time.

"Thank you," Amber told him. "And look, this was fun, but I do think I'm gonna get going."

Probably better that you don't stay around. Might ruin Kai's good mood, just by being in a five-mile radius of him.

"Yeah, no problem," was what he said instead.

They left the room together with Zach stopping to punch in the lock code on the door.

They were about to go their separate ways when Amber stopped at the top of the stairs and looked back at him. "Oh, and I'm sorry that you kept HJ waiting because of me. I know she's not exactly the most patient person," the redhead explained.

"Yeah. It's cool though. She'll be fine."

She nodded and left, and Zach went into a bedroom and locked the door. And although he knew his girlfriend was patiently waiting for him to finish "bonding" with one of his estranged family members, that was not at all the person Zach was actually bonding with …

Chapter 40

KAI

I DESERVE LOVE. RIGHT? I MEAN, I think so.

When Amber had wanted him to stay over the night of the party, there was only one obvious answer, and he felt as though the gods had rewarded him for following the little rules she'd set. He never did anything more than make out with her that night. It was hard—really, *really* hard—but he had kept reminding himself that if he could do exactly what she had asked, then maybe, just maybe, this time, things would actually stick for them.

As usual, he was wrong.

The morning had been like a dream … a dream that you got abruptly woken up from. He had gone over everything that had happened in his head countless times, and the only thing that he could come up with was that something horrible had happened.

He'd actually gone to check on her one night that week, and he thought he saw her little sister, Fleur, in the window. But he knew that was crazy because she was at their home in Charleston.

That was the moment he knew he had been obsessing over the situation way too much.

Instead, he'd placed an order for Cookie Dude to be delivered to her apartment and didn't give them his name even though he was pretty sure she'd know it was from him.

Everything was different after that day though, and it wasn't just Kai who had noticed—Dawn and Hanna June had both asked him if she was okay after their little post-snooping meeting at her apartment.

She'd switched most of her classes to online delivery, which was a battle she'd fought with the administration. She stopped going downtown with them and instead went back home every single chance she got. A few times, she'd even leave campus on Thursday night, and wouldn't come back until early Monday morning. When she was on campus, she pretty much stayed in her apartment.

The only reason she had shown up at Zach's frat's Halloween party was because Kronos had basically told them attendance was mandatory.

"Episode seven premiered last night, and seeing as social media plays a major part in the show's growing popularity, it is imperative that you all at least make an appearance."

She had already been there when he got to Greek Row.

She and HJ were taking a picture in front of the doorway with some random girls when one of the guys facing the entrance announced, "Hey, Newport's here!"

That was promptly followed by a series of cheers and hollers and HJ pulling him right in between her and Amber for *another* photo op. Shortly after that, Dawn and Damon showed up, and a few pictures were captured, sans Damon. Turned out, most frat guys were terrified of Richard's oldest spawn.

A while later, he caught a glimpse of her sitting on the bottom of the staircase, anxiously checking her phone. Then, she dropped it in her lap, picked up her drink, and took a long sip. Pick up her phone, put it back down, and on and on.

So, he texted her from his stance in the overcrowded common area.

Kai: You okay?

Amber: Yeah

Kai: You don't seem like you are

Amber: I am

Kai: Are we okay?

She didn't answer. He watched her pick up her phone, look at the text message, and start typing out an answer. She paused to stare at it, her thumbs ceasing any motion, and then deleted whatever she'd started texting back to him and dropped her phone back into her lap.

That was when Kai had taken the bottle of Bacardi outside to the front porch.

Which, admittedly, as he looked back on it, probably hadn't been the most productive idea.

Honestly, none of his choices after that were things he wanted to own up to, which only made him feel worse.

But ever since that morning when she'd woken up *in his arms,* she'd been rattled. He wanted to help her in any way he could, if only she would let him in.

Obviously, she's just going through something. And it probably has nothing to do with me. She'll come back to me when she's ready.

But …

What if she doesn't?

What if the thing she's going through is me?

What if that night didn't mean as much to her as it did to me?

What if she found someone else?

Before he could redirect his fine motor skills to stop and think about what he was doing, he whipped out his phone and was texting her.

Kai: Hey, are you busy?

Her answer came two minutes later, after Kai started pacing outside his RV.

Amber: Not really. Just working on a Lit paper. What's up?

How could she be so casual about this?

He felt like his heart was beating so fast that it was going to lift off and take flight out of his rib cage.

Kai: I really need to talk to you.

Amber: Okay… you wanna come over?

Kai's feet were already moving down College Road, in the direction of her apartment complex, where it sat perfectly separating downtown and the edge of campus.

Kai: Be there in a min

He passed the visitors parking lot—which was never full, even on Parents' Weekend—the back of the Rec Center, and a cluster of residence halls, including the one where he'd lived his first two years. After practically sprinting across the street, he made a beeline for the parking lot, where her car was, and began taking the steps two at a time up to her one-bedroom apartment.

She opened the door just as he reached for the handle. She must've been waiting or seen him coming, and that thought alone flooded his body with some much-needed serotonin.

"Hey," she greeted him as the wind from the door opening sent her auburn hair flying back away from her face. "Come on in. Do you want anything to drink?"

He sank down into a chair, only emotionally tired from the last five or so minutes, and asked her for water. He downed the whole glass within seconds, set it down on the table, and looked up to meet her gaze. Her eyes were this alluring hazel color, and Kai wanted to just stare at them.

"Kai? You okay?"

A sad smile painted his lips. "Does anyone on the show know your middle name? Or where it comes from?"

Her delicate face screwed up, but she still looked so pretty to him. "What kind of question is that?"

"Just answer it, please."

Amber glanced down at the edge of the table in front of her, picked at a piece of the peeling paint that it had been decorated with, and responded to his question with a short, "No." She paused, biting her lower lip for just a split second. "Well, they have access to it. I just don't think anyone cares enough to look it up."

"I know it."

"That's because I told you."

"And you told me the meaning behind it too. And I remember it."

Her eyes finally flicked up to meet him. He couldn't quite read her expression, but he could tell it wasn't happy. She wasn't grateful that he remembered the small talk they'd made long ago, and she wasn't grateful he was bringing it up now.

"Kai …"

"Every moment we've spent together has meant something to me." He couldn't stop the words from tumbling out.

Her mouth snapped shut, and she blinked at him.

"And I'm really worried that they haven't meant anything to you."

She still didn't answer.

"I really care about you, Amber. I did before this stupid show, and I'll keep caring about you after it all ends." He leaned back in his chair, hoping she'd pick up on his signal that he was done, and he'd really like it if she said something back in response.

For two minutes, she didn't though, and it drove him crazy. He wanted to keep going, to say whatever he could to try and win her over. But he could also see her eyes roaming across the table and drifting toward her hands in her lap as she mulled over how to answer him.

He was considering getting up and leaving and hoping she'd be on board with just pretending the whole interaction hadn't happened when she cleared her throat.

"I care about you too, Kai. I know that doesn't always translate, but I do."

He bit his tongue to keep from asking *why*, knowing that interrupting her would only make this worse, and let her continue.

"I knew what I was doing when I asked you to stay that night, I promise. I had very different plans for how the next day would go, but … things just came up. Plans change. My family needs me, and I'm sorry if you can't understand this, but they will always come first. If the show ends, if I fail out or drop out of school, they will still be there for me. I have to put them first, over everything else." She blinked, and he could see the tears hazy in her eyes. "I'm really sorry, Kai. But I can't give you what you want. Not right now."

He wanted to hug her. He wanted to run to the other side of the table and scoop her up in his arms and do anything and everything he could to take all her stress and her troubles away and tell her that she didn't need to choose between the two—that she could be there for her family *and* he would be there for her.

But he knew that wasn't what she wanted.

Not right now.

So, he stayed in his seat and just nodded, understanding what she was saying. He should be grateful that she was admitting it to him. That she had recognized that she wouldn't be able to give one hundred percent of herself to a relationship and that she was really doing him a favor. He should be happy that it was a mature conversation.

But he didn't want to be mature, and he sure as hell wasn't happy.

So, he stood up, pushed his chair in, and fixed the collar on his shirt. "Thanks for being honest with me, Am."

She smiled up at him sadly and blinked some more tears away.

"Maybe we should pretend this didn't happen. You know, for the sake of the show. Personally, I don't want people asking questions and stuff."

She tucked her long hair behind her ears and nodded. "No, that makes complete sense. We'll just go about everything normally."

He was halfway out the door when he stopped and looked back inside at her.

"Amber?"

She was watching him leave. "Hmm?"

"For what it's worth, I would've loved you so hard."

And then he shut the door.

And then he flew down the steps.

And then he walked toward campus as fast as he could without drawing too much attention.

And then he crossed back over busy Court Street, which was technically Fifth Street at this point—the cutoff line was the center of campus, but most people didn't know that. When he thought he was far enough away, he slowed down to a tortoise pace as he came upon the fountain.

He sat on the edge of it and really wished it were dark outside, so he could submerge his whole body.

Why did I have to say that? Why couldn't I have just left it alone? I said way too much as it was. Why add to it? Lit everything up in flames. Might as well just dump some gasoline on it. Great job, Kai. Great fucking job.

He stared at the flow of the water coming out the top of the structure. He wasn't sure how long he'd been sitting there—it might have only been three minutes, but it might have been thirty—when he heard a high-pitched voice.

"Kai?"

He turned around and saw a girl from his Fishery Science Fundamentals class. *Kendra? Kelly? What the hell is her name?*

He gave a nonchalant wave in her direction as she came over to where he was seated. She stood in front of him, the breeze rustling the edges of her flower-printed skirt.

Amber likes flowers.

"Hi there." She smiled at him.

"Hey."

An awkward silence settled in as she shifted her weight from one foot to the other. "I'm Karolyn. We have Fish Sci with—"

"With Anders. Yeah, I know who you are."

Thank God she said her name.

She stood up a little straighter and smiled bigger at him. "You're on that TV show they're filmin' on campus, right? *The Olympians?* I started watchin' it, like, two weeks ago." Her Southern accent was thicker than HJ's.

"Yeah, that's me." He leaned back on the palms of his hands and just looked at her. She definitely wasn't bad looking.

"So, what's going on? Why are you sittin' all by yourself?"

"Just, uh …" He glanced back at the aqua water behind him. "Just thinking."

"Hmm." She nodded back at him, then proceeded to eye him up and down twice. "Well, if you want somewhere quiet to think, I live in Myrtle, just right down there." Karolyn leaned over to point to the three residence halls closest to where they were, and her skirt flipped up slightly as the wind swept by.

"That sounds good to me."

"Great!" She bounced on her toes. "So, let me give you my number so that, sometime, we could—"

Kai stood up and held out his hand to her. "Actually, I was thinking I could use some quiet time right now."

Her eyes doubled in size, and her jaw quivered slightly, like she wanted to say something but she wasn't exactly sure what. After a second, she composed herself once more and took his hand.

And for twenty not-so-quiet minutes, Kai didn't think about Amber.

Well, at least not the whole time.

Chapter 41

AMBER

**Fleur: is my dark red top at your apt? the one
with the little flowers on it?**

Amber had looked high and low for her shirt for the last half hour, tearing her apartment apart. It was a good thing she lived alone. But she had yet to find the shirt.

Fleur texted back that it wasn't a big deal and didn't seem too upset about it, but Amber could feel the anxiety building in her chest.

Was it a stupid thing to be getting *this* worked up over? Yes. Did that make her feel any better? Absolutely not.

**Amber: Still no sign of the shirt, but you left
your phone charger here**

Fleur: keep it, I have two more here

Amber's charger had suddenly stopped working that morning, so she promptly plugged her phone in … only to find that charger also didn't work.

That's two phone chargers and my laptop charger that just crapped out on me in, like, four days.

She paced back and forth down her tiny hallway for the umpteenth time, fixing minor things that she'd knocked sideways during her search, and returned to where she'd left her laptop open at her dining room table. She tapped on a random key to light up the screen and tried to refocus on what she was studying—Geology. Which typically wouldn't interest most people, but Amber loved it. She normally could sit down and do her coursework, no problem.

But with the show picking up and strangers constantly staring at her and wanting pictures and autographs from her on top of her dad disappearing *more*—according to Fleur—and the way Fleur had been taking longer to answer her texts since she had come to stay with her, Amber was so stressed out that nothing could redirect her focus. Switching the majority of her classes online hadn't even helped. Her mental list of things to stress about was ongoing ... which was *another* thought that stressed her out.

She thought about the little pills Zach had so nonchalantly handed over to her.

Unless ...

No.

No, she couldn't take one. She'd been selling them, which, yes, was illegal, but it was illegal for Zach to have given them to her in the first place.

But maybe ...

The show is really popular. Kronos just offered us all five-figure salaries, which is more than any college kid is making. And if my grades drop, I'll get kicked out, and then I can't be on the show since it's tied to the scholarship program ... so I need to pass this class.

The logic seemed flawless to her, so she slid down the hallway, stopping to turn a potted hibiscus slightly, and grabbed the bottle from where she'd hidden it in her underwear drawer. She'd already sold half of them since Zach had given her the bottle a few days before.

She had a small handful of people who bought from her, and when she'd offered the Adderall with the weed for a "bulk price," they'd all jumped at the opportunity.

Holy shit, I'm a drug dealer.

She stared down at the circular pill in her hand and contemplated for a moment before her internal debate kicked in again.

Could be worse. You could be selling coke or heroin. Ninety percent of college kids smoke weed, and the amount of people who go without Adderall and actually need it but can't get a prescription because they can't go to the doctor because they don't have insurance is probably huge.

That's probably not statistically correct.

But it definitely sounds right.

She walked back to her laptop, popped the little orange pill into her mouth, and swallowed down some Diet Coke as her phone buzzed on the table.

Unknown Number: You the chick who can get me addies and grass?

It wasn't like she could keep taking them anyway. She had paying customers who wanted them, and Amber hated letting people down.

Chapter 42

DAWN

"NO, NO, NO!" SHE WAS talking out loud to herself. "This is not the time!"

Her laptop had frozen, then unfrozen, then given her the blue screen of death, as her dad referred to it. She didn't know what it meant, but she knew it was bad.

What made it worse was that she had been in the middle of a paper for her Legal Foundations of Planning when it happened.

Her classes last year had definitely been more enjoyable—even fun, like her Historical Architectural Styles course. This current semester, however, was *rough*. As passionate as Dawn was about what she was learning and her whole plan she had, some of it was so *boring*. She'd finally gotten going on this paper though, and she was so close to being done … but now, it looked like she didn't have a laptop.

Guess my time in the library is done.

Dawn: Daddy, my laptop gave me the blue screen of death again…

Dad: Again? That's the fourth time this month

Dawn: Yeah, I know. Maybe I should get a new one?

Dad: Nope

Dad: Mama and I will get you a new one

Dawn: No, no, I don't want you to buy me one. I can afford it.

Dad: Consider it your graduation present :)

Another text came in at the same time her father's arrived.

Amber: Dawn, I have a favor to ask

Dawn: Go for it!

Amber: Can I call you actually? It's kind of a lot to text

Dawn: Sure! I'm just leaving the library now.

Amber: Wait, the city library or school one?

Dawn: The school one.

Amber: I just left SciTech, can we meet at the Student Center? I wanted to get Chick-fil-A for dinner.

Dawn: That sounds good! See you in a few minutes.

Dawn got there first and spotted an empty table toward the back. There were only a handful of students in the building, and all of them immediately turned their heads to look at her as she came around the corner.

Two girls came up to her and asked if they could get a picture. As long as they were polite, Dawn always obliged. The rest of the people turned to whispering, either about her or the show most likely, but several people just ignored her.

She didn't necessarily like the fanfare, deeming it nothing more than a distraction, but she didn't shy away from posing with fans for a selfie or signing an autograph.

The first time they had been approached, it was all six of them, as a group. They were leaving this same building, heading out a different exit than the one she'd just entered. It had only been a handful of days after the show first premiered, and they'd all finished an interview when Kronos asked them if things had changed for them. For the most part, they'd all said no, stating only that people stared at them more than they had before.

Ten minutes later, that all changed. They were about to split up and go their separate ways when they were swarmed.

"That's them! That's the Olympians!" a girl's voice yelled out in the middle of the day, and then there were students everywhere around them. Dawn couldn't see straight for a few seconds, highly overstimulated and not sure where to look.

"HJ, I love your style! Where do you get your clothes?"

"Zach, you're so hot!"

"Kai, I love you! I love you so much!"

There was one girl who just kept crying Damon's name over and over even though Damon had somehow managed to escape before the crowd got to them.

"Dawn, can you sign my planner?" A pen was shoved into her hands suddenly, and without much thought to it at all, she signed a big *DS*, with a heart next to it. And then she did another. And another. She'd lost track after the eighth one, but by that time, the fanfare around her was dying down. Several people were taking group selfie pictures.

Zach and HJ found themselves right at home, posing and answering pictures and signing their initials and giving advice, and at some point, nearly every crazed student turned fan redirected their attention to the two of them.

At that same moment, Damon shifted his Lincoln into neutral and rolled down the little street on campus. Dawn had grabbed Amber and Kai, and the three of them had made a run for it into their getaway car, then gone to a sandwich shop on the opposite end of the city to hide out and decompress.

Now, Amber silently slid up next to her as she waited in line, lost in thought as she stared at the menu. "Hi."

"Oh, hi! I was just deciding if I want fries, or fries *and* a cookie."

"Get the cookie. Always get the cookie," Amber coached her. "Yeah?"

"If you don't, you'll wish you had."

That was true. She offered to let Amber go in front of her, but the redhead declined. They both placed their orders and waited for them to be ready.

As they walked over to the table Dawn had mentally saved when she got there, she noticed a young guy in the opposite corner with his phone camera pointed at them.

"We're being watched," she whispered to Amber and tried not to move her lips.

She dropped her head down so onlookers couldn't see her face and replied, "We always are now."

Dawn sent a silent thank-you to whoever might be listening that the table was still available as they sat down at it. Before the show, she would have set her backpack down on a chair to save it without hesitation. She didn't really have that simple luxury anymore.

Amber unwrapped her chicken sandwich and bit into it, sliding a pickle out between her teeth. Dawn liked how little Amber cared about how she was publicly perceived. HJ, on the other hand, had to look perfect all the time. When *she* ate in public, it was tiny bites of perfectly cut-up food, so she didn't accidentally end up with a mouthful. She had even told Dawn that she tried to only eat "clean" foods in public, which mainly consisted of salads.

"So, nothin' with sauce, like nothin' that might make me messy, ya know? And I usually stay away from finger foods if there's a lot of people 'round. Wouldn't want to look like a slob!" Eating with Amber was refreshing, to say the least.

"So, what's up … what's Zach's nickname for you?"

"Grain Brain," she answered with her mouth full.

Kind of gross but refreshing.

"Why does he call you that?"

"Uh, I think it's because my family owns an agriculture company, like wheat and grains and stuff."

"Ah, that's actually clever. And he came up with that?"

Amber chuckled as she nodded and stuffed a fry into her mouth. "Yeah. So, okay, here's the deal. I need to buy a house."

Dawn's eyes doubled in size, and the movement of her head made her septum piercing wiggle slightly. "Sorry, what?"

Amber rolled her eyes. "Well, not *me*. But my dad."

"Is he moving?"

"Not exactly." She plucked another fry from the cardboard box and tossed it into her mouth. "See, he's been traveling for work a lot, and my sister is only fifteen, so she technically can't be left alone for more than a few hours. I would gladly watch after her, but, you know, I'm here. So, what my dad and I agreed upon is him buying a house up here, in town, just to live in for a few years, until Fleur is old enough to go to college and actually be responsible for herself—you know, legally."

"Huh, okay. That doesn't sound like a bad plan at all."

"Right? And so, while we lived there, we'd fix it up if it needed to be, and then we could just resell it."

Dawn broke off a piece of her cookie, the half-melted chocolate stretching slightly as she pulled it apart. *Good choice on the cookie, Amber.* "I'm not usually one to make assumptions, but I take it, you'll be living there with them?"

"Absolutely."

"So"—Dawn saw the picture being drawn out in front of her as the scenario played out—"that would make market value go way up since I'm pretty sure you're considered a celebrity now."

The other pickle slid out the back of her sandwich and landed on the wrapper with a dull thud as Amber stared at her. Her lips were pursed, and her gaze was strong but empty. "Oh shit," she muttered.

There was a short laugh from the other side of the room, and the young man with the phone earlier looked as if he'd just captured Amber at that right moment, in shock, on video.

"Great," she mumbled but turned her attention back to Dawn. "So, anyway, umm, I thought of you because your dad is in real estate, right?"

"He is! Yeah, I'll tell him your dad is looking. Let me get his number."

They exchanged contact information for their fathers and went back to their meals. After they were done, Amber went up and ordered another cookie, and the two of them split it.

"I feel bad. You didn't have to stay and eat with me. I know your parents are at home."

"No, don't feel bad! I'm glad to switch things up a little and spend time with you away from the cameras. Well, mostly. And they're happy to see me go out with a friend."

Amber's green eyes lit up. "Okay … this is gonna be weird. But we *are* friends, right? Sorry, I know that's stupid." She let out a short laugh as her cheeks started to turn the same shade of red as her hair.

"That's not stupid at all, but I completely understand why you'd think it was. We were kind of forced into spending time with each other, but honestly, I'm really glad that we were. I definitely consider you a friend. One of my only ones actually," Dawn told her.

"Look who it is," a voice boomed into the café area of the building.

Kronos was walking in and apparently wanted to make sure everyone knew it.

Several long strides in front of him, Damon was making a beeline for the girls. He pulled up a chair from the table next to them and sat on it backward as their audience watched Kronos walk up behind him.

"What are we having, ladies?" His teeth were so white.

"Christian chicken," Amber offered, glancing up at him.

He burst out laughing at her response, holding his audience.

I don't think that's entirely necessary.

"Well, I'll let you all get back to it. Mr. Montclaire and I just finished another very closed-off interview."

Damon gave Dawn an annoyed look as Kronos placed a hand on his shoulder.

"Maybe you ladies can put him in a better mood?"

"No promises," Dawn replied, making the man laugh obnoxiously again.

"Understandable, Miss Sutherland. Completely understandable. Well, I should be going. Sorry to interrupt. Have a nice night, everyone!" And with that, he left.

"I don't like that man." Damon hunched over the table. "Sorry, by the way. I didn't think he'd follow me in here."

"It's fine." Amber pulled a piece of the cookie off. "Cookie?"

He stared at the melty, chocolaty goodness for a second before sitting up. "Actually, yeah."

"Okay, good 'cause I can't eat anymore." Dawn leaned back in her chair, making the edge of her skirt fan out around her foot.

Amber pushed the cookie toward him. "Just finish it, Damon."

"You sure?"

"Yeah, I don't need any more."

Damon pulled pieces of it apart as Amber dusted the crumbs off her hands and onto the floor.

"Do you think she told him?" Amber asked, not lifting her eyes from her dead ends she was picking at.

"Who told who what?" Dawn asked.

"If HJ told Zach."

"About what?"

She turned to look at Damon. "About what the two of you are doing … you know." Amber raised her eyebrows and slightly tilted her head toward the open area of the room. She didn't want to say it, just in case someone was listening, and Dawn didn't blame her.

Damon shook his head. "I don't think so. Oh, speaking of, I got in."

"Into what?"

"The computer file. HJ's in class, so I haven't had a chance to talk to her about it yet."

Amber fiddled with the ends of her hair. Again. "You can tell us if you want," she suggested.

Damon glanced around the dining area and leaned in. Dawn and Amber copied his movement. "We need to go somewhere else."

Chapter 43

DAMON

"WHY DOES ALL THIS STUFF have these initials on it?" HJ whined for the fourth time in the last twenty minutes.

"I don't know, Hanna June." He always gave her the same answer, and yet she still continued to ask.

The files *were* huge, like Zach had told her, and they were all marked with the same three letters on the top—*TAP*. Some of them had a number after it, but nothing higher than three. Their files all had a one.

What made it even more confusing was the computer file. There was nothing on it. *Nothing.*

When he'd finally figured out his password and logged on that first day they snuck into his office, he hadn't found much—an internet browser with no search history, one picture of the six of them on the city library steps, and a few files. Mostly just documents and presentations for Parthenon, but there was one that was locked and titled *TAP*—the same letters that appeared on their files.

"What does that mean?" Hanna June had incessantly asked him after making the connection.

"If I could open the file, I might be able to answer your question."

Damon had copied every file over onto his flash drive, but when he got back to his apartment that night, there was nothing in the TAP file. He assumed maybe it had some complicated encryption protecting it, so when the two of them went back the following Tuesday, he'd logged back on. He opened up the file … but just like how he'd opened it at his apartment, there had been nothing there.

Which made no sense.

Opening it on my laptop would make sense, but why would there be nothing in the file on his own computer?

He was pulled from his thoughts by Hanna June's thick drawl.

"Wait, I got somethin'." She spoke up from her cross-legged position on the floor.

She had finished going through the files with their names on it last week, finding an alarming number of photos and articles about them from back when they had all been in high school. There were two files with *TAP2* scrawled across the top in black permanent marker, so she had decided that going through those next was the smartest idea.

After the janitor had come into his office that day, they agreed that it would be best if they spent as little time there as possible. Instead, they reserved one of the study rooms in the library on Tuesdays. They'd only gone back two other times—for Hanna June to take pictures of everything she could. Damon decided to see how useful her constantly tapping away on her phone actually was. Considering the amount of documents she had snapped pictures of and how fast she went through them all, she'd actually proven to be helpful—to his surprise.

Dawn and Kai still played lookout and made sure that Kronos and Zach didn't decide to cut their lunch short one day. She had informed Damon that he was really opening up to her, and she honestly looked forward to their Tuesday stakeouts.

Aside from not wanting to get caught in his office, what had also freaked out both of them—not that Damon would ever admit it to her—was Mr. Henkles. Damon had done a faculty search to figure out his name, and then he had used some of his contacts to get his medical record. He wasn't blind.

He had looked directly at Hanna June—Damon had seen it through the slits in the closet door—and yet he had seemed completely unaware of her presence.

Damon got up from the desk chair and stepped over the piles they'd sorted. "What is it?"

"Look." She held a file closer to him and pointed to the header. "Both of these two files with the two on top are students here already. Well, technically, only one is actually. Heath Blackburn-McHugh. And Astrid Radzilowicz is at UCLA right now, but she'll be transferring here next semester." She pulled a few documents from the manila folder and shoved them into his hands.

Damon scanned the information that had been forcefully handed to him, effortlessly committing it to memory. Heath was a sophomore, from Honolulu, worked in the campus body shop, and was a declared mechanical engineering major. Astrid was the same age, from LA, an intended sociology major, and had a pretty popular social media vlog channel.

"I think Zach knows the guy. I mean, Heath's not a very common name. And she has to be that YouTuber—how many girls named Astrid do you know?"

Damon grunted in agreement as he kept reading.

"Then, I found these also—Alexia Chang and Gunner McHugh. He's got one of the same last names as Heath—isn't that weird? He's in the Army, but he's supposedly coming here in January. And then Alexia is at a community college in Texas right now, but her transfer papers are right here." She handed him some more papers. "And they say she'll be starting in January."

"Jesus."

"They didn't have a number on top, but I'm assuming they should all be marked with a two. There're two files with a three and then two more unmarked folders, but those students are the same age, so I'm assuming they all go together. Four new students in the program next semester, four more the semester after that."

Damon stared at her. Yes, he had made quite a few judgmental assumptions about her in the beginning. But ever since they'd started their Tuesday afternoon snooping sessions while Dawn and Kai were on stakeout duty, he'd learned a lot about her. Mainly because she talked a *lot*, but also because they were forced to work together. He would've liked to get everything done on his own and not have to worry about trusting another person, but he had enough going on.

Not only was he working on a master's degree, but he was also on a TV show that was causing far too much fanfare for his comfort.

Paulina was breathing down his neck from over seven hundred miles away, and *her* brother had been asking him if he could pick up some jobs down here. And to top it all off, David's competitor in the ranks, Harold Braun, had people trying to bribe Damon into selling secrets even though the election had been last week and David had won by a landslide.

"They only adopted you to make themselves look good, right?"

"He's probably a terrible father, never around and always focusing on his work."

"He knowingly married into a family of assassins, so how mentally stable is he really?"

Honestly, the normal stuff was just too much, and then when you threw everything else into the mix … he was glad to have someone to do the digging with.

Even if it was Hanna June.

"And look at this," HJ kept going on as she reached back into the file, pulling out paparazzi-looking photos and passing them over to him. "They've even got pictures of them. How creepy is that?"

He pulled the first two pictures Hanna June had handed him and began to study the two confirmed students who'd be joining them. Heath was a pretty big guy, not nearly as tall as Damon—few people were—and he was muscular. Astrid was gorgeous—that wasn't even up for discussion. She had long legs and incredibly curly, short black hair.

"Gosh darn it, she's pretty." HJ was looking past his bicep at the picture of Astrid in his hands.

"Hmm."

"You know," she began as she held up the photo next to his face and glanced back and forth between her image and him, "you two would make a cute couple."

Damon gave her a look. "Don't even start, Hanna June."

"I'm bein' serious! I don't know why you don't date."

"I'm not interested," he replied and hoped she'd drop the topic.

Every once in a while, she'd bring it up, and he'd just shut her down.

"I think you are though. You're tall, you're hot, you're smart, you come from money—you check so many boxes for so many girls. I don't know why you don't want to at least entertain yourself."

"Hanna June," he warned.

"What?! I can say all that because I'm happily taken, and I feel like we've become friends. Maybe not as good friends as you and Dawn, but still. I know there're girls in your DMs, and I see the comments they leave on your Instagram pictures. By the way, I'm sure you know this already, but your most recent post is from April. You really should put up something more updated."

"I'm going to leave if you don't stop talking."

She huffed out a breath, stared at him for a moment, sat back down among her stacks of files, and got back to work, glaring at him from the corner of her eye.

He hadn't even gotten the chance to refocus before his phone went off on top of one of the stacks he'd shoved under the desk.

Fleur: I just finished Good Will Hunting, it was SO GOOD! Thanks for telling me to watch it

Damon smiled. She had been so adamant about not watching movies from before she was born the last time they'd talked, but he had gotten her to cave and watch one of his all-time favorites.

Damon: I'm glad you liked it. Pretty sure all my favorite movies are from before 2000.

Fleur: I don't think I have a favorite movie…I'll have to think about it…

Damon: Let me know so I can watch it

Fleur: Lol deal

"Oh Mylanta."

Damon jolted his head to face where the voice had come from. His texts with Fleur had gone back and forth within seconds, both of them obviously seeing the bubbles, indicating the other one was typing a response. He'd forgotten where he was and what he was doing.

Until Hanna June had somehow seen his phone screen. Now, Damon wasn't sure what to do, so he just stared back at her. She had obviously seen that he was texting someone, but he didn't know how much information she had past that, and he definitely wasn't about to offer it up.

Too many awkward, silent moments passed while they stared at each other.

"Are you texting Amber's little sister?"

Shit.

Damon had never really been big on lying to people, and he didn't feel like now was an appropriate time to start. As much as he didn't want to admit it, she was right.

"Yeah."

"Why?" Her big brown eyes stared at him, almost as if they were afraid of what his answer would be.

Damon took a deep breath and just let the truth roll off his tongue. "Because she's one of the very few people I *don't* strongly dislike."

It was quiet again as she cocked her head at him. "Do you … like her?"

"I like talking to her." *Not a lie. Not the whole truth, but not a lie.*

HJ only nodded, choosing to keep her thoughts to herself. She had a strange expression on her face, but Damon couldn't tell what she was thinking by it. "Does Amber know you talk to her?"

"No." It came out hard and sharp and much too quickly.

"I'm going to assume you want me to not tell her."

"I want you to not tell anyone."

She stared back at him for a long minute before agreeing. "Just don't … don't screw her over. Amber will most likely kill you."

Damon swallowed a scoff. None of them had any idea what he was capable of.

Chapter 44

GROUP INTERVIEW WITH ALL SIX.

Kronos: All right, this is the last group interview that we're going to put on this season. Once we finish this, that's it; you're done.

HJ: [*confused look*] Wait, what do you mean, done?

Kronos: I mean, that's a wrap on the whole season. We got the green light back in March for a ten-episode season, and it's about to be over!

HJ: Oh …

Kronos: Are you disappointed, Miss Pruitt?

HJ: I mean, yeah. I know it wasn't everyone's cup of tea, but I really liked everything about being on *The Olympians*.

Kronos: Then, you're in for a surprise. [*to the crew behind him*] Cameras rolling?

Crew Member: Since you sat down, sir.

Kronos: Wonderful. We'll cut in right here.

Kronos: Thank you all for sitting down with me before you go home for Thanksgiving break. I just have some exciting news to share with you before you depart.

HJ: Oh my God, wait …

Kronos: There are three things that the network wants you all to be aware of.

Kronos: Number one: You obviously know the show is a massive hit here in the States, but you have also gained a huge following over in Europe and Japan. The network is working on organizing some sort of multicity tour over there.

Kai: Japan? Fuck yes.

Kronos: There's also talk about a *meet-and-greet panel* type of situation taking place back here in the States after that, similar to Comic-Con.

Amber: Oh God.

Kronos: The second thing is that the show has become such a massive hit in the last two months since we started … that you've been renewed for another season!

HJ: [*happy, ear-piercing screams*]

Dawn: [*mellow voice*] That's so exciting!

Zach: Fuck yes! [*pulls HJ closer to him and kisses her on her forehead*]

Damon: Shit.

Kronos: [*chuckling*] Okay, okay, settle down. I'm glad you're excited. The last thing—are you ready for it?

Damon: No.

Dawn: [*glaring at Damon*] Yes!

Kronos: We will be adding four new cast members at the beginning of the new semester!

Amber: More of us?

Zach: Yes!

HJ: Who?

Kronos: Two young women and two young men. One of the young men is already a student here, in his sophomore year. The other male joining us has been recently discharged from the Army. He'll be starting as a freshman, but he's slightly older than Miss Hargrove and Mr. Newport. And as for the young ladies who will be a part of our group, one is transferring here from UCLA as a sophomore, and the other graduated from her high school a year early but attended her local community college in Texas for her first semester. She turned eighteen in September.

Kai: Isn't ten of us going to be a lot?

Kronos: [*chuckles*] We'll be adding some more chairs around the table, Mr. Newport.

HJ: Are we going to meet them before we start filming together? Or maybe can we meet the one who's already here?

Kronos: [*smiling*] Slow down, Miss Pruitt. Of course you'll meet them all before you start working together. That surprise is something I can't quite divulge yet though.

HJ: Kronos, I hate surprises.

Kronos: Get used to them, Miss Pruitt. If things go the way I'm anticipating they will, then you're in for a whole lot of them.

Chapter 45

HANNA JUNE

HJ: room 204

Not thirty seconds after she sent him the text, she heard the door shutting behind her. She jumped in her seat, turning around to meet his chiseled face. His five o'clock shadow was clearly visible, and she remembered how much older he was than the rest of them. Dawn was actually the oldest, but at least sometimes, she joined in on the fun. Damon was always more closed off, holding himself more properly and staying in the corner when they were all together.

"I didn't even hear you come in!"

He pulled up the extra chair in the small room and sat beside her. Kronos and Zach had had their last Tuesday lunch the week before, and she and Damon had agreed they still needed to go through everything they'd found. Mainly because it was a lot ... and they still couldn't figure it out.

The meetings at Amber's had ceased after that first afternoon with Dawn suggesting that maybe they shouldn't meet up again until all the information had been collected and gone through. They had all agreed, noting that some of Amber's nosy neighbors had seen the five of them together that day.

Two of them meeting up was much easier to hide.

"Have you found anything else?"

"Nothing new. I've got basic info about all eight of the incoming students, but there's still all these weird notes about the six of us *and* them that I can't decipher."

Damon pulled his glasses out of his bag, put them on, and stuck out his hand. "Let me see."

HJ's eyes got huge. Well, they were actually always huge. "When did you get glasses?"

"When I was fourteen. Hand me the papers."

"What? I've never seen you wear glasses before!"

"Well then, it looks like this is a very exciting moment for you," he deadpanned back to her and took the papers out of her hand to begin studying them.

She silently shook her head at him but went back to some other files.

Not ten minutes later, he picked up his head and looked at her. "I have a thought."

Hanna June dropped what she had been in the middle of reading. Damon never willingly offered up his thoughts about anything, so this was, yet again, another exciting moment for her.

"Okay." She opened up the floor for him.

"It's going to sound insane."

"Doubt it," she argued.

"Hanna June … you know that I would never say something like that if I didn't honestly think it. Trust me, it is going to sound insane."

She didn't like the tone of his voice; it worried her. A lump formed in her throat, and she tried hard to swallow over it. "Okay."

A silent, solid minute passed between them before he finally spoke up. "These notes … the abbreviations … they're the exact same as the Greek Olympian gods."

The laugh that left her mouth was loud and abrupt, shrill even. She doubled over in her chair, holding her stomach. She kept going and going because it felt good to laugh really hard, but also because he couldn't be serious.

"You can't be serious," she finally pushed out in one breath, wiping a tear away from the corner of her eye.

"I'm completely serious." His mouth was in a straight line, and his eyes were black and dead inside.

Holy shit, he's completely serious.

"Can I explain my reasoning behind it, or are you going to laugh at me again?"

"I was only laughin' 'cause I thought you were jokin'!"

"I never joke," he argued back and scooted in closer to her, pushing the papers in between them. "See this? The letters next to both yours and Zach's names—*H* and *Z*?"

It was Hanna June's turn to give him an annoyed stare. "Those are the first letters of our names."

He was shaking his head at her before her sentence was finished. "That's what I thought at first too, but"—he shuffled through the papers before pulling one from the middle out—"look at Amber's."

She scanned the paper before identifying what he was trying to point out to her and slowly lifted her chin. "It's a *D*."

"Exactly." He nodded.

Another quiet, awkward moment settled between them—it was so common for the two of them that she wasn't really sure if you could still call them awkward silences—before HJ had to admit to something.

"I don't actually know anythin' 'bout Greek mythology, so ..."

Damon's head fell as he let out an exasperated sigh. "You didn't learn about the ancient Greeks and their deities in any history class?"

"No ... we learned normal American history things. The Civil War, Revolutionary War ... I'm pretty sure we were taught about the French and Indian War ..." She tried to recall exactly what she'd learned in any of her history classes.

"Please tell me you're kidding."

"Damon, I went to public school below the Mason-Dixon line, and you went to private school in New York City. We had very different educational upbringin's."

His face said that he was trying really hard to hold back an eye roll. "Okay, crash course: The ancient Greeks had a lot of gods, hundreds of them. The king of the gods was Zeus. He was the god of the skies, lightning and thunder, and the weather. He was basically the main guy in charge. With me so far?"

"Yeah," she answered as she nervously glanced down at the paper in between their elbows.

"Zeus was married to Hera. She was the queen of the gods, but also the goddess of marriage, women, family, and childbirth. Zeus cheated on her constantly, but she couldn't ever lash out against him because the one time she did, he hung her from golden chains in the sky for everyone to see. She promised to never act against him again as long as he let her go. He did but continued to cheat on her, usually having to turn into an animal to do so, which is beside the point. So, Hera would redirect her anger toward the women that Zeus cheated on her with."

Hanna June could feel her mouth go dry as she listened to Damon's summarized version of the king and queen of Greek mythology.

"Doesn't that sound the least bit familiar to you?" He raised his eyebrows at her, patiently waiting for her rebuttal.

"You're saying he's Zeus and I'm Hera? Is that what you're getting at? Because if it is, then, yes, Damon, you do sound insane."

"I know; I know, but—"

"You're saying we're Greek gods? Is that it? You and me and Zach and Kai and Amber and Dawn are all reincarnated Greek gods and goddesses, and we have magical powers, and we're immortal, and we live in a beautiful kingdom above the clouds. Is that it?"

"Hanna June—"

"Damon, just … just leave it alone. Okay, yeah, I agree. All this stuff is weird. Creepy even, especially the pictures. But suggesting that we're somehow modeled after Greek gods is ridiculous, especially for you. That kind of shit doesn't happen in real life."

Once more, the silence settled, and after a few motionless moments, Damon began packing up the papers and sliding them back into their file folder. He pushed it over toward her and got up out of his seat when she spoke again.

"Sorry, I—" she mumbled. "It's a possible thought. I didn't mean to shoot you down. We can keep looking into it after break, but maybe … maybe let's not tell anyone about any of this until we've figured it out for sure?"

Damon cleared his throat as he reached the doorknob. "Agreed, Your Majesty." And then he left.

Chapter 46

THE REST OF THE SEMESTER *was fairly quiet, compared to the fanfare the six had caused during filming. They all attended their final classes, studied for their finals—Amber had saved a few Adderall—and passed their exams … for the most part. Kai failed one of his Biology exams, but a girl he'd been hooking up with offered to do some extra credit for him, and he ended up passing the class once he turned that in.*

Kronos thought it would be a good idea for Zach, HJ, Kai, and Amber to attend commencement, as Damon and Dawn would be walking. They brought a small camera crew and told everyone to dress nice and to sit together.

Zach: [*looking through the graduation booklet*] What the hell is Dawn going to do with a masters in architecture? Doesn't she have a teaching degree or something?

HJ: Her bachelor's is in educational leadership, but she doesn't have a teaching license.

Zach: How do you know that?

HJ: Because I talk to people about their lives.

Zach: [*raises his eyebrows and gives her a snarky look*]

Amber: [*reading the graduation booklet*] Damon James Montclaire. Master's of science, forensic psychology. [*looks at Kai*] Damon's middle name is James?

Kai: [*lost in thought*] I feel like I did know that …

HJ: Sounds so regal.

Zach: Do you think he's a virgin?

HJ: What? No. No way.

Zach: No? Think about it. He's said he's interested in girls, and I totally believe that. My gaydar has not gone off once for him.

Kai: I'm pretty sure you have to be gay to have a gaydar …

Zach: No, that's not true.

Amber: He's straight, but he's not a virgin. There's no way.

Zach: No, just listen. He's with Dawn, like, *all the time*. They both claim they've never hooked up with each other, which I think is true 'cause there's no, like, weird sexual tension between them. But he's never been seen talking to any other girls aside from that one time they flanked him right after episode three aired over fall break. His mom did that whole speed-dating thing for him, and he wasn't interested in any of them, and I saw these girls—they were *fine*. No offense, baby. You're still my number one.

HJ: [*skeptically smiles*] I know.

Zach: I think he's just so emo and closed off and shit that everyone was scared of him for a long time, and now that he's in the spotlight, all these girls want him, but his *lose your virginity* window is gone 'cause he knows that if he goes to hook up with a girl, it could get brought up that he's never done it before. She's gonna be like, *What the fuck?* Am I right, or am I right?

Kai: [*stares*] No, you're not right. You're fucking stupid.

Amber: You've put a lot of time into that theory.

Commencement music begins. About fifteen minutes in, Zach turns to Hanna June.

Zach: [*whispers*] This is so boring.

HJ: Shh. In three and a half years, that'll be us.

Zach: Yeah, but right now, it's not. You wanna, like … go to the bathroom?

HJ: [*eyes him up and down*] No. There're cameras watchin' us right now. Later though.

Zach: Ugh, whatever. I'm taking a break from this. [*gets up and goes to the restroom*]

He comes back ten minutes later with a small hickey on his neck peeking out from under the collar of his shirt. Hanna June sees it but doesn't say anything about it.
After graduation is over, they all go outside of the football stadium to find Dawn and Damon and take some pictures with them. Both sets of their parents are there in attendance as well.

Amber: [*running up to Dawn*] Congratulations!

Dawn: Thank you! We need to get some pictures together—one of you and me, one with all the girls, and one with all six of us!

Chantel: Yes, come on now! Get together! I can't wait to frame this for Nana and Poppy, Dawnie.

Paulina: I need one of just the graduates too! I can't wait to put this on Instagram

Chantel: [*to Paulina*] You know, Dawn is not only the first person to go to college in our family, but to also graduate with a master's degree. This is a huge deal.

Paulina: Oh, you must be so proud!

Damon: Paulina, take the picture, please.

David: Sweetheart, take it. He's actually smiling. We have no idea when we'll get this opportunity again.

Paulina: Oh, David, stop it.

Lawrence: You got a real nice smile there, son.

Chantel: He does, doesn't he?

Paulina: [*scoffs*] If only we saw it more.

David: Okay, now, can we get one of all the Olympians?

Everyone shuffles in to pose for the photo. The girls are all in the front with Damon and Dawn in the middle, Zach and Hanna June on the right, and Kai and Amber on the left.

Paulina: Oh my, these are perfect. Such a good-looking group. Ah, I love it! These are going to Papa, too.

Damon: Paulina …

Other graduates and guests come pouring in and start taking pictures of them.

Amber: Oh no …

Damon: I'm not doing this.

HJ: [*grabs on to Damon's robe as he starts to leave, whispers to him*] Humor them. Pose for another ten seconds, and then you can leave.

Damon: Why should I?

HJ: [*through gritted teeth*] Because these people are the reason you're about to have a paycheck.

Damon: I have a trust fund; I don't need Kronos's money.

HJ: [*rolls her eyes*] Don't say that.

Damon: Well, they're also the reason I have no privacy.

HJ: You agreed to this …

Damon: [*glares at her but slinks back to his position with the group*]

After a minute, David and Lawrence step in and thank everyone for the pictures but ask for some privacy. Most of the crowd obliges while a handful of onlookers linger. Several of them take out their phones and start recording.

Zach: [*leans in close to HJ's ear*] What was that all about?

HJ: What?

Zach: You talking to Damon like that.

HJ: I was just trying to convince him to stay. I'm not going to let him ruin a good photo op for the rest of us just because he's antisocial.

Zach: Looked like you guys were pretty close …

HJ: What's with the hickey you didn't have before you went to the bathroom?

Zach: Holy fuck, this shit again?

HJ: Well, it's *another* hickey that I swear on my mama's life I didn't put on you, so, yeah, *this shit again.*

Zach: [*annoyed*] Jesus Christ. [*runs his fingers through his hair*]

HJ: I'll let you come up with a response. [*pats him on the pec and walks away to stand with Amber, who links her arm with HJ's*]

Paulina: We should all go out to eat!

Chantel: Actually, we're having a big barbecue at our house with the family, and you're all more than invited! It's beautiful today, and we've got plenty of food!

David: [*to Lawrence*] I'm good with that. Means I don't have to open my wallet! [*laughs*]

Dawn: But now, that means that you're gonna be having real Southern food, I'm not sure if your fancy New York palates can handle it! [*nudges Damon in the ribs*]

Damon: [*looks up from his phone*] What?

Paulina: Son, get off that thing.

David: [*whispers to Paulina*] Honey, wait. Look, he's smiling again.

Paulina: Huh …

Dawn: [*sees what they're talking about and leans in*] I think it's a girl.

Damon: [*without looking up from his phone*] I can hear all of you.

Chantel: Come on, y'all. I got a pig roastin' away back at the house!

Chapter 47

KAI

"OH, MY BABY IS HOME!" Leticia came running off the dock, the *Buoyant Mortgage* rocking on the tiny waves in the marina. Her arms were outstretched, and her smile reached the edges of both sides of her face. "There's my superstar college boy!"

She pulled him in for the biggest hug Kai had ever gotten in his life. He sank into it. He had missed his mom so much more than he'd thought.

"I'm gonna bring his bags in, Letty," Kris informed his mom as he squeezed past their reunion on the wooden planks beneath their feet.

"Thank you for going to get him!" she called to him.

Kris had gotten to Olympia last night and crashed on Kai's couch after catching up with Mr. Caffrey and taking his nephew out to dinner. Only two girls had come up to them in their back booth at Philomena's, thankfully. Kai really just wanted to catch up with his uncle.

He loved getting to talk to Dawn on Tuesdays without having to worry about cameras or any of the other four being around. She was so receptive and understanding, and she never judged him. But there were still some things he just felt like he couldn't talk to her about, simply because she just wouldn't get it. Dawn had both her parents, and from the few interactions he'd had with them via FaceTime and once in person, they were both great people, and they just wanted the best for their daughter.

Kai hadn't wanted to go to college in the first place, and even beginning his third year, he still didn't want it, but he could never tell his mom that. And talking to a family member about that made him feel better.

The two of them listened to music and talked the entire drive back to Beaufort, where his mom had docked for her workload over the next three days. Kai had arranged for Kris to take her out tomorrow and give her the day off while Kai cleaned Dr. and Mrs. Hannon's yacht. He desperately wanted to spend time with his mama, but he knew she needed a day off more.

They'd be getting salaries starting in February, so Kai was already planning to buy a car. That way, he could drive to wherever his mom was on the weekends and spend time with her. That would definitely save him from doing more stupid things that ended up on TV.

Or maybe I could just get a flight …

Or a private jet.

An hour later, the three of them had finished dinner, and his mom had broken open the photo albums.

"Oh, look at this one!" She pointed to a picture of him at his fourth birthday party.

His mom and uncle had rented one of those pontoon boats with a waterslide on it and invited the rest of his family over. The picture had Kai in his little life jacket, not that he needed one—he was a naturally strong swimmer—at the top of the slide, turned around and showing off his little muscles.

They flipped through a few more pictures, and Kai heard a sniffle.

Oh my God, she's crying.

"Mom?"

"I'm fine." She wiped away the tear beading up at the corner of her eye.

He pushed the photo album away and bent down next to her. "Mom."

"It's just … things are just very different now. You're this big TV star," she began to explain.

But Kai let out a laugh. "Mom, I'm not a star."

"You absolutely are! I have clients askin' me things about you and the show and Mr. Kronos! Everybody knows who you are, baby."

Kai's dark eyebrows furrowed together. He didn't want to believe what she was saying and definitely didn't want to accept it.

"She's right. I was in Winnipeg last weekend, and this couple came up to me around the lake, telling me I looked like this American reality star."

"That didn't happen."

"It absolutely did! Son, you're everywhere."

Kai stayed quiet, understanding what he'd been told. Strangers were approaching his family about him.

That didn't make him feel good.

If he'd been more like Zach, he would have loved the attention, no doubt. But he wasn't when it came to this. He was more like Damon. Damon, who had known better to switch his classes all online so he wouldn't have trouble completing his coursework. Damon, who already had family security but decided to talk to his parents about stepping up the precautions. Damon, who was getting out of this as soon as he could.

But Damon also scared him; made him feel like he wasn't good enough, like he didn't have things nearly as half together as he should by now.

"Baby," his mom started as she gently placed her hand on top of his, "this thing is already huge. And I'm—we're worried it's going to go to your head."

"Mom, no, no, not at all."

"Sweetheart, your face is all over the world. Your ... very drunk face, crying over a girl."

"Mom, ugh, okay. Look, I made some stupid decisions, but, like, I'm almost twenty-one. It's kind of expected."

His mother's expression changed as she deadpanned to him, "Not every twenty-year-old has their life broadcast for other twenty-year-olds to watch."

"Mom, it's just entertainment. So much of that isn't real. It's organized and edited, and it's not real and—"

His mom interrupted him, "You know that, right? You know it's not real?"

"Of course I know that, Mama. I promise. I know that, and I won't forget it."

"Okay." His mom smiled just a little, and it looked like she was really trying to believe him.

He cleared his throat. "But there are, uh, there're some things I want to talk to you about."

"I'm gonna go wash dishes," Kris excused himself, knowing where the conversation was going, having helped Kai plan out what he was going to say to his mom.

"Kronos told us that we're going to get paid, starting in February."

"Oh, baby! That's so exciting!"

"Yeah, yeah. So, I really think that some of that money needs to go toward security for you."

Leticia's delicate face morphed into confusion. "What are you talkin' about?"

"So, I've been thinking about it the last few weeks, but especially after *both* of you just told me that people are coming up to you now. I think it's the best idea to get you some protection."

Only a half a second passed in silence before it was his mom's turn to erupt in laughter. "Oh, baby, ha-ha! Can you imagine? Me, flanked with a bodyguard! Ha-ha!" She looked like she was nearing tears as she shared her apparently hilarious mental images.

"Mom, I'm being serious. This isn't a joke."

"I am absolutely not getting a security team, Kai. Don't be ridiculous."

Kai was on the border of being offended.

Why the hell does she think this is funny? I've honestly been in a semi-panic over something happening to her more than once.

"Where did you even get this idea from?"

"Damon," Kai offered, about to go into an explanation when his mom jumped ahead again.

"That's understandable, although that young man does not come off as the most inviting. I hope he isn't mean to you."

"No, Mama," Kai sighed, "he isn't mean to me."

"Okay, good. Although that's how his family is. They've had a security team since before that boy was on this show because that's the life they live."

"I know that, Mama, but that's kind of what my life is turning into too," he tried to explain to her.

"Well, just as long as you don't listen to anything that Alexander boy says. He's just like his daddy—conniving thing he is."

Kai just grumbled in agreement, not wanting to feed into the conversation.

Thankfully, his mom picked up on it. "Look, sweetheart, I don't need protection. I work alone, and nobody bothers me when I'm not working. You know what I started doing? Harris Teeter lets you order your groceries online! I don't even have to get out of the car! They bring 'em right out to me and load 'em up! You know how much time that saves me?"

He gave her a weak smile. "That's great, Mama. I'm happy for you."

She reached forward and closed the photo album, saying, "Now, if you don't mind, we've got a week until Christmas, and I really didn't want to decorate without you. So, if you can get the tree out of the storage. Kris got the tinsel out, so I'm going to start wrapping it on the deck." She flashed her smile at him, crow's-feet around her eyes, as she got up and began to decorate her floating home for her favorite holiday.

She's the same. She doesn't seem freaked out by this, and neither should you.

You need to calm down.

Let it go.

You're all going to be fine.

Chapter 48

HANNA JUNE

Was she a bitch? Probably. Some of the things she did sure made it seem like she was. For instance, not an hour ago, she'd taken to Twitter to share, *It only took one semester of college for KE to get knocked up. Guess I was right all along.*

Kelly Engers had hooked up with Zach during their eleventh-grade homecoming game, and everybody knew it.

"You are such a whore!" HJ screamed at her in the middle of the cafeteria the following Monday while her boyfriend held her back, whispering to her, "She's not worth it."

"Wrong. Whores are stupid and end up pregnant."

"Oh, trust me," she had spat back at her, "you will. I guarantee that by sophomore year of college, if you even get in, you'll get knocked up by some skeezy stoner. Just you wait."

Kim Driver had texted her as she got back from Christmas shopping with her mama.

Kim: Guess who's preggers???

HJ: Omg no

HJ: Pls tell me ur joking

Kim: Salina just told me and asked if you knew

Kim: I had to beg her to let me be the one to tell you

HJ: Omg thank you, that just made my day hahaha

HJ: when's she due?

Kim: I think April?

HJ: Omg wait who's the baby daddy???

Kim: …you're gonna lose it

HJ: Kimberly…

Kim: Eddie DeSantis

HJ: HAAAHA OMG

That conversation had been like an injection of serotonin for her.

Her post had only been up for forty-three minutes, but it already had four hundred and eighty-three likes. Some were from people she had gone to high school with, but most just seemed like they were fans of the show, from the brief overview she'd done of their profiles.

HJ loved looking into her fans on social media. She had only followed maybe a dozen of them, and they'd all freaked out when she did.

OMG HJ FOLLOWED ME. YOU GUYS, SHE KNOWS I EXIST.

I was made to have my own fan base.

"June Bug, dinner's about to be ready," her dad called to her as he walked down the hall past her room.

"Be right there, Daddy."

"Do you want a glass of the white for dinner?"

"No, thanks, just some water for me," she answered, making her father back track his steps and appear in her doorway.

"Are you sure? You always have wine at dinner," he questioned her, his forehead wrinkling in confusion.

"I'm sure." She would be drinking more at school now—after Kronos had basically told them it was okay as long as they didn't commit any felonies while inebriated. She couldn't be consuming *too* much alcohol. She had appearances to keep up with after all.

"All right, I'll go pour you a glass. Come on down though. Mama made your favorite," he told her as he started to back away from the doorframe.

"Spaghetti?"

"With lots of oregano!" he called to her from down the hall.

Without the cameras around, she didn't have to worry about accidentally looking like a mess on-screen.

She was closing her laptop when her phone buzzed again. *Please be sending me a baby bump picture of slut-face Engers.*

Amber: Have you guys seen this?

Amber: YouTube: Cast of The Olympians as Full House Video

Dawn: This is so cute!

Kai: Why'd they make me Joey?

Amber: Because if they made you Jesse, then Damon would've been Joey, and we all know THAT doesn't make any sense

Zach: Damon as Jesse doesn't make sense either tho

Amber: He at least somewhat resembles him

Damon: Stop talking about me.

Dawn: Well, you don't talk about you, so someone's gotta do it

Hanna June already missed them. It had been a week since she'd heard Amber annoyingly talk about her family, and she felt like something was missing in her life.

It was weird how much she'd learned about all of them in such a short amount of time. They really had become like a little dysfunctional family, each person with their quirks. Kai, who dressed like a Florida tourist with his printed button-down shirts and flip-flops whenever he could. Amber, whose diet consisted of Cookie Dude deliveries and cheap Mexican food. Damon, who carried around pepperoni sticks in case he switched positions too fast and was about to pass out because of it. Dawn, who put *way* too much sugar in her coffee—and consumed too much coffee for that matter.

What's Zach's flaw?

Oh wait, don't go down that road.

He … oh jeez, uh, let's see. He …

He can't decide on a major! One day, he's business, and the next, he's poli-sci. He's very indecisive.

Now, what's my flaw? Hmm …

My roots are showing.

Sure, that sounds good.

After dinner, she wanted to go look at Christmas lights in their neighborhood with Zach, but he texted back, saying he was taking Skye and Keanu shopping to get their parents Christmas presents.

He's such a good big brother. He's going to be a great dad someday.

So, Hanna June resorted to doing what any bored teenager would do—aimless scrolling on social media. Posts from stay-at-home moms, sorority sisters, and girls who had hooked up with Zach filled her feed. She switched apps, closed them out and reopened them, and refreshed the pages until she saw something that made her thumb stop mid-motion.

QUIZ: WHICH GREEK GODDESS ARE YOU?

Uh, no.

She scrolled down … but then back up. She stared at the ad for what she knew would be a complete waste of her time but clicked on the hyperlink anyway. Pointless questions filled her phone, and although she didn't want to answer some of them honestly, she did.

YOUR RESULT: HERA.

Which was followed by a description of the goddess.

Queen of the gods—that sounds good.

Goddess of marriage, women, and childbirth—also good.

Wife and sister of Zeus—wait. Wife AND sister? That ain't right. Moving on …

Jealous and vengeful—oh great, I'm a bitch, apparently.

She should've closed it out, and she knew that, but something made her keep reading.

And reading.

And reading and reading and reading.

She was deep in a story about some prince named Paris choosing between goddesses—Hera, Aphrodite, or Athena—to be "the fairest one" when there was a knock on her door. "Bug, dear?"

HJ jumped. She had never before gotten sucked into reading about something that she completely forgot where she was. "Uh, yeah?"

"Dear, are you going to bed soon? I know you're on break from school and all, but we both have work in the morning, so we were just wondering—"

"Yeah, I'm 'bout to," she called back to her mom as she got up and walked over to the door to open it.

Her mama was standing in her old robe, her fuzzy slippers on her feet. There was a smile on her face, but anyone could tell it was forced, especially by the tired look in her eyes.

"Love you, Mama. I'll see you in the morning. I'll come over, and we can have lunch together," she suggested.

The lines next to her eyes crinkled as her smile morphed into a genuine reaction. "I'd love that, Bug. Get some sleep. I know TV stars stay up late and don't listen to their mamas, but you're still my baby, and I need to make sure you're taken care of."

Sally Ann kissed her on the cheek and squeezed her hand before turning around and retreating to her room. HJ waited until the door was shut before she closed her own door as quietly as possible, turned off her light, and then dived under her covers. She unlocked her phone, and the tent she'd just made for herself was immediately illuminated by the horribly bright screen.

"Okay, now, where were we?"

The next evening, Zach had taken her out to dinner and then on the walking tour of the holiday displays in their neighborhood. They only lived a few streets away from each other, which had made sneaking out easy when they were younger.

Not that they ever should've needed to do that—it was their parents who had set them up in the first place.

They were looking at the McGregors' massive garden display, HJ's head resting on his shoulder, when she felt his phone vibrate. It wasn't even leaning against her—she was just that in touch with him.

And unfortunately, with his text delivery.

He slid it out and glanced at the screen, and then something happened. Something that was so simple and yet so rare that HJ actually got a serotonin high from it.

He showed her his phone.

She felt like an elated idiot every time he flipped it around and let her in on what was really happening on that stupid little screen of his, but it also made sense.

Which she knew was pretty sad.

"Look what I just got."

Kronos: Hope you and Miss Pruitt are enjoying your time with your families! Wanted to have you be the first to know that we will be seeing each other again in a few days. Keep a lookout for travel instructions!

Kronos: And yes, you can tell Miss Pruitt :)

She looked up at him, feeling a smile stretch across her cheeks. "What do you think he means by that?"

"I don't know." He shrugged.

Thoughts flew around in her head at warp speed as she put it together. "Wait … you don't think … no," she thought aloud as she zoned out, staring at the little piles of snow crunching underneath her UGGs.

"What are you thinking?" Zach was turned, fully facing her. She had his undivided attention. She'd never admit it, but sometimes, she would "think out loud" without really saying what she was thinking, just to pique his interest.

Which, again, was pretty sad.

"I just … well, we wouldn't all be meeting at Olympia because campus is closed until after New Year's."

"Yeah, so?"

"So"—she pulled at his hand, halting their stroll—"if we're not going to be summoned there, where are we going?"

She watched the wheels in his head turn as he tried to get to where she was.

Come on. Put it together.

His eyes started to grow, and his words came out slowly, like he was very unsure of what he was thinking. "Wait … you don't think …"

She couldn't wait for him. "We're going to LA."

"No …"

"Ask him."

"What? No!" His curious demeanor was gone, the expression replacing it mirroring nervousness.

"Zach, baby, he loves you! Just ask him. What's the worst that could happen?"

Eyes shifted down toward his phone as he contemplated. He hesitated a little too long though, and HJ tried to push it.

"I can do it for you," she offered.

"No, that's okay. I got it." The words flew out of his mouth, and suddenly, he was responding to the big, bald man in charge. He spoke out loud what he was typing as his thumbs tapped away. "*Are we by any chance going to Los Angeles? Just want to know so we can start looking for tickets.* That's good, right?"

"Yeah, that sounds good. Do you want me to check to make sure you spelled everything right?"

"Nah, it's fine." And he hit the Send button.

Dammit.

Kronos's reply came only seconds later.

> **Kronos: Actually, you'll all be flying private out to the City of Angels. Do you and the future missus want to fly out from Dulles, Reagan, or Baltimore?**

Chapter 49

ZACH

IT WAS SIX DAYS UNTIL Christmas, and he still didn't have a gift for HJ. Not only that, but he also didn't even have an *idea* of what to get her.

He'd walked around the mall with Skye in tow at least three times and was still coming up empty-handed.

"She likes jewelry," she offered another suggestion.

"Nah, I get her jewelry all the time."

"What about something she needs for school?"

"No, I need something that's going to mean something to her," he answered her as they sat in the massage chairs.

I need something that says, Yes, I pay attention to you every second of the day and think about only you.

She was quiet for a few minutes, putting more effort into actually coming up with an idea than he was.

"Was there anything that you said to each other, like, a long time ago? Something that she'd remember too? Because, like, if you bring that up in your present somehow, I think that would definitely qualify as meaning something to her," she proposed to him.

Shit, she's right.

That's kinda genius actually.

"Skye, I think you just came up with the best possible idea."

His little sister sat up a little straighter, and a big smile danced across her face. "Well, Mom and Dad say that I *am* smarter than you were at my age."

"Shut up." He laughed at her.

She gently kicked his leg. "So, what are you getting me for Christmas?"

"Can't tell you," Zach answered her, starting to scroll through Amazon.

"That's because you don't have a present for me, isn't it?"

"Wrong. I actually got yours and Key's, like, a month ago."

"Liar."

His head snapped toward her, his joking demeanor gone. He hated being called a liar.

Even if he was one.

Well, he was a purposeful liar. If he wasn't telling the truth, it was more than likely because he knew the truth would just disappoint the other person. Maybe it was because they expected a better answer; maybe it was because they would only end up mad or upset with him. Either way, neither reaction was productive, so Zach thought it was just better to avoid the possibility altogether.

"I'm actually *not* lying, brat. But if you don't believe me, guess you won't be getting your present." He tapped away on the online shopping site, adding two go-karts into his cart. He went to check out and chose the faster shipping, not bothering to check the extra price of it.

Her expression changed harshly too. "I'm telling Mom and Dad you called me that!"

"Oh my God, Skye. Calm down, okay? Jeez."

"No! Sometimes, you say mean things, and then you tell me to just *feel better* even though you made me upset. That's not fair!"

She was right.

But she was also eleven.

"Skye, what do you want from me? Do you want me to buy you something? We can go back to Abercrombie and get you that sweater you were looking at. I'll get it for you in every color," he suggested, trying to put out whatever fire he'd apparently started in her.

"No, I don't want a *sweater*." She was almost yelling.

Some people were starting to look, and of course, once they looked, they saw him and couldn't pull their gaze away.

"I *want* to spend time with my big brother, but he's too busy on his phone!" With that, she got up and stormed off toward the pretzel shop.

Jesus Christ.

He started to get up and go after her when a group of high school girls stepped in front of him.

"Oh my God, you're Zach! From *The Olympians*! See, Tara, I told you it was him," a girl with dark hair said.

He flashed his smile at them. *Thank God I got my teeth whitened the other day.*

"That's me. What can I do for you ladies?"

"Oh, uh, well, we really just wanted a picture, but you should probably go and check on your little sister," a very short girl with blonde hair suggested to him, the rest of her friends nodding.

Dammit. That could've been my first foursome.

"That's so sweet of you all. Thank you. Yeah, she's going through a tough time right now. Maybe I can still get your number though?"

The girls giggled.

The dark-haired one spoke again. "Which one of us?"

"All of you, of course."

There was even *more* giggling, but Zach didn't walk up to the pretzel counter, where Skye was ordering a cup full of nuggets, until he got all three of their phone numbers.

"Listen, I'm sorry you got upset when I called you a brat." He leaned down on the counter next to her, getting on her level.

She didn't answer him.

"I do have a present for you, I promise. I could never forget about you too."

She turned to eye him, realizing what he had said.

"Not that I forgot about HJ!" The words rushed out of his mouth. "It's just that me and her have been together for so long that getting her presents is really hard. 'Cause, ya see, I have to get her at least three presents a year."

"Three?" she asked as the employee behind the counter handed her a cup of greasy pretzel nuggets, doused in cinnamon and sugar.

Gross.

"Yeah, three—her birthday, Christmas, and our anniversary."

"Oh, okay." She plopped one into her mouth as they sat down on the edge of the fountain.

Zach hated sitting near the water, but he knew she liked it, and right now, it was just about making her feel better, so she didn't rat him out for being a shitty big brother again.

"The other tricky part is that I can't repeat any of the presents I've already gotten her, and since we've been together for a really long time, that's kinda hard to do."

"Pretzel?" she offered him.

"I'm good."

"So," she began, talking with her mouth full, "why don't you get her something that, like, you can add to every time you need to buy her a gift?"

That's not a bad idea …

"Like, they have those Pandora bracelets. And like I said earlier—because, if you remember correctly, I am very smart—she likes jewelry. Plus, she'd be able to show it off, like, on the show every time you get her something new to put on it. Maybe it could turn into a sponsored deal or something."

That's a genius plan. Why the hell didn't I come up with that?

"Yeah, I guess that'll work," was how he replied to her instead.

He let her finish her sugar-covered rolls of dough and then dragged her to a jewelry store and picked out the bracelet with three charms for HJ.

"Don't give her it with just *one* charm."

They were about to check out when Zach saw dainty little rings that looked like a crown.

That's perfect. And I found it by myself.
Kinda.
I wouldn't be in here if it wasn't for Skye, but still.

"I also need that ring in a size … eight, I think."

He would be using Skye's sloppy little handwriting to create a note from when they had been younger that he wrote for her but never gave to her … until now. He had the bracelet that Skye had also come up with the idea for. But the ring was all his idea. And he knew that the only thought in her head would be that he had given her a *ring*.

I'm so getting laid after she opens this.

Chapter 50

THE CAST OF THE OLYMPIANS *had not had plans to get back together until a few days before the spring semester began.*

However, Kronos received some last-minute news from the network and flew all six members out to Los Angeles to meet with the network professionals, have a wrap party, and meet the new program members who would be joining them in mid-January.

Zach and HJ were flown in from Reagan, Kai from Raleigh-Durham, and Damon from JFK. Amber and Dawn met in Charleston and flew in together.

Their pictures were taken by both fans and paparazzi as they arrived at LAX and were ushered into cars with blacked-out windows.

At Parthenon Headquarters, the six of them were reunited after two weeks of being apart. They were being held in a separate room until Kronos was ready to finally introduce them to the executives responsible for making the show.

Dawn: [*runs up to Damon and hugs him*] Happy birthday!

Damon: [*immediately annoyed*] Dawn …

Kai: It's your birthday?

Amber: Is today the twenty-second? I haven't had to write dates down anywhere, so I guess I forgot. Happy birthday, Damon!

Damon: [*mutters*] Thanks.

Kronos: [*walks into the room*] Mr. Montclaire, happy twenty-fifth birthday! Don't think I forgot about you! Both Miss Sutherland and Miss Pruitt made sure to remind me that today is a special day.

Damon: [*stares at Dawn and HJ, deadpans*] Thanks.

HJ: [*proud smile*] You're so welcome.

Kronos: But first, before we start the party or even meet the people who are responsible for putting you all on TV, I want you to meet three very important people. [*backs up from where he came, sticks his head around the corner, motions for the others to come in*]

Three people enter the room—two girls and one boy. Damon and Hanna June immediately recognize two of them and make eye contact with each other. The last person to enter is new to them though, and she pushes past the other two with her hand extended.

Alexia: [*shakes hands with Kai*] Alexia Chang, nice to meet you.

Astrid: [*smirking behind her, whispers to the guy next to her without looking at him*] Is she serious?

Zach: Alexia? Cool. So, we can call you Lex.

Alexia: Alexia is fine.

Zach: Oh … okay, well, I'm Zach.

Alexia: [*nodding*] I'm aware of who you are. Kronos gave me a binder with a cheat sheet about all of you, which I then used to make flash cards.

Zach: Oh … well, that's very … organized of you.

Alexia: Thank you.

Dawn: Kronos, I thought you said there'd be four new members coming in?

Kronos: There are, but unfortunately, Mr. McHugh couldn't make it. You'll all meet him at our first meeting back in January. [*turns to Heath*] Except you, Mr. Blackburn-McHugh.

Heath: [*grunts*]

Zach: You know him?

Heath: He's my stepbrother.

Kai: [*doing a Will Ferrell impression*] I know you touched my drum set!

Zach: [*laughs*]

Heath: Nah, I wish it were like that. I haven't seen Gun since I was eleven, I think …

Kai: Shit …

Astrid: [*waving her hand and taking a step forward*] Hi, I'm Astrid, if anyone cares.

Zach: [*mutters*] Whoa.

HJ: [*hits him gently on his chest*]

Astrid: Hi. Just wanted to make sure I wasn't left out.

Kai: Nope. We wouldn't do that.

Kronos: All right guys, let's take the conversation up to the penthouse to meet the people in charge!

Everyone begins shuffling out of the room and following Kronos.

Astrid: [*waits for Damon, who's the last one*] So, I hear you're the birthday boy.

Damon: I'm twenty-five. I definitely don't qualify as a boy anymore.

Astrid: [*eyeing him up and down*] No, you don't.

Damon: [*rolls eyes, ignores her*]

Astrid: [*leans in to him as she's walking*] I'm Astrid.

Damon: I heard.

Astrid: So, what did you get for your birthday?

Damon: I've been on a plane most of the day. I haven't gotten anything.

Astrid: [*steps in front of him and puts a hand on his chest to stop him*] Well, you can unwrap me.

Damon: [*grabs her hand, pulls it off his chest, and grips it hard*]

Astrid: [*trying to hold her composure*] Ow.

Damon: I wouldn't touch you with a ten-foot pole if you paid me. [*shoves past her*]

He storms into the room, picks up a glass of wine off the tray of a waiter passing by, and steps out onto the balcony. Astrid sulks into the room, holding her hand, and pauses at the threshold.
Dawn is talking with Heath and Kronos. Amber is almost done with her glass of wine while Alexia drones on next to her. Kai is eating hors d'oeuvres he's never heard of and trying to casually choke down the ones he finds disgusting. HJ is standing in the middle of a group of people in formal business attire with all eyes on her.

Zach: [*saunters over to Astrid*] Hey.

Astrid: Hey.

Zach: You okay?

Astrid: [*looks at him, confused*] Yeah. Why wouldn't I be?

Zach: [*looks out the wall-to-wall glass window at Damon on the balcony*] I heard.

Astrid: Oh … well, [*fakes a laugh*] that's embarrassing.

Zach: No, don't be embarrassed. He's just, like, this … super-antisocial king of darkness. His behavior has nothing to do with you, I promise.

Astrid: Really?

Zach: Uh, yeah. Look at you!

Astrid: [*giggles*] Thanks. It's Zach, right?

Zach: Yeah. You're from Los Angeles?

Astrid: [*flashes him a smile, her confidence quickly coming back*] Born and raised. What about you?

Zach: DC.

Astrid: [*nodding*] Is your family in politics?

Zach: Yeah, yeah, my dad's the mayor there.

Astrid: Oh, wow! That's so coo—

Zach: Yeah, it is. Listen, you look really familiar … have we met before?

Astrid: [*smiles slyly*] I'm on YouTube.

Zach: [*tilts his head, trying to picture her*] Are you, wait … no.

Astrid: [*making weird faces at him, trying to figure out if he's placed her yet*]

Zach: Oh my God. You're *AskAstrid*!

Astrid: [*big smile, shakes her shoulders*] That's me!

Zach: Wow. You, uh … you talk a *lot* about sex.

Astrid: Well, yeah, but that's the whole reason I have my channel. They teach us in school that sex is bad and only bad things can happen if we do it, but that's just so, so wrong. So, I decided it was my job to educate people.

Zach: Well, on behalf of anyone who's ever watched any of your *very informative* videos, I would just like to say thank you for taking your job so seriously.

Astrid: You are so welcome.

Zach: The forum thing is a smart idea too—answering people's anonymous questions like an old newspaper column or something.

Astrid: Yeah, I really like doing those! I'd do more each week, but the videos would just get so long.

Zach: [*stepping closer to* her] I'd still watch them.

Astrid: Oh yeah?

Zach: Yeah.

Astrid: [*stepping closer to him*] Something tells me you don't need to be watching my videos.

Zach: [*small shrug*] That's probably true, but the way I see it, you're, like, the expert on the topic, right? You're the best of the best. Just, like, based off your vids. So, *if* I'm going to learn anything, why should it be from anyone aside from the professional?

Astrid: [*staring at his mouth*] That makes sense. [*arches an eyebrow*] I would love to give you some pointers ... but your girlfriend is right over there. [*gestures toward HJ with her head*]

Zach: She's in her element. She won't even notice I'm gone.

Astrid: There's a bathroom back down the hall next to the room we were waiting in.

Zach: Perfect.

They both leave the party.

Epilogue

DAMON

Damon could remember sitting in a doctor's office, high up above Seventh Avenue, and listening to Paulina cry when the family was told the physicians thought he had diabetes.

Her dramatized sobs had proven to be unnecessary, as his postural tachycardia syndrome diagnosis came not two minutes later, paired with a nervous, laughter-filled apology. This meant that he got to carry around jerky in his backpack, and as a skinny thirteen-year-old, he'd figured that was a pretty good deal.

What had stuck with him though was the little miracle hormone the endocrinologist had mentioned to a hysterical Paulina—insulin. Damon had made sure to research it when they returned home from their visit with his new stock of overly salty rescue snacks, only to find out that the right amount of it could save someone's life and that too much of it could end it.

And that was exactly what he'd used on sweet, old Sylvia Herrera. It wasn't entirely untraceable, but that didn't matter to Damon.

They won't find her body.
And if they do, they'll thank me.
If they can even identify it.

There was nothing happening out on the freezing water tonight. The Gulf stretched out as an untouched indigo sheet as he sped back to Key West. It was well past midnight, but no part of him was tired. His soul was awake; he felt ignited from within, every part of him. Fireworks could be set off from the ends of his fingertips—he was sure of it. It was adrenaline that a caffeine surge couldn't provide him, satisfaction he hadn't had in years, a warm, gooey mixture of having conquered a phantom like terror. And he didn't want to share the news with anyone. Not Ernesto, not the FBI or the CIA, definitely not Fleur.

Not that Damon told her any of this. It was something that would forever stay hidden in the deepest crypt inside him, kept as far away from her as possible, where every other terrible thing that belonged to only him lived.

A small splash jumped up over the bow, and he smiled in spite of himself.

I did it. I fucking did it. I single-handedly took out the most miserable excuse of a human, who had just so happened to also be running the most notorious international human trafficking ring in the world. In the whole fucking world. Completely by accident, if you ask some, but to me, it was fate.

The lead he'd been given on a drug runner stocking up at the country's southernmost point had turned out to be fake. Lost in his thoughts, annoyed and frustrated, he turned quickly and bumped into a woman, pacing the length of the sidewalk and warning passersby in a doomsday-like way. Desperate to get away from her, he ducked into the closest bar a few doors down, greeted by a man behind the counter who had his eyes glued to the door.

"That woman still goin' crazy on Caroline Street?" the bartender had asked him.

When Damon confirmed his suspicion, the man shook his head, his eyes still fixated on the entranceway.

"She talkin' nonsense, saying, 'She's back. She's here. She come all the way here. Don't go out after sundown. You best be lockin' your doors and windas. She's back.' "

Glancing between the bartender and the spot where his gaze stuck, Damon was struck with a flicker of curiosity.

Venturing back out into the futile December sun—as fate would have it—he learned that the woman on Caroline Street was not crazy. Incredibly high and in desperate need of a shower, but not out of her mind. And her bizarre directions led him to an old, shut down, dilapidated storefront, only to find Sylvia Herrera. She was right there, with a handful of idiot goons and about a dozen captives, ready to ship them off to Havana at nightfall, and then who knew where next?

Getting her unconscious was the easy part—she never even saw him coming. Her pack of henchmen were stunned, and the local police had been called.

I'll let them escalate it from there, he had thought.

He knew that if it had been Ernesto, he would've had SWAT there in minutes and would've done something dramatic about her disappearance from the group, like write on the sand-covered floor, *I took care of the kingpin,* as some sort of big mystery.

But Damon didn't do that. *Let them keep looking for her. Let them think she got away. She's outsmarted every intelligence agency on the planet since 2003, and I found her in Florida, just days after Christmas.*

All is calm.

He pulled into the dock just after two, freezing cold and still riding high on the thought that he had done what no one else could.

His resort wasn't far from the marina, and despite the wind, the walk back was actually pleasant. Multicolored lights hung on several boats and wrapped around lampposts.

As the waves crashed against the wall beneath him as he walked along, he couldn't help but picture her face the way he had last seen it—covered in her own blood as he slipped her body over the side of the cramped fishing boat, knowing the water would be deep enough to host vicious creatures and the scent would pull them right to her lifeless body like a magnet.

"Good evening, Mr. Montclaire," he heard as he stepped into the lobby.

Thank God I always have a change of clothes with me, he thought, acknowledging the young girl behind the counter.

Having to explain the gruesome mess to her was not on his agenda. He figured she was probably already terrified to be working the night shift, and he was glad he didn't have to make it worse.

Nodding at her, he made his way to the elevator. The chime sounded as the doors opened, and he jumped.

"Damon."

She's been waiting for me.

He got in silently and stood next to her. They traveled up to the top floor without saying a word to each other, and when the doors opened, she got out first.

Taking long strides down the hallway, she headed right for his room.

I shouldn't be surprised—he's had me followed for the last four years. Which makes it really hard to do all the jobs he keeps tossing my way.

She opened the door with her own key card, and he followed her inside. Her fingers grazed the body of a wineglass she must have left there as she sauntered over to the corner.

Damon stalked into the bathroom and turned the shower on, not willing to start the conversation.

"He's not happy."

Big surprise. "I had things to do," he answered as he took off his shirt.

"He gave you an assignment, one that *should* come naturally to you. Well, at least more naturally than … this."

Damon was used to conversing with Rhianne, but he knew it would shock the other five if they knew she did more than just coordinate a filming schedule around his doctorate classes.

"I had things to do," he repeated louder, stepping under the scalding hot water.

Letting the steam fill up the space around him, he closed his eyes. *Don't let her take the light off your win. You fucking did it.*

As he began his monotonous shower routine, the bathroom door creaked slightly, and he figured she had come to stand in front of it, not ready for their conversation to be over.

"Rhianne, I'm on his mission, okay? I just happened to come across something that needed to be taken care of."

"I understand that. He understands that too. But he needs you to get back on track. Especially because his office has been ransacked."

Shutting the water off quickly and reaching for a towel, Damon jumped out to face her. Standing there, dripping wet, he looked at her. Her eyes were huge and round, like flying saucers, as they stared back at him.

"What?"

"His office was ransacked," she repeated, but this time, she added, "Nearly everything inside was stolen."

Damon felt his knees wobble.

Every ounce of triumph, every little bit of euphoria he'd felt over the last few hours, was gone without a trace. He felt the hope leave his body, and in place of it something dark and heavy and cold filled in.

"How?" It was all he could manage to get out.

The words seemed to flood his brain, but everything felt like it was fighting for dominance, like the questions swimming around were arguing with each other that they were the most important and therefore should come out and get asked first, but instead, they just seemed to all back up and clog the exit where his mouth was.

Rhianne shrugged her bony shoulders. "No idea. It couldn't have been a mortal—they wouldn't have been able to get past the charms or jinxes or whatever it was that Jade put on it. It had to be one of us."

Damon stormed out past her, leaving wet footprints on the floor as he yanked open the door to the refrigerator and slid the bottle of bourbon out.

After pouring himself a glass and taking in what was probably too much on a normal night—but what seemed appropriate for the situation—he looked up. The confident expression Rhianne had shown in the elevator was long gone as she leaned against the wall, her hands wrapped around themselves like she wasn't sure what to do.

Damon spoke up. "When you say 'nearly everything' … you mean—"

"The files are gone. Every single one of them."

Silence flooded the space between them, and although Damon could feel the alcohol rush through his body, he felt horridly sober.

He knew that she knew the question he was about to ask, and he had a horrible feeling the answer he dreaded would follow, but he asked anyway. He had to be sure.

"What about Fleur's?"

Rhianne didn't pause, and although the madness surged through him when she confirmed his thoughts, he was thankful she hadn't prolonged it.

"Every single one of them, Damon. Someone has it—has them all. Someone knows."

Acknowledgments

Before I get started, let me first say that I've never done one of these before. Apologies in advance.

The first group of people I need to thank are the lovely individuals who made this book as pretty as it is. Jovana, first of all, I'm sorry I made you work so hard for your money. Second of all, thank you doesn't even cover it. In case you couldn't tell, I was rushing to make my own deadline and clearly did not give this thing a reread initially. Thank you for turning my very complicated storyline and chaotic characters into something that actually makes sense.

Juniper, I have no words. That's a lie; I have a lot of them. I came to you with complete chaos and told you I basically didn't have a clue what I wanted and to just make me something. And, wow, you did. You took my original cover and morphed it into this epic foundation piece, and I am itching to see what you do for the rest of the series. I can't wait to see all five of them lined up together. Thank you times a million.

Maggie, thank you immensely for bringing my six best friends to life in the book and for allowing me to share them with the world.

Glory Byrd, I am in love with the map. Thank you for bringing my little city to life and for including directions how to print it properly to display on my wall because that most definitely will be happening.

I need to say thank you to my parents for not pushing me to work on this, but encouraging. I still don't think you anticipated me actually finishing it because, let's face it, I've never seen anything through the way I have with this.

Kimberly, thank you for being the first one to take it all in. Your notes were incredibly helpful. There's no one I would rather have be the head of my fan club.

Harley Rae, you're the love of my life. You'll never read this, but I'm including you in hopes that you don't rip up any of these copies, like you've done to other books I own.

The last person I need to thank is myself. I have started countless endeavors, but this is the first one I've ever finished. Why that is, I have no idea, but I'm going with the thought that I've never been as passionate about something; never truly enjoyed what I was doing, until I created this world and these characters and their stories. I am so proud of myself … which are words I really don't think I've ever said before. I did the damn thing—somehow—and there's a tangible product to prove it.

The most important acknowledgment goes to you—the reader. None of the joy I feel from sharing this story with the world matters without your presence. I hope you'll stay along for the ride. Thank you endlessly.

About the Author

HALLIE GETS BORED EASILY and likes to experience new things, which is why all her characters are so different. She is most definitely living vicariously through them.

When she's not writing, she likes to rewatch shows she's seen dozens of times; spend time with her dog, Harley Rae Skywalker; and listen to music that she relates too much to.

Hallie is a graduate of East Carolina University and currently lives in New York.

The Ambrosia Project is her debut series, originally publishing Book 1 as *Theories and Tape Sessions* in December 2022, but rereleasing it in February 2025 as *The Clandestine Dawning of the Gods*. Book 2 can be expected spring 2025.

Follow her for updates, playlists, and chaos on social media.

Instagram: @hallieparkerwrites

TikTok: @hallieparkerwrites

Pinterest: @hallieparkerwrites

Spotify: @hallieparker

9 798987 323625